LOST RUNES

A Montague & Strong Detective Novel

ORLANDO A. SANCHEZ

BITTEN PEACHES

ABOUT THE STORY

What some call lost, others call hidden.

By returning to the foundations of the magical sects, Monty and Simon must locate one of the main sources of magic.

The lost runes.

There's only one problem. The runes were never lost—they were hidden, kept away from mages and humanity because of the mind-numbing destructive power they contain.

The Keepers of Arcana, who hid them, want them to remain that way. They will destroy anyone who tries to harness their power—starting with Tristan Montague.

Now, Monty and Simon must find a way to unleash and control the power of the lost runes, accelerate Monty's ability, avoid being disintegrated by the Keepers and pull all this off without obliterating, well...everything.

"The most precious things are always invisible; they are always kept hidden."
— *Sunday Adelaja*

"All information belongs to everybody all the time. It should be available. It should be accessible to the child, to the woman, to the man, to the old person, to the semiliterate, to the presidents of universities, to everyone. It should be open..."
—*Maya Angelou*

DEDICATION

To the keepers of the secrets,
to those who hold the whispers
in the shadows of the night
as something precious.

This is for you.

ONE

I stood across the street from the Moscow and looked up.

Dawn was fast approaching, which would make the damage easier to see. Blue energy crackled on the building's surface, running up and down its length.

I thought taking the practice session across the street to the 14th Street park would minimize any collateral damage.

I was wrong.

I should've realized I was dealing with a mage—and, even though she was young, minimizing collateral damage doesn't exist in their vocabulary.

"Are you sure she had something to do with this?" I asked, examining the large, gaping, frost-covered hole in the side of the building. "We do have more than a few enemies who are capable of this kind of damage."

Monty, who was standing next to me, gave me a look that clearly said: *You must be joking*. He turned back, narrowing his eyes and looking at the newly perforated Moscow.

He slowly shook his head and frowned.

"That may be true," he said, "but the damage, while

extensive, was not aimed at our home. That, and the fact that a displeased Olga is currently standing in the entrance of the building, looking our way, seems to indicate this may have something to do with my young apprentice."

"That and the ice everywhere?"

"Well, there is that," he said. "Fortunately the structural integrity of the building seems intact. We won't have to evacuate anyone."

"I don't know," I said. "Looking at Olga, I may want to evacuate the immediate area. It was so fast, I didn't even see it happen."

"I'm sure Olga saw and felt it," Monty said, still focused forward. "I am surprised her power has advanced this much."

"You haven't really been teaching her much," I said. "Could be you missed her power increase because you've been distracted. Verity has been keeping us busy."

"Indeed," Monty admitted, still looking at the building. "However, I have been remiss in my duties as her instructor. I knew her power was increasing; I just didn't expect her to start creating new exits in the building."

"What *did* you expect?" I said. "She's a kid with power, more power than she knows what to do with. She's going to try using that power. Actually, I'm surprised the building is still standing. She has more self-control than some adults, present company included."

He gave me a look and then turned back to focusing on the building.

"I expressly forbade her any major casts while inside the building," Monty said, glancing behind us. "It was a clear instruction."

"Forbade her? Really?" I said. "It must be a mage thing, then."

"How so?"

"It's the Wet Paint Syndrome."

"I've never heard of this Wet Paint Syndrome," Monty said. "Elaborate."

"If you ever see a bench or a wall with a Wet Paint sign, it won't last five minutes before there are fingerprints somewhere on the wet paint. Never fails."

"How is that related to anything we are discussing?"

"Well, every time I hear about something that's forbidden in the magical world, there is always that one mage who can't resist trying to use that same forbidden thing. You know, like lost elder runes."

"That is not the same thing at all," he said with a huff. "The lost runes cannot remain hidden forever. What if someone with evil intent finds them?"

"What if someone with evil intent only finds them because a curious mage uncovers them?" I said. "Some things need to be classified; some things need to remain hidden. Don't you think?"

"No, I do not," Monty said. "Information like the elder runes should be available to mages. Much good can come from the dissemination of ancient knowledge."

"Even if that knowledge consists of world-ending runes of power?"

"I am a pragmatist," he answered. "I don't believe I am the only one searching for the elder runes. You heard Albert —it was my uncle Dex who stopped him when he was close to locating them.

"Are these blood runes, too?" I asked, concerned. "If they are, you should walk away now."

"Not to my knowledge," Monty said. "These runes require a different catalyst—power. Even unto his death, Albert was looking for them. His sole pursuit was power."

"It was," I said. "Which is probably why they should remain hidden."

"At the very least, she seems to have followed my instruction about not casting inside the building," he said, looking up again. "All the damage appears to be external."

"She did," I said. "That damage, and the angle of attack definitely indicates the impact came from outside of the Moscow. Are we still convinced it was her, though? Maybe it was a freak atmospheric blast?"

I glanced back to look at a very sheepish Cece, who stood out of earshot some distance behind us. Her guardian, Rags, sat by her side in a defensive position.

Cece had grown a bit since I last saw her. Her white-blond hair was longer and tied back in an intricate braid. She had switched her Vader shirt for one with a very young-looking Yoda, who, I recently learned, was now called Grogu.

Her blue jeans were sporting holes over both knees, which I realized was not the result of a battle, but the current fashion.

Around her, the air was charged with energy that was slowly dissipating.

"At least she's come over to the light side," I said, more to myself than Monty. "That new Baby Yoda is cute."

"A freak atmospheric blast? I'm sure Olga will accept that as a reasonable excuse for the damage to the building," Monty said. "Is that how you would like to explain it?"

"Why am I explaining anything?" I asked. "She's *your* apprentice, not mine. Do I look like I want to explain anything to our resident ice-queen landlord?"

"I was not out here encouraging her to—how did you put it? '*Go for it. Let's test the dawnward. Unleash the beast.*'"

"I didn't tell her to punch a hole in the building," I said. "If she—allegedly—did it, then it was an accident. I'm sure Olga will understand that. Accidents happen all the time."

"There is one thing Olga does not seem to tolerate well," Monty said, "and that is damage to her domain. She takes it personally, which means she will take it out on us —personally."

"She does seem pissed. What did she say...exactly?"

"Fix hole or find new place to live," Monty said in his best Olga imitation. "I believe that was verbatim. A woman of few words but of immense power. Care to explain what exactly happened?"

"I wanted to see how much damage the dawnward could take, and *you* said to push her," I countered. "I pushed, she unleashed. The dawnward held. Her blast ricocheted off the shield. I didn't see it punch into the Moscow, though."

"I also told you to wait until I was downstairs."

"You were taking too long," I said. "You tell her she can cut loose, and then you tell her to wait. Were you ever a child? That's a recipe for certain disaster."

"No, it was an exercise in patience," he corrected. "She was—you both were—supposed to wait until I was present, to prevent just this sort of thing from happening."

"An exercise in patience?" I said, staring at him in disbelief. "I really don't think you were a child...ever."

"Of course I was a child," he said. "Now, we need to repair this before Olga becomes more agitated."

"Judging from her expression of barely controlled fury, I'd say that's about five minutes," I said, glancing over to where Olga stood fuming inside the lobby of the Moscow. "She looks like she could cause some major bodily damage right about now."

"I best get to the repairs before she feels the need to act on that anger."

"That is your department," I said. "I'll go talk to Cece while you do your finger thing. Your track record with her is spotty at best."

"Please tell Cecelia to refrain from casting until after

I have repaired the damage," Monty said, shaking out his hands and moving closer to the building. "The last thing we need right now is more damage."

"Sure, it's not like she's feeling bad about blasting a hole in the building," I said. "I'll just crush her feelings a little more, tell her she's a major screw-up and that if she dares cast again, it's just going to mess things up further. That should do wonders for her self-esteem."

"That is not what I meant at all," he said. "I only meant to—"

"Save it," I said, raising a hand and shaking my head. "Just do your finger-tango thing and see if you can fix it. You have the bedside manner of a brick. An angry brick. I'll talk to her."

"It is not a finger thing," Monty said. "Actually, I can use a variant of the Restoring Palm. It will allow me to—"

I walked away before he got carried away with how he was going to fix the Moscow. I had an idea of how the Restoring Palm worked, but right now there was a little girl who had broken a building because I had pushed her to unleash the beast—not that there was any actual proof of said action taking place.

She was feeling horrible, and Monty, even though he was phenomenal as a mage, truly sucked when it came to speaking to children. I wondered if it was a product of age. He was pushing over two centuries; there had to be some residual crankiness there.

I had to make this right.

The first step was not letting Monty address the situation with Cece. He was too proper and set in his ways. He would begin the conversation with correcting her and lecturing about how this was all the result of her disobeying his express instructions not to use a major cast.

Basic mage grumpiness.

He didn't realize how much she looked up to him. He would think he was helping her understand the consequences of the misuse of power. All she would hear is that he was angry with her and that she had messed up.

"Hey, Cece," I said as I approached, "how you holding up?"

She looked up at me, worry etched into her expression. I could tell she had been crying, but had rubbed the tears away in an effort to appear brave and calm.

"I broke the building. I am in so much trouble," she said as her eyes began to water. "I didn't mean to. I really thought I could get through your dawnward."

"Not your fault," I said, crouching down to make our eyes level. "If anyone is to blame, it's me. I shouldn't have told you to unleash the beast."

"Can he fix it?" she asked, looking at Monty, then glancing at the lobby of the building. "Olga looks so pissed."

"Well, he is usually better at taking things apart," I said, turning to look at Monty, "but he has been known to fix things from time to time."

"Really?"

"Yes, really," I said, standing. "Why don't we step back a bit and give him some room to work? I'm sure he can handle this before Olga comes out."

"Will he be able to?"

"Well, if we stand far away, at the very least, we'll have a head start in case Olga wants to turn us into icicles."

"You're not very funny, Mr. Simon," Cece said. "You don't know how strong she is. She could stop us from where she is now."

I turned and looked at the entrance of the building where Olga stood, emanating waves of violence through her eyes at us.

"That's good to know," I said, putting a hand on her

shoulder and guiding her away from the building. Rags let out a low rumble. "Easy Guardian. Just trying to keep her safe."

<As am I, bonded one. No one will harm one under my charge—no one.>

TWO

My hellhound nudged me in the leg, nearly throwing my hip out of joint as we put more distance between us and the Moscow.

<Will the angry man be able to fix the hole? Should I help him?>

<How are you going to help him? You aren't exactly skilled in fixing, well, anything. You plan on doing...what? Biting the building or punching more holes in it with your eye-beams of doom?>

<Anything that demonstrates I am the Mighty Peaches in front of the Guardian. She is looking, isn't she?>

<Not really, no. She seems focused on Cece.>

<She is probably worried about the cold girl.>

<Breaking a building is kind of a big deal. I'd be worried too.>

<You never seem worried when you break buildings.>

<I never break buildings. That's you and Monty. I just get blamed by being associated with the two of you.>

<Don't worry. When you become mighty, maybe you will break a building on your own.>

<I have no intention of breaking any buildings, boats, bridges, or vehicles in the near or distant future, thanks. Let's focus on letting Monty fix that hole.>

We kept moving until I felt we were far enough away—which, if I was being honest, meant anywhere out of Olga's line of sight. Still, we were on the opposite end of the 14th Street park as Monty got into the heavy-duty finger-two-step.

He raised a hand as the other gestured, and even from where I stood, I could feel the increase in his energy signature. Olga must have sensed it, too, because she stepped out of the Moscow.

She crossed into the park, keeping a healthy distance from Monty, and turned to look at the Moscow. Monty unleashed a lattice of violet light. It raced toward the Moscow, covering the hole Cece had created.

With another series of gestures, I saw the building repair itself—except it wasn't really a repairing action, but one closer to rebuilding. It was like watching a movie in reverse.

The bricks reformed back into place and the facade restored itself as if it had never been hit by Cece's blast. Somewhere in the pit of my stomach, I had an a uneasy feeling. I didn't get the same vibe I'd had when Monty used a dark cast, but this was considerably stronger than anything I had seen him cast lately.

What concerned me more was that it wasn't a struggle for him to cast it. From the expression on his face, we could have been sitting in the kitchen while he sipped tea.

That definitely worried me more than the actual cast.

After a few more minutes of finger-wiggling, the building appeared unscathed. Olga approached Monty as I closed on him with Peaches, Cece, and Rags in tow.

Olga reached Monty before I did and had started speaking to him before I could catch the conversation. Judging from her body language, she wasn't chastising him; it seemed more like she was genuinely curious about the cast he had just executed.

"This palm is timecast?" she asked as I stepped closer. "It controls time, da?"

"That is a good question," Monty answered, rubbing his chin. "I suppose the argument could be made that if it restores, it is, in the strictest sense of the word, a type of timecast. However, I am no chronomancer. I don't know how to manipulate time."

"How far it restores?" Olga asked, before glancing at me. "Good mornink, Stronk."

I nodded in her direction, but remained silent, curious to see where her line of questioning was going. I also kept my mouth shut because she still looked pretty pissed off at having had a hole in her building. Her greeting sounded more like a threat than an actual greeting.

"I don't know," Monty said, admiring the repair work on the building. "I have recently acquired this cast."

"This is good," Olga said with a nod after a pause. "You have more power. I go to visit sisters now. Cecelia and Guardian stay with you. She will be safe."

"You're *what*? Excuse me?" Monty stammered as he whirled on Olga. "You're leaving her here alone?"

"No," Olga said, stepping closer to Monty as the temperature around us dropped suddenly, from dangerous to menacing with an expression to match. "I leave her here with *you, Prepodavatel*—her teacher. She will be safe with you."

"I must disagree," Monty began, as Olga crossed her arms and just stared down at us the way I imagined a mother eagle would observe a flailing worm that was about to become food for her eaglets. Monty took a few seconds to notice the frigid stare of doom and death, so he kept speaking. "Leaving her here with us—"

"Yes," Olga finished. "I leave her here with you. I leave now. Any questions?"

By now Monty realized that Olga wasn't really asking for

questions, suggestions, or comments. She was merely stating what was. I felt that was my cue to ask a question, of course. Because living life dangerously had become the only way to live.

"How do we contact you in case of an emergency?" I glanced up at the building. "Not something like this," I added quickly, pointing at the Moscow as Olga narrowed her gaze at me. "I mean a *real* emergency. What if something happens with Cece and we need to get in touch with you?"

"What is *real* emergency?" Olga asked, turning to give me her full attention. The sudden realization that I didn't want that much attention gripped me by the neck and choked me slowly, making the formation of words difficult. "If building is okay, no emergency. No more practice in park, or street, or close to building. You keep Cecelia safe and go to other park to practice."

"Other...other park?" I asked once I got my voice under control, not knowing what she meant. "What other park?"

"Central Park," she said, pointing north. "You practice with Cecelia there. Far from Moscow."

A good forty-five blocks away from the Moscow, in fact.

"We understand," Monty said. "It is concerning what happened this evening, but you can't presume to leave a child in our care. We are not proficient in taking care of children. In addition, we are in the midst of some dangerous activities. Verity—"

"Bah! Baby mages," Olga said, dismissively. "Much talk, no power." She looked at me again and gave me a once-over. It was like being disapprovingly X-rayed by a machine that clearly felt you were an inferior life form, and the mere act of gazing upon you was doing you a favor. "Even Stronk can stand before them. He has more power now. They cannot hurt Cecelia."

"That doesn't mean—"

"Cecelia, here," Olga said, cutting Monty off with a gesture. "We talk."

Cece approached meekly.

"Yes, Aunt Olga?" Cece asked, her voice low as she tried to hide behind Rags. "I'm sorry about the building."

"Building fixed," Olga said, raising a finger to point at Cece. "You do not break again, no more."

"I won't," Cece said, with a vigorous shake of her head. "I won't break it again."

"If you do, I break your teacher and his good friend. *Persiki* is good dog—he, I will not break," she said, glancing from Monty to me, then back to Cece. "You must practice more, control power, grow more power."

"Are you sure that's a good—?" I started.

Olga fixed me with her glacial stare of mild obliteration.

"Is very good little Cecelia grow more power," Olga finished for me. "Her teacher will teach, Cecelia will learn. Good. This is very good talking. Andrei, now building manager, will watch Moscow, you will watch Cecelia. I come back in two weeks. No problems, da?"

"No problems," Monty said, resigned to losing the conversation before I could open my mouth. "Have a good visit with the family."

Olga nodded and glided away.

THREE

A few minutes later, we approached the Moscow with Cece and Rags in tow.

"Do you know anything about watching children?" I asked as we stepped into the enormous lobby. I managed to see a nervous-looking Andrei step away from the door. "Andrei looks spooked."

Andrei gave us plenty of room once he saw Peaches and Rags approach the entrance. He stepped back from the door and found important things to do behind the massive reception desk, avoiding us entirely.

"It would seem the presence of both your creature and Cecelia's guardian has him slightly rattled," Monty added glancing at Andrei. "Do try to behave, both of you."

"I thought he was just scared of Peaches," I said to Cece as I watched Andrei beat a hasty retreat behind the large desk. "Is he scared of Rags, too?"

"I think he doesn't like big dogs," Cece replied, nodding to Andrei and patting Rags' head as we passed him in the lobby. He shrank back a bit as we stepped close. "I think he knows or senses that they aren't regular dogs."

"Oh, I'm sure of that," I said, thinking back to Andrei's regular encounters with Peaches. "Still, maybe we don't terrorize him?"

She gave me a look.

"I don't terrorize him…much," she said, touching Rags on the shoulder, who then proceeded to pounce on the reception desk, placing both of her huge paws on the edge, giving Andrei a low growl and a near coronary. "See? Rags is super friendly."

Andrei stepped back and put on a brave face as Rags shoved the reception desk forward a few inches. I had the distinct feeling he was going to need medical attention if she kept that up.

"Let's go," I said, trying to maintain a serious face and failing. "So sorry, Andrei."

Andrei, who had gone pale, failed to acknowledge my apology as he fixed his gaze on Peaches. He probably expected something worse from my hellhound. I made sure Peaches just kept walking.

Last thing I wanted was an angry Olga interrogating us to explain why her building manager dropped dead of a heart attack in the lobby.

"Please…keep…keep away," he managed. "Good dogs. Keep away. Thank you."

We entered the stairwell, leaving a shaken Andrei staring after us.

"Monty, this is a bad idea," I said as we climbed the stairs to the second floor. "I know she's powerful, but she's too young to be around us while we look for"—I gave Cece a sidelong glance—"those *things* that are lost."

"I'm right here, you know," Cece said as we reached the door to our space. "You do know I can hear you?"

"Sorry, Cece," I said as Monty disabled the defenses on

the door. "We're in the middle of some tense situations. Being around us right now is dangerous."

"Really?" she said. Her face lit up as she smiled. "How dangerous? Real dangerous as in deadly, or just mildly dangerous, as in I could lose an arm?"

I stared at her and shook my head in disbelief.

"No," I said, shaking my head. "No way. She can't come with us. Did you hear what she just asked?"

"My hearing is functioning quite well, thank you," Monty said. "She is a mage. I would say her inquiries are practical. It's wise to anticipate potential threats."

"She wasn't anticipating," I countered. "She was looking forward to the danger."

"That's anticipating," Cece volunteered happily.

Cece smiled at me: a scary smile of barely controlled mayhem.

"Better to look forward to it than to fear it," Monty said. "It is always a good policy to face the danger."

"You are *not* helping," I said. "Stop encouraging her. We can't take her with us. You know this."

"We may not have a choice," Monty said. "We certainly can't leave her here alone. Olga would be most...displeased."

"You mean Olga would blast us to icicles," I said, "after she broke us."

"Yes," Monty said, opening the door. "Her reaction would very likely be one of extreme violence. Don't forget Cecelia is her ward and has been entrusted into her care. Any harm befalling the child would be viewed as weakness on Olga's part, even if it were by proxy."

"Meaning?"

"If we let harm come to Cecelia," Monty explained, glancing at Cece, "Olga's reputation could be damaged. She would be perceived as weakened."

"Olga? Weakened?" I asked in disbelief. "Did you feel her energy signature outside? That would be a hard sell."

"Be that as it may, I cannot claim to be privy to all the nuances of the politics within her domain," Monty said, moving to the kitchen. "I can only presume that the appearance of inability to take care of a mere child would factor negatively in her life as well as ours, if we let any harm befall my apprentice."

"Mere child?" I said. "This mere child punched a hole in a building."

"With your help," Monty added. "It only lends weight to the fact that we have to keep her safe." He gave her a stern look. "She still has much to learn regarding the control of her abilities."

"So we have to protect Cece," I said, nodding. "I can understand *that*. What I don't understand is why you didn't explain to Olga that Verity won't hesitate to h-u-r-t little Cece if they could. Just to get to you, to us."

"You heard her," Monty said, reaching for a tea cup. "It seems Olga thinks little of Verity's capabilities in regards to presenting a credible threat towards us, or Cecelia."

"I don't know; Edith felt like a credible threat when she was trying to erase us."

"Indeed," Monty said, still in the cupboard. "Have you seen the digestives? I left them right here. Did your hellhound devour them again?"

"Over there," I said, pointing to the top shelf next to the cabinet he was rummaging in. "He doesn't eat your crackers—"

"Biscuits," Monty corrected. "And he does. I have seen him disappear an entire package in one gulp."

"Doubtful. Your cookies aren't meaty enough for my hellhound," I said, rubbing Peaches' massive head. "He has very discerning taste."

"Discerning?" Monty scoffed. "If an item is edible, or even *slightly* edible, it's in danger of consumption around your creature."

I heard Cece get comfortable in the reception area and held my breath. Cece was currently getting cozy on the Hansen as Rags curled at her feet. To my knowledge, Cece was the only person, besides Roxanne, who was allowed to sit on that sofa and survive.

How she managed this, I still didn't know.

"Who wants to h-u-r-t you?" Cece asked from behind us. "I can spell, you know. I'm not a baby, Mr. Strong."

"I know that," I said, turning to her. "I never said you were. We just have some nasty people after us at the moment. I don't think it would be a good idea for you to hang with us right now. These people wouldn't think twice about hurting a little ki—er, a young mage, if they felt threatened. And right now, they are feeling very threatened."

"Is that Verity?" she asked. "I heard Aunt Olga call them baby mages."

"Yes, you did," I said, realizing Cece was sharper than I gave her credit for. "Olga thinks they aren't much, but we don't want to take that chance. Not with you."

"Rags would protect me," she said, extending a hand to rub her guardian's thick coat of fur. "She always protects me."

"I have no doubt about Rags being an awesome guardian," I said. "I'd rather not have to find out just how awesome she is. Know what I mean?"

"I do," she said pensively. "What's lost? Maybe Rags and I can help you find it? We are really good at finding lost things."

I felt the energy signature fill the space as I was about to answer and looked down at the door that led to Dex's room. If it was Dex, I hoped—really hoped—he was dressed respectably...or at the very least, dressed.

"There are a series of runes that are classified as lost," Monty began. "We have been instructed to find and harness them."

"Lost runes?" she asked, curious. "That sounds like fun. Can I help? We found Mr. Simon when he was lost."

"I was never *lost*," I said, clearing my throat as Monty turned to hide a smile. "I was kidnapped."

"And valiantly made your escape."

"Yes, I did."

"With the assistance of a young girl, two canines and a lizard," Monty continued. "Such bravery in the face of danger. The valor. How did you ever make it out alive?"

"We don't discuss that event, ever."

"Right, we'll file that under top secret and classified," Monty said with a nod, still smiling, before turning serious. "Careful. We have a guest."

"I know," I said, matching his nod. "I really hope he decided to wear—"

My heart nearly leapt out of my chest as Dex materialized next to me in the reception area.

Dressed in bohemian casual mage, Dex had his hair back in a loose braid, and was wearing a light green dress shirt paired with dark jeans finished off with a Zegna jacket that pulsed with soft green runes along its surface. He padded over to the kitchen, his bare feet making no sound.

"Hello, Uncle," Monty said. "You're someone who may have some insight into the lost runes."

"They're not lost, they're hidden," Dex said with a growl as he headed for the kitchen. "For good reason."

"I have to find them," Monty said, his voice firm as he glanced at Cece. "And we may need your assistance with a certain young mage."

"Ach," he said, shaking his head. "Are you planning on taking her with ye?"

"I don't see we have much of a choice," Monty said, laying on the guilt with a little extra drama. "Her Aunt Olga left her here with us. I am her guardian while she is away visiting family, but I couldn't, in good conscience, take her with us. It's simply too dangerous."

"Too dangerous?" Dex asked with a chuckle. "She's stronger than most Jotnar her age. She'd probably be protecting you."

"Be that as it may," Monty continued, "I would rest easier if we had some place safe she could wait for her aunt. A place where she could be taken care of and perhaps even taught..."

"You're laying it on a little thick there, nephew," Dex said with a sigh. "Fine, the lass can come to the school until her aunt returns. Mo can even show her some things regarding her power."

"A school?" Cece asked. "What kind of school?"

"A school for battle magic," Dex said with a wicked smile. "Want to learn how to become even more dangerous?"

"Monty...?" I started. "Are we sure this is a good idea?"

Cece smiled back and I realized she was giving Dex the exact same smile back to him. How this could end up any way besides disastrous escaped me.

We were creating a dangerous ice-mage terror.

More dangerous than she was at the moment.

Cece gave it thought for a few seconds and then nodded.

"Yes! That sounds like fun. More fun than looking for crusty old lost runes," she said. "When can we go?"

"In a moment, lass," Dex said, raising a hand. "I need to talk to these two for a moment, then we'll be off. That okay?"

Cece nodded and sat practically vibrating in place. Whatever skill Dex had with relating to children the way he did, Monty needed to learn it. It was probably partially a product of Dex's own age—maybe the fact that he looked like everyone's most fun and mischievous grandfather allowed him to relate to children the way he did.

Dex turned to us.

"The lost runes are not lost," Dex said. "You know this, yes?"

"I had an idea it was a term being used to dissuade the curious," Monty said. "Can you lend us any assistance as to their location?"

"No. They are constantly being moved," he said, shaking his head. "Finding the one you did was more luck than anything else. Ziller is very careful with the elder runes."

"How did Monty find that area?" I asked. "Maybe we can start there?"

"It's no longer accessible," Dex said. "Ziller saw to that. It's gone."

"You mean he secured them?"

"I mean, the room my nephew managed to stumble into is gone," Dex said. "Non-existent. Ziller removed it from this, or any other plane of existence, along with the runes it held."

"But the Caretaker told Monty to—"

"I don't care what the Caretaker told you," Dex snapped. "The Keepers of the Arcana will try to kill you if you start this."

"Keepers of the Arcana?" I asked, concerned. "Are they part of Verity?"

"They predate Verity by millennia," Dex said. "Not a group to get on the wrong side of. If you try to uncover the elder runes, I guarantee you they will notice."

"Can it be done without them noticing?" Monty asked. "Can it be done with subterfuge?"

"By me, perhaps," Dex said, staring at us. "You three? Impossible."

"Are these Keepers mages?" I asked. "Are they stronger than you?"

"Are ye daft, boy?" Dex asked. "Of course they're mages! Powerful ones who will try to remove you from existence. What part of my words are failing to get through that thick skull? What does it matter if they are stronger than me—they aren't, but they are stronger than you...all of you."

"If you help us, will they try and take you out, too?"

"Trying to eliminate me is one thing," he said with a crooked smile before growing serious again. "You two facing off against them is a death sentence, one you can't escape. They will do everything in their power to keep those runes hidden; it's their purpose for existing. If that means eliminating the two of you, they won't lose any sleep over it. This is a bad idea."

"I don't see how we have a choice," Monty said. "The instructions were specific."

"Oh, so *now* you are following instructions?" Dex asked, throwing a hand in the air. "Every time *I've* given you specific instructions, you've gone out of your way to ignore them, but now the Caretaker tells you to throw your life away and you can't hurry off the cliff fast enough, is that it?"

"Not at all," Monty said, pouring hot water into his cup. "We—I—need to do this."

"Why?" Dex asked. "This is suicide. Don't you have enough to deal with as it is? Why unleash a world of pain upon your heads?"

"Our heads?" I asked. "*I'm* not looking for these runes. I'm looking for a cozy vacation spot away from angry mages looking to blast me out of existence."

"Don't fool yourself, boy," Dex said, looking at me. "If he"—Dex pointed at Monty—"takes on looking for the elder runes, they'll be coming for the *both* of you. It's that simple."

"I'm not a mage," I said. "What am I going to do with lost elder runes? I'm not a threat."

Dex looked at me for a few seconds before laughing.

"Imp...impressive that you can say that with a straight face, Marked of Kali and bondmate to a hellhound," he said between chuckles. "Not a threat you say? Who was it that initiated the stormblood? That must have been some other immortal hanging about the Wordweavers that day."

"That was a move out of desperation," I said. "Edith was going to end us. She felt we were a threat."

"And Verity *still* feels that way, boy," Dex said, becoming serious. "They haven't suddenly forgotten about you. You try to uncover elder runes, and Verity will treat you like the major threat you are. You don't want that."

"You mean they've been taking it easy on us?" I asked. "Well, I'd hate to see them pissed off."

"Do not underestimate them," Dex warned. "You've bloodied their noses, but they still have plenty of fight left in them. There will be no turning back once you step on this path. You need to be clear about this course of action."

"We are," Monty said, his voice low and filled with a simmering anger. "I'm not a dark mage, nor is Simon a dark immortal. We need to acquire the runes to dissuade those who would paint us as threats worthy of elimination. We need to show them they are wrong."

"There is a danger here, lad," Dex said. "In your quest to prove them wrong, you can become exactly what they fear. Do not lose yourselves in this. Do not give them the satisfaction of seeing you fall to darkness."

"We won't," I said as Dex motioned to Cece. "I've seen the dark side up close. It's not a place I want to visit, much less live in."

"Aye," Dex said with a nod as if making up his mind about something. He glanced at me before turning to Monty. "If you insist on this course of action, you're going to need help."

For Dex to suggest help meant we were swimming in

deep, murderous waters. Judging from his expression, he wasn't kidding.

"If what you say is accurate, we can't really count on any assistance," Monty answered. "If these Keepers are as powerful as you've described, I doubt anyone will be willing to confront them."

"True, none of the sects will assist you in this," he said. "Don't waste your breath asking. Not even the White Phoenix will cross the Keepers—officially or unofficially."

"Dark Council?" I asked. "Maybe they can—?"

"Neither Dark nor Light Council will so much as look in your direction," he said. "If you pursue this and end up ablaze because of it, they would warm their hands with the flames you gave off as you burned to ash."

"The Ten?" I asked, hoping against hope. "Can we call them?"

"The Ten is best reserved for some world-ending cataclysm," he answered with a shake of his head. "This is way below their pay grade. If you call them, it's as a last resort and the world better be at risk of ending. I'm serious, boy."

"And you can't help?" I asked. "Can you lend us the Morrigan?"

"*Lend* you the Morrigan?" he asked with a crooked smile. "As if she were some kind of specialized weapon?"

"Well, that's not exactly—"

"I'm going to pretend you didn't say what you just said," he said, cutting me off with a growl. "Be thankful she wasn't here to hear your words. She may have taken offense. You do not want to encounter her when she is offended...ever. The worst thing you could do is face off against an angry goddess of death."

"Making a mental note to never bring this up around her."

"Wise choice, boy, and no, I cannot *lend* her to you," he

said. "She has her hands full at the Forge, among other things...like being a goddess."

"Then we do this the way we always do it," I said, my voice determined as I glanced at Monty, who nodded. "We go it solo."

"Are ye daft?" Dex said, stepping close and poking me in the chest with each word. "Have you not heard a word I said? You can't do this alone. You three are not enough. You need help."

"You just told us no one will help us," I said, throwing up a hand in the air in frustration. "Who are we supposed to call if no one is insane enough to help us?"

"One group will."

"Who?" I asked. "Who's insane enough to help us?"

"Treadwell," he said, looking at Monty. "They're just crazy enough to take this on with you, or at least set you on your way."

"I'd rather we didn't," Monty said. "Besides, he prefers to remain in the shadows. He won't risk his organization for us. Not for this."

"He will," Dex said. "They're your only option at this point."

"Treadwell?" I asked. "Who or what is a Treadwell?"

"My uncle is referring to the Treadwell Supernatural Directive," Monty said. "They have no affiliation to any of the known organizations in the magical world."

"No affiliations?" I asked. "How did they manage to pull that off?"

"Because of Sebastian Treadwell," Dex said. "He's strong enough to avoid getting entangled with any organization."

"They must be huge," I said. "Is this Treadwell that powerful?"

"Aye, but more than powerful, he's cunning," Dex said.

"The true numbers of the Directive are unknown, but his core group is only twelve strong."

"Twelve strong? Are you kidding? You want us to face off against these Keepers with the Dirty Dozen?"

"Why would he agree?" Monty asked. "He has refused all calls for assistance in the past."

"All depends on who's doing the asking, don't you think?"

"You didn't," Monty said, pinching the bridge of his nose. "Tell me you didn't."

"I did," Dex said. "Like I said, lad, you only have two options here: certain death if you do this alone, or a slim chance at life with Sebastian's help. Both choices are bad, but only one choice gives you a chance at walking away from this."

"I'd almost prefer we do this on our own."

"I don't," Dex said, his voice as soft as tempered steel. "He will reach out to you soon. Try to bury the hatchet, and make sure it's not in each other."

"This is unwise."

"This is your only choice."

"Who exactly is Sebastian Treadwell?" I asked. "Anyone care to clue me in?"

"I'll let my nephew fill in the details," Dex said. "Make this work, Tristan. I do not want to have to get involved. The repercussions of my confronting the Keepers would be...unpleasant."

"You shouldn't have called him," Monty said. "You know how he is. Ever since the Golden Circle, his priority has been to prove his superiority as a mage."

"This could be the perfect opportunity to demonstrate how you've matured," Dex said. "I'm sure he has put such pettiness to one side."

"I find that highly unlikely," Monty said. "Treadwell has

been known to move in less savory circles. Rumor has it that he's a criminal."

"We're going to get the help of a criminal?" I asked. "That doesn't sound smart."

"Hear him out," Dex said. "Listen to what he can offer, and then make a decision."

"I'll hear him out, but I won't agree to any of his terms," Monty said. "If he helps, it's because he chooses to do so. This is not a quid pro quo."

"Agreed," Dex said. "That could get you into a tight spot. Give him the benefit of the doubt and hear what he has to say."

"I will."

"On your word as a Montague and a mage," Dex said, "no violence shall arise between you two."

"On my word as a Montague and a mage, I will not initiate any violence between myself and Sebastian."

"I saw what you did there," Dex said. "I suppose that is good enough."

"It will have to suffice," Monty said. "As long as he refrains from violence, there won't be any."

"Don't start none, won't be none?" I asked. "Really?"

"Hear him out and then decide," Dex said. "You two"—he glanced at Peaches—"you *thre*e aren't enough to deal with a Keeper."

"Don't you mean Keepers?"

Dex gave me a dark look and shook his head.

"Keeper—singular, boy. They're nearly as strong as Archmages; some are stronger."

I glanced at Monty.

"We may want to reconsider this whole elder-rune mission," I said. "I'm not really in the mood to face off against anyone that can hang in Archmage levels of power."

"Aye, one of the Keepers is enough to make you a bloody

memory," Dex said. "You intend to go after all of the elder runes. There's a good chance you'll be facing more than one."

"Maybe we can postpone this op?" I said, still looking at Monty. "Say, for three or four centuries, when you're much stronger?"

"We will still have to face the Keepers," Monty replied. "Time is not the issue here—not losing our lives to them is."

"See that you don't," Dex said with Cece and Rags in tow. "I'll inform the ice queen her young charge is with me and Mo while you two make some new enemies."

Peaches gave off a low whine as Rags walked away without so much as a glance in his direction. Dex touched the frame and the area around the door flashed green. He opened the door to reveal a familiar sight.

The courtyard of the Sanctuary.

The scene was a tranquil one. I saw the stone road surrounded by the bamboo trees that wound its way deep into the forest. A young woman was waiting for Dex. She was dressed in a gray combat uniform with a dark green insignia on her left shoulder and chest area.

When Dex opened the door, she gave him a short bow, which he returned. He gently ushered Cece and Rags onto the road. The woman silently led Cece away, and both disappeared into the forest.

FOUR

<You'll see her again, boy.>

<But she won't see me being mighty. How will she know I am mighty?>

<I can always call you the Mighty Peaches.>

<You are my bondmate. You will not impress her. She needs someone impressive to call me the Mighty Peaches. Then she will be impressed.>

<Did you just call me unimpressive?>

<Being my bondmate makes you impressive. But she is a guardian. I need someone even more impressive than you. One of the women with the dark blades would be impressive enough.>

<The Valkyries. You mean the Midnight Echelon?>

<The one you call Nan. She would be impressive. She is powerful. She called me the Mighty Peaches. That would be acceptable.>

<Right. I'll make sure to ask her to call you the Mighty Peaches in front of Rags the next time we are facing off against some monsters or running for our lives. Should be no problem.>

<Thank you, you are my favorite bondmate.>

<I'm your only bondmate.>

<That is why you are my favorite.>

"Thank you for watching over her," Monty said. "I'm sure she will enjoy her stay at the school."

"Mo will keep her busy and I'm sure she'll make some friends," Dex said. "Unlike you two."

"We intend to undertake this without acquiring new enemies," Monty said. "I would say we have plenty as it stands."

"It's always good to have a dream," Dex said. "It's been my experience that your ability to make enemies is outstanding."

"Maybe we could use diplomacy with the Keepers?" I said. "Explain the situation to them. Mention the Caretaker and the instructions Monty was given?"

"Aye, you're certainly welcome to try," Dex said, shaking his head. "If I recall correctly, the Keepers aren't keen on non-lethal diplomacy. They like to open with deadly force."

"Are you sure you can't help us?" I asked, thinking about how dangerous these Keepers could be. "It would certainly make our lives easier."

"No, it wouldn't," Dex said, looking at Monty. "Tristan only managed to avoid the repercussions of wielding Nemain because it was a blood matter. Make no mistake though: being associated with me or the Harbinger will make your lives harder—now, and especially in the future."

"That sounds promising," I said. "Nothing more cheerful than knowing impending doom is on its way."

"I know, right?" Dex said, with a smile. "Exciting, isn't it?"

"I think we have different definitions for excitement," I said. "My definition doesn't involve death."

Dex let out a short chuckle before clapping me on the shoulder.

"You two be careful," he said, glancing at the scene beyond his door. It had begun to grow fuzzy at the edges. "I may not know where the runes are now, but if I were you, I would try Ziller first. If anyone knows where the elder runes have gone, it would be him."

"Will he tell us?" Monty asked. "He may know, but not wish to impart the information."

"You'll have to be extra convincing," Dex said, placing a hand on the handle to his door. The frame around the doorway gave off a brighter green glow, coming into sharp focus again. "Maybe explain to him how you feel about hidden information. I'm sure he shares some of your beliefs; if not, he'll probably just blast you out of the Living Library. Nothing ventured, nothing gained."

"Thank you, Uncle," Monty said. "We will be careful."

"You'll need to embrace your role as an Aspis more than ever, boy," he said, looking into my eyes. "I hope you're ready."

"I'll do my best."

"See that you do," he said with a low growl. "I'll not be burying either of you."

Mage morale building at its best. I remained silent and took a step back, nodding to him as he crossed the threshold.

Dex nodded, gave me a look that said, *Don't you dare screw this up and get killed*, and then stepped onto the stone road. He pushed the door to close it before walking away.

I made sure the door was completely closed before speaking.

"Nothing ventured, nothing gained?" I said as the glow around the door slowly vanished. "That's his advice? Go ask Ziller, and *maybe* he won't blast us out of existence?"

"It *is* solid advice," Monty said. "A little light on information, but instructional. Professor Ziller has been known to blast a student or two, especially when they display a lack of understanding of his basic concepts."

"His basic concepts are probably brain melting to everyone else."

"Well, there is that, but I don't think he will be entirely forthcoming considering my recent acquisition of the elder rune of seals."

"You mean, breaking into the Living Library and borrowing one of the elder runes may have left him pissed off at us?"

"At me," he said. "He didn't expect I could access the area where the rune was being kept."

"I'm guessing he didn't expect *anyone* to access that area," I said, thinking. "Why not use that?"

"Use what?" Monty asked. "His anger at my subterfuge? Sounds potentially life-threatening."

"His curiosity," I said, shaking my head. "He will want to know *how* you did it. I'm pretty sure he's at least curious—maybe curious enough to trade the location of the lost runes for your information?"

"You're suggesting I barter with Professor Ziller in order to get him to comply?" Monty asked. "It's a risky proposition."

"Better than the less-than-helpful advice Dex gave us," I said. "Nothing ventured, nothing gained? Why not just tell us to cross our fingers and hope for the best?"

"Don't be ludicrous," he said. "Crossing your fingers rarely works."

"*I'm* being ludicrous?" I asked. "Dex gave us nothing. Less than nothing."

"In my uncle's typical fashion, he gave us much, if you know how to listen," Monty said, raising a finger. "Think back to my uncle's words."

"I'm having a hard time trying to recall anything past the 'blast you out of the Living Library' part of the conversation. Oh wait, yes, these 'Keepers of the Arcana will do their very best to eliminate us' if we try to uncover the elder runes. I remember *that* part, too."

"There was more," Monty said, after taking a sip of tea. "Think back. How old are the Keepers?"

"Older than Verity," I said, reluctantly. "Older by millennia."

"Which means?"

"They've had extra years to build up the crankiness?" I said. "I've yet to meet an old mage that isn't cranky and just plain angry."

"It's more than that," he said. "The threat presented by the Keepers, from my understanding, is considerable."

"Have you ever run into them?"

"No," he said, shaking his head. "There was no reason to encounter them before now."

"Not even after you removed the lost elder rune?"

"It would appear that the elder rune of seals is not a major rune," Monty said. "Or else they would have paid me a final visit."

"The *Keepers of the Arcana* sound like a group of angry librarians," I said. "How dangerous are they?"

"Think of them more like very dedicated librarians entrusted to keep extremely powerful runes from those who would abuse them to gain more power and thus endanger this entire plane," Monty managed in one impressive breath. "They take their duties seriously...very seriously, from what I've learned about them."

"How seriously? Are we talking lethal response or a strong talking to?" I asked. "I know what Dex said, but he could just be trying to convince you to not go through with finding the elder runes."

"My uncle is not prone to exaggeration, unless he is discussing his escapades with the Morrigan," Monty answered, with a shake of his head. "In those instances, I think his adherence to the truth is a bit thin. However, if he says they will come after us with lethal intent, they will. We need to prepare for their response."

"So we're going to have angry librarians after us," I said, with a shake of my own head. "I can't believe that's a thing."

"Angry, *powerful* mage librarians—yes. It is a thing, apparently."

"But they haven't come after you for the elder rune, you know," I said. "Why not?"

He rubbed his chin in thought. I could tell he had thought about it as well. If they were as serious as they sounded, the Keepers should have crashed the party when we faced Mahnes, but they didn't. This made me think they were waiting to see how Monty would use the elder rune.

It was not a good thought.

"That is perplexing," he said. "It would stand to reason that my acquisition of an elder rune would trigger some kind of response."

"Unless they're giving you rope."

"I beg your pardon?"

"Giving you rope," I said. "It's an old saying: giving someone enough rope to hang themselves. They could be waiting and watching to see what you're going to do with the knowledge."

"That would be a dangerous game," Monty said. "What if I were a dark mage with intent to do harm?"

"They'd probably come down on you in force," I said. "They must be aware of our fight with Mahnes by now. Why not pay you a visit?"

"A good question. One I'm certain we will answer, once we speak to Professor Ziller. He will possess more insight into the Keepers."

"I don't like the idea of getting the attention of old mages," I said. "Most of them are either angry, have some plan to destroy everything, or want take over the planet," I said. "Or all of the above: destroy everything while they angrily take over the planet."

"The Keepers, while old, have no intention of taking over the planet."

"How can you be sure?"

"If they had wanted such power, who could have stopped them from taking it?" Monty asked. "They are the guardians of some of the most powerful runes in existence. If they wanted it, it was at their fingertips."

"That's a good point, but I still don't trust elderly mages," I said. "What if one of them decided being a librarian is overrated and now it's time to be a ruler? That's the issue with living so long. Eventually, these beings get bored after doing everything."

"I don't think it's simply a matter of being long-lived," he said. "My uncle is considered advanced in age, yet is neither angry nor a maniacal megalomaniac with delusions of world conquest."

"True, Dex is just regular insane," I said, "and also the personification of the Harbinger of Death. Not dangerous at all, no."

"I never said he wasn't dangerous, just that he wasn't bent on world domination," Monty replied. "It's a matter of character."

"What was he referring to when he mentioned Nemain?"

"I explained it to you," he said. "Don't you recall?"

"Vaguely. My last visit to Haven was a heavily medicated experience, thanks to Roxanne," I said. "She said something about not trusting just my curse for my recovery. The details are fuzzy. Can you share, or is the fine print a blood matter too?"

"In order for me to wield Nemain, even for a family blood matter, I had to agree to the terms of the Harbinger," he said. "It's not very complicated."

I could tell he was avoiding the subject, so I pressed him. Starting awkward conversations was one of my major strengths, right up there with knowing which buttons to push in a crisis.

"Then explaining it should be easy," I said. "Go on, I'm all ears."

He let out a small sigh and took another sip before continuing.

"When my uncle passes, I will have to serve as the Harbinger in his stead, until a permanent replacement can be found," Monty said. "In the case of a supernatural conflict, such as a war, I will take up the mantle of the Harbinger until said conflict is resolved, providing the earlier conditions are met."

"That Dex is dead?"

"Yes, and that no replacement has been found."

"So, while Dex is alive, you won't become the Harbinger or need to use Nemain?"

"I hope to never *need* to use that weapon ever again," he said with a small shudder. "But you are technically correct—while my uncle lives, only *he* can be the official Harbinger of Death."

"If he dies, do you automatically become the Harbinger?"

"No. I can serve as the Harbinger and wield Nemain, but it is neither automatic nor permanent," Monty said. "Death would have to choose me in a specific instance to serve as the Harbinger."

"Would Ezra pick you?" I asked. "Somehow I can't see that happening. Then again, it's hard to see Ezra as Death —capital D."

"True, especially when we visit him and he plies us with food."

"Not just food—delicious, mouthwatering food," I said, glancing at my hellhound. "But there have been moments I've felt a part of his energy signature. I can't see a situation where he'd need to pick you, or anyone, for that matter."

"I think the Harbinger is the less nuclear option where Death is involved," Monty replied. "The Harbinger is a force to be reckoned with, but pales in comparison with Death—hence the title of Harbinger."

"Dex I can see. You, not so much," I said. "You're not on the edge of psychomage enough. I don't see Ezra choosing you."

"It's unlikely but not impossible," Monty said. "It would depend on the arrangement he has with my uncle as Harbinger. I don't think my uncle would take kindly to my wielding Nemain, or becoming the Harbinger in his stead. He said as much when he let me deal with Uncle Albert."

"Why *you* though?" I asked. The question had been on my mind since Monty had told me about how he'd dealt with Albert. "Why didn't Dex do it himself?"

"He did," Monty said. "Allowing me the use of Nemain was him making himself present as I took the mantle of the Harbinger in his place. I could never wield Nemain on my own, not even for the short amount of time it took to dispatch Albert. It would have driven me mad had I attempted to do so of my own volition. The power required to wield that weapon defies explanation."

"That doesn't explain why it was you."

"I know," he said. "The simple answer is that I requested to do it. The more complicated answer is: My uncle was too close to Albert. Doing something like that would have destroyed him. He loved Albert, looked up to him—even after Albert betrayed him."

"The same way you feel about Dex?"

He nodded.

"Albert betrayed the Montague Code of Mages," Monty said. "The punishment was clear and inevitable. My uncle knew it, as did Albert—it was why he fled to the Black Forest. He knew there was nowhere he could go that he wouldn't be found and brought to account for his actions."

"Nowhere? Really?" I asked. "What about off-plane?"

"There was *nowhere* he could go to escape the Harbinger, or his fate," Monty repeated. "His blood would broadcast his location. This was why it was a blood matter. Only a blood relation could locate him and mete out this particular punishment."

"Why the Black Forest?" I asked. "He could've gone anywhere. I would've hidden under an active volcano. Why make it so easy?"

"The Montagues have ties to the Black Forest that span generations," Monty clarified. "It made sense he would await his end there. He wasn't trying to hide. He was waiting."

"Waiting for the end."

Monty nodded.

"He knew it and my uncle knew it, but I don't think my uncle could have ever brought himself to do it, not even as the Harbinger."

"*That's* why he spared him the first time," I said, finally seeing the obvious. "He cared too much. That's why he gave him a second chance."

"It was unheard of," Monty said. "The Harbinger doesn't give second chances, much less send targets to the Living Library for rehabilitation. My uncle did both."

"Didn't Death get pissed?" I asked. "I mean, Albert was supposed to be eliminated."

"Death is patient, it seems," Monty said. "Eventually, everyone meets Death. He was willing to allow my uncle some latitude in this matter."

"Mighty generous of him," I said. "I guess it helps when you're the Harbinger. Despite all that leniency, Albert still screwed it up."

"The lure of power is a difficult desire to overcome," he said. "I have seen its destructive influence many times over."

"Same here," I said, thinking about the times I'd had to refuse power. "I can see why Dex tried to help Albert."

"My uncle may be many things—unfeeling is not one of them, especially when it comes to his family," Monty said. "And so, I requested the burden of becoming the Harbinger for that instance, to mete out the consequences to Albert, a burden I have no wish to ever carry again."

"I hope it never comes to that," I said, shaking my head. "That weapon is scary. I have faced some scary things in my life lately, but nothing has come close to that weapon when Dex held it."

"I know," Monty said. "I held it. The power and madness it exudes..." He shook his head. "I don't know how my uncle contains it."

"Contains it?" I asked "What do you mean, contains it?"

"Where do you think he keeps a weapon of death like that?" Monty asked. "It's not sitting on a rack somewhere. That would be too dangerous."

"I have an idea," I said, thinking about Ebonsoul. "I'm sure it's not hanging on some weapon rack in his home. I just figured a weapon like that would be better kept somewhere external—maybe with the Morrigan?"

"He keeps Nemain the same way you hold Ebonsoul," he said, confirming my suspicions. "He holds it within, to keep it away from potential abuse. Could you imagine that weapon in the wrong hands?"

"*That* is a scary thought," I said. "How hasn't he gone crazy?"

"He is extraordinarily powerful," Monty said. "Now, to the Keepers of the Arcana." I could tell he wanted to change the subject, so I zigged when he did. I could always push him on the subject later. "What do we know?"

"Older than Verity and powerful mages."

"We know more than that."

"We do?" I asked, at a loss. "If we do, you're going to need to illuminate me, because this is the first time I've heard of them."

"Not surprising," Monty said, looking down at Peaches, who was giving off a low whine while looking at Dex's door. "What's wrong with your creature?"

"He misses Rags," I replied, patting my hellhound on the head, while looking down at his sad face. His puppy dog eyes were next level, capable of making anyone bend to his will. "She'll be back. She barely looked at you while you were next to her. Stop being so dramatic."

"Cecelia's guardian is very focused on her role as protector," Monty said, heading away from Dex's door and back to the kitchen. "Perhaps you can engage your creature in his role as your bondmate? That should distract him sufficiently to reduce his pining for the guardian."

"His role as my bondmate?"

"Surely you don't think his sole purpose is to devour copious amounts of meat while engaging in arbitrary destruction?" Monty said, heading to his room. "Professor Ziller may be reluctant to allow us entry to the Living Library. I'm going to ascertain the fastest way to locate it."

"It's lost?"

"Not exactly. I've been informed that Professor Ziller has increased the security measures since my last visit," he said. "It will take a concerted effort to locate an entrance now."

"I'm sure that has *nothing* to do with your last unauthorized visit there," I said with a small smile. "Maybe he's just making sure things are safe and kept away from nosy mages?"

"Since you have some time, and we are currently *not* fighting for our lives," he said, "why don't you try some basic transposition with your creature? We can discuss the

Keepers further at the Living Library, once I gain authorized access."

"Are you sure he will grant it?"

"He will," Monty said, with a certainty I didn't share. "He will not be so petty as to hold a grudge. He is, after all, a scholar. The pursuit and preservation of truth is his prime motivator."

"If you say so," I said, making a mental note to avoid being next to Monty when he had *that* conversation with Ziller. "You want me to do some basic *what* with Peaches?"

"Do you recall when I mentioned you should be able to access your creature's senses, being his bondmate?"

"Yes, I remember something about using his sense of smell, something like that," I said, recalling the memory. "You want me to try transfiguration with him?"

"Do you want to become a hellhound?"

"What?" I asked. "Why would I want to become a hellhound?"

"It's either that or you want to be transformed into some kind of deity."

"Can you speak English?" I asked, confused. "You were the one that said transfiguration, not me. Now you're talking gods for some reason. No one mentioned deities of any kind."

"I said *transposition*, not transfiguration," he corrected. "Transposition, the act of exchange—in this case, your sense of smell with that of your creature, not your sublime transformation into some spiritual or divine being."

"Oh," I said, glancing at my hellhound. "Transposition. Got it. Maybe you can explain it in case Peaches is unclear— you know, just to make sure."

Monty shook his head.

"Transposition," Monty said, pointing at me, then at Peaches. "You're bonded. With practice you should, in theory, be able to become one along the bond you share. Try something simple, like sharing his sense of smell. What he smells, you should be able to as well."

"Just to be clear, this doesn't mean I end up smelling like him, right?" I asked. "I should be able to smell like him, without actually smelling like him?"

"If done correctly, you should acquire his sense of smell temporarily," he said, giving me a look that clearly said he was beginning to regret suggesting this to me. "You should be able to smell like your creature, without...smelling like your creature." He waved a hand at me as he shook his head. "You know what I mean."

"Is that even a thing?" I asked, glancing at my hellhound dubiously. "Really? Do I even want to? Somehow that sounds like a recipe for disaster."

"It should be perfectly safe," he said. "You are considerably stronger now."

"Should be safe?"

"There is a reason bonded hellhounds and their bondmates are so feared," Monty said. "When they truly become one, it is nearly impossible to stand against them. Think about it. If you possessed a tenth of his actual power—which you don't—as well as the ability to plane-walk at will, to unleash a baleful glare, and to have nearly indestructible skin...?"

"That sounds like something I would never want to face," I finished. "We would be a major threat."

"More so than you are now," he said, leaving the kitchen with another cup of tea and a tray of chocolate McVitie's Digestives. "A word of caution. I have no desire to face a livid Olga...again. Do not destroy our home."

"Understood, no home obliteration," I said with a nod. "Just one thing." I held up a finger. "Do you know how I'm supposed to tap into his sense of smell?"

"I'm not the one bonded to a hellhound," he said. "I

would imagine it would be similar to the way you communicate with him. How do you do that?"

"I just do it," I said. "He's in my head and we can speak to each other."

"Well, I'm sure it's similar," Monty said, creating a large sausage and handing it to me. I immediately had my hellhound's attention. "Instead of getting into his head, try getting into his nose? That should help."

"Get into his nose?" I said, looking from the sausage I held, to my now very focused hellhound. "Are you listening to yourself right now?"

"I don't know how it's done," Monty said with a huff before starting to walk away. "Only practice tapping into his sense of smell, nothing else. That should be safe enough."

"Got it, only tap into his sense of smell," I said, glancing down at my salivating hellhound. "Sounds safe enough. How bad could it be?"

FIVE

Turns out, it was pretty bad.

And dangerous.

I sat down in the conference room with my hellhound, sausage in hand. If I was going to smell what he smelled, I figured we needed an item *to* smell.

A large sausage sounded like the perfect item to get his full cooperation.

That was my first mistake.

I should have known better, but in my defense, there are no manuals on how to initiate the transposition of senses between an ever-hungry hellhound and his bondmate.

<Is that for me?>

<Not yet, no.>

<Why not? Are you going to eat it?>

<No. It's for you, but first we have to—>

<Can I have it now? I never got to show the guardian the Mighty Peaches. I should have been mighty when she was here.>

<Somehow, I don't think Rags impresses easily. Besides, what were you going to do? Use your baleful glare to blow up a car, or punch another hole in the building?>

<Do you think that would have made her understand how mighty I am?>

<Absolutely not. I doubt guardians are impressed by things that could put the people they're supposed to protect in danger. Rags would be upset if you did those things to impress her.>

The last thing I needed was a hellhound going around destroying the city in an attempt to impress his crush. I couldn't even begin to imagine how many agencies and groups would be after us for a rampant hellhound. Somehow, I didn't think telling them he just had a crush on another canine would go over well as an explanation...if they even waited for an explanation before attempting to blast us off the face of the earth.

<I need to find someone powerful to speak to her for me.>

<More powerful than your bondmate? You do realize it's rare to be bonded to a hellhound? It takes a special person to be able to bond to a hellhound, you know.>

<You are special.>

<Thank you. I like to think I am.>

<But you are not special enough.>

<Really? Not special enough?>

<No. She will not consider you very powerful. We had to rescue you. Very powerful people do not need to be rescued.>

Wonderful—now I was being insulted by my lovesick hellhound.

<Well, let's worry about that when we see her again. Right now, I need to smell like you.>

He stepped close and sniffed me.

<You smell like my bondmate. You cannot smell like the Mighty Peaches. You are not a hellhound.>

<I mean—be able to smell like you do. How does the sausage smell to you?>

<Delicious. Can I eat it now?>

<No. I need you to focus. I want to smell the sausage the same way you smell the sausage.>

<Why? Is your nose broken?>

I needed to explain this in a way that he could understand while I distracted him from the sausage I held in my hand. The drool was getting out of control. If he kept it up, I'd have to swim out of the conference room.

<No, but we are bondmates, right? If I can connect to your powers, I can smell the bad people coming to attack us. If I get strong enough, maybe I could even use a baleful glare like your omega beams. With enough practice, maybe I could even become mighty like you.>

He gave me a look and chuffed.

<Your nose is not strong enough, but we can try. If I can eat the sausage after we break your nose.>

<We are not breaking my nose.>

<You are not a hellhound. If you try to be mighty like me, we will break your nose.>

<Let's give it a try.>

He chuffed again and sat on his haunches, staring at me.

<Do you know how to smell with our bond?>

<No, not really. I've finally gotten comfortable being able to speak with you in my head. Do you know how to do this?>

<Yes, but you are not strong enough yet to become mighty.>

<Can you teach me?>

<I can show you, and we can try, but I cannot teach you how to be stronger. You must be stronger—like me.>

<Don't know if I will ever get that strong, but if you can show me what it takes to smell with our bond, that would be enough for now.>

He gave off a low rumble with a growl and then slapped me in the face with his tongue. I wiped the drool from my cheek.

<What was that for?>

<My saliva can heal you.>

<I'm not hurt—I don't need healing.>

<You will.>

I was about to respond when my hellhound, who was already in my head, shoved me to one side. Not physically, but mentally.

It felt like being pushed out of my own head. I could see and sense I was still in my body, but at the same time, I was watching myself through his eyes.

<What is this?>

<I have pulled you into me with our bond.>

<My mind is in your mind?>

<No. Your mind is too soft, too young, to be in my mind. That would break your brain. I am a hellhound. I am letting you see with our bond. Do you understand?>

<Not even a little. I'm seeing me through our bond?>

<Yes. I am helping you because you are not strong enough to do this alone. When you are older and stronger, you will do this without my help, but not now.>

<You sound different in here. Like when you are Peaches XL. You sound smarter.>

<I sound closer to my true self, but I must still take precautions so as not to damage you.>

<Basically, you're making this easy so I can understand you without melting my brain?>

<A rudimentary but accurate description. Brace yourself. I am going to try and senseconnect with you. This may be the painful part.>

<I'm ready.>

<No, bondmate. You are not.>

He was right.

There was nothing that could've prepared me for the sensory bombardment that overwhelmed me in the next moment.

A few seconds later, a very distant part of my brain noticed that I had begun groaning in pain. It was a surreal moment. I saw myself through his eyes. I could see the blood pouring from my nose in a steady flow and distantly felt the pressure on my head.

It felt as if my brain were about to implode. A few moments later, the curse flushed my body immediately with a moderate inferno of heat.

It felt like holding a small sun in the center of my chest as my sense of smell exploded, magnified exponentially as I smelled...everything.

It was beyond anything I could've ever imagined.

SIX

<This isn't good. I'm bleeding.>

<The connection will be severed before any permanent damage is done. What do you smell?>

<Everything. I smell the sausage. It smells delicious.>

<Yes, it does. Do you smell anything else?>

<I smell everything else. I smell me, I smell Monty, I smell the energy in the air around us. I smell your scent. I smell the residual energy of people who have been here in our space. I smell it all. It's amazing. How do you keep it all straight? This is just too much.>

I saw myself raise my hands to my head.

<The angry man is coming. He thinks you are in danger.>

<I probably am. This is beyond sensory overload. I can't process all...all of this. It's...it's too much. Feels like my head is going to explode.>

<It will not, but you are not strong enough...yet. He is here.>

I looked up and saw Monty through Peaches' eyes. His body blazed with an aura of violet and black power. With a gesture of his hand, I felt myself violently shoved back into my body. I was airborne a second later and headed for a painful impact with the nearest wall.

I could still see through Peaches' eyes, but the image was fading, as if the connection was being cut off. It was similar to looking at myself through a split screen, and it nearly gave my brain a spasm. The last thing I saw Monty do was give Peaches a look and point at me as I took flight.

Peaches growled and blinked out.

He reappeared behind me and intercepted my collision with his massive head. I want to say that bouncing off the steel that doubled as his skull was softer than impacting the wall at velocity, but I would be lying.

Hellhound heads are hard—harder than any surface I've ever been slammed or thrown into.

I grunted with pain as Peaches diverted my path into the floor while leaping off the wall with an agility I could never hope to match. I bounced on the floor a few times, before sliding into the opposite wall, coming to a stop with a solid *thump* as I crashed into the very solid, immovable, and sturdy wall.

"Ow," I said, with a groan. "That felt excessive."

I sat up and rubbed my side, feeling for any broken ribs.

"You're bleeding," Monty said, handing me a handkerchief. "How did that happen?"

My vision was still blurry. As everything came into focus, I turned to where I heard Monty with an answer, but then realized he wasn't talking to me. He was looking pointedly at my hellhound, who gave off a low whine as he stared back with enormous puppy dog eyes of innocence.

"It wasn't his fault," I said, getting unsteadily to my feet, feeling around 105. My curse was warming my body and dealing with the damage, as the bruises forming all over screamed at me. "I didn't anticipate the connection to be that strong or that taxing on my body."

"Having no prior experience myself, I didn't think there was any harm in your attempt, considering your growth in power," Monty said, still looking at Peaches. "It would seem I underestimated the power your creature possesses. This bears further investigation."

"Not today it doesn't," I said with a groan. "I need a new brain after that."

"That would be, by all accounts, a marked improvement," he replied, looking at me. "Did you at least manage a transposition?"

"Yes," I said, ignoring the barb. "It blew my mind, almost literally."

"What did you smell?"

"Everything," I said, leaning on the conference table for balance, at least until the room stopped acting like a ship in the middle of stormy seas with the swaying. "I don't even know how to put it into words."

"As challenging as it may seem, give it an attempt," he said. "It will further your understanding of the bond."

"I smelled the sausage," I said, pointing at the sausage on the floor. "I can understand the hellhound fixation with meat a little better now."

"That would make sense," he said. "I'm certain there are nuances we can never hope to achieve with our limited sense of smell compared to that of a hellhound. What else were you able to smell?"

"Energy. I could smell energy signatures: yours, mine, those of people who had visited us. Their signatures left traces here."

"Fascinating," Monty said, narrowing his eyes and looking around the room. "You could smell the signatures of guests, even though they are no longer present?"

"Yes," I said, waving an arm around. "All around us, there are traces of energy signatures. It was...intense, and too much to take in all at once."

"I wonder how long these signatures persist to your creature's senses?" he said. "This could be invaluable, if you could somehow learn how to harness this aspect of your bond. We will need to test the outer parameters of his ability to see how long a signature remains detectable."

"Not before my brain takes a major break," I said. "My brain couldn't handle five minutes of that much sensory overload. Testing the outer limits sounds like an express trip to Haven. Don't think I can stand prolonged exposure to his unleashed senses, at least not through the bond."

"I doubt many could," Monty said. "Your bond facilitated and protected you from any lasting damage."

"No kidding," I said, holding my head with one hand while I wiped my nose with the other. "I have a massive migraine incoming."

"Be thankful that's all you have incoming," he said, narrowing his eyes at me. "Invasive sensory overload has been used as an attack among mages. It can cause severe and permanent brain damage."

"And you felt I should just give it a try with my hellhound?" I asked, incredulous. "Thanks for the warning."

"You are bonded," he said, waving my words away. "The risk to you was minimal, and to your creature, non-existent. It's why I instructed you to focus on one sense and what I assumed was the most powerful he possesses, though I may have been mistaken in that assessment. We really need to have a conversation with Hades about him, your bond, and the potential that exists therein as you grow stronger. This is unexplored territory for me."

"I think that would be an excellent idea," I said. "Maybe we could take a few days off—"

He gave me a look.

"Fine," I continued, raising a hand in surrender. "Let's consider it readiness training. The more we know about the bond and what Peaches and I can or can't do, the better prepared we are when we face some being wanting to rip our faces off because we got on their bad side."

"Or they think we are going dark."

"Or that," I said, glancing at Peaches. "Although, wouldn't my forming an advanced battle duo with a hellhound put me right at the top of the dark immortal list?"

"How so?"

"Well, how many immortals are bonded with a hellhound?"

"You mean outside of Hades and Cerberus?"

"Yes, outside of Hades and Cerberus the nightmare," I said, with a slight shudder at the memory of our recent encounter with the gatekeeper of the Underworld. "Any others?"

"None to my knowledge," he said. "A hellhound—in this case, a scion of Cerberus—would be disqualified as a bondmate for any perceived light immortals, and no one in their right mind would gift a dark immortal a hellhound."

"Why?"

"Aside from the danger? Because of the perception. Hellhounds are viewed as inherently evil. Gifting one to a known dark immortal would be seen as having a premeditated intent to wreak havoc on a massive scale."

"That would be bad," I said. "How bad is it if a hellhound gets out of control?"

He glanced at Peaches for a few seconds before replying.

"Catastrophic," he said. "If it's unbonded, it can be neutralized with overwhelming force. If it's bonded, the pair is exponentially stronger and nearly unstoppable."

"What the hell was Hades thinking?"

"An excellent question," Monty said. "One, I think, you should ask him when you get the opportunity. In any case, the odds of encountering rampaging hellhounds are slim. They aren't being sold in a pet store. The only way to acquire a hellhound is to go to the source."

"Cerberus?"

"Hades," Monty said. "The god, not the place. He was the one who gave you your creature. Presently, it is the only way to get another hellhound. They aren't exactly roaming the streets."

"Does Verity really assume Peaches is evil because he's a hellhound?" I asked in disbelief. "You must be joking. He's the sweetest hellhound I know."

"But not the only hellhound you know," Monty corrected. "Would you describe Cerberus as a sweet hellhound?"

"Only from a distance," I said. "Several planes worth of distance."

"It's not just a perception," Monty continued. "Hellhounds aren't necessarily evil, but in the distant past they have been bonded to mages who have exploited their power for nefarious deeds."

"So it's more than a PR problem," I said. "Hellhounds have a shady history."

"Closer to black, not shady," Monty said. "Every act involving a hellhound is tainted by death and destruction on an immense scale. It's another reason they are feared on sight. The stories of their deeds precedes them and have only been embellished over the years. That stigma will follow your creature, and *you* endlessly."

"That explains Verity's animosity toward him."

"And you as his bondmate," he said. "If he's evil, then it stands to reason that his bondmate must be evil as well."

"They're just going to pass judgment without even getting to know us?" I asked as the anger rose. "How is that even remotely fair?"

It's not," he said with a nod, "but we are dealing with a

group mired in tradition and bias. They will not embrace change willingly. We will have to teach them."

"Wow, we're off to a great start by electrocuting Edith," I said, shaking my head, realizing the problem. "Somehow I don't see them losing the dark-immortal narrative after the light show at the Cloisters."

"True, that does make it more of a challenge."

"More of a challenge?" I asked. "They accuse us of going dark, so what do we do to change their minds? We unleash a stormblood—"

"*You* unleashed the stormblood; Quan and I were there as support in that moment, just to be clear," he said, interrupting me. "Details do matter."

"Let's just say it was a group effort, done by the group they declared as going dark."

"We hardly classify as a *group*," he argued. "Quan, you, and I hardly comprise a group—persons of interest, perhaps, but not a group."

I stared at him and shook my head.

"Semantics," I said after a pause. "Bottom line is, they called us dark and we did one of the darkest things possible. We electrified Edith to dust."

"What course of action do you think we should have taken?" he asked. "Edith wasn't there to exercise her diplomatic skills. She was intent on killing us."

"I know," I said, resigning myself to the truth. "I'm just saying they are going to view us as dark no matter what we do or say."

"I don't believe we can do anything to change Verity's opinion of us," he said. "We must operate under the premise that they consider us a threat and act accordingly to defend both ourselves and those close to us."

"Which means learning exactly what I can do through my

bond with Peaches," I said. "I think we do need to pay Hades a visit."

"Yes," he said. "Though somehow I don't think Hades will be as forthcoming as we wish him to be."

"Why wouldn't he share openly?" I asked, rubbing Peaches' massive head as he padded over to where I stood. "The last thing anyone wants is a dangerous hellhound and his bondmate on the loose."

"That is a rational assessment, but not one I completely agree with."

"What are you saying?"

"Not everyone benefits from you learning more about your bond with your creature," he said. "To do so means you would have to increase in knowledge and power."

"You think Hades is one of those who would prefer I stayed in the dark?"

"I don't know," he answered. "That's what concerns me."

"Me too," I said. "Did you locate an entrance to the Living Library?"

"I did," he said with a nod, glancing down at Peaches. "We're going to need to visit the Hellfire Club."

"What for?" I asked, warily. "You think Eric wants to see us these days?"

"No choice. Ziller has made access…difficult. We can use the Hellfire to leapfrog the defenses, gain entrance to the Argosy Bookstore, and enter the Living Library proper."

"Ziller will be overjoyed at that move."

"Actually, I rather think he will be livid at the unauthorized intrusion," Monty said, "but needs must."

"This is going to royally suck, isn't it?"

"In a word, yes," Monty said, "but we've faced worse. You've just narrowly avoided having your brain liquefied. I'd say after that, anything else that happens today is a positive."

"I need coffee," I said. "No more words or thinking until then."

I headed to the kitchen with my hellhound in tow.

<Can I have the sausage? I'm starving.>

<Of course you can. Bring it to the kitchen while I make some coffee. I'll drink, you eat, and I'll try to get my brain back in working order after that Vulcan nose meld of ours.>

He padded silently after me, leaving a small river of drool behind him as he refrained from inhaling the sausage until we entered the kitchen.

SEVEN

"Why do we have to do this two-step to get to Ziller?" I asked. "Can't we just activate a door from here?"

Monty shook his head.

"Under normal circumstances, yes," he said. "However, these are not normal circumstances."

"When are we ever under normal circumstances?"

"A valid point. These are extraordinary circumstances, to say the least," Monty rectified. "Ziller rarely shuts off direct access to the Living Library."

I nodded.

"How much flak are Erik and the Hellfire Club going to catch if we do this?" I asked. "Wouldn't it be better to avoid getting him involved with Verity?"

"As the leader of the mage contingent in the Dark Council, Erik is, and has been, involved for some time now," Monty said, rubbing his chin. "But you make a strong case for minimal involvement. Our presence at the Hellfire will bring him unneeded and unwanted attention."

"Can we avoid it?"

He thought for few seconds.

"Yes," Monty said, with a slow nod. "There is a way."

"I'm not going to like it, am I?"

"Not entirely, no."

"Does it involve blood, or you going so far over to the dark side that I'll be forced to bring you back by nearly ending you?"

"Absolutely not," Monty said. "I am not, and never will be, a dark mage—any more than you are a dark immortal."

"Just making sure," I said, raising a hand in surrender. "It's always better to ask these things up front so it doesn't come back later as lethal fine print."

"Wise, but unnecessary in this case."

"This method you're going to use, does it involve the elder rune you know?"

"Yes," he said, after a moment of hesitation. "My main concern is that my use of the rune will get the Keepers' attention this time."

"Why? What would be different this time?"

"This time I would be using the elder rune to force an entry into the Living Library," he said. "Think of how that might be perceived."

I gave it some thought and then realized what he meant. If he used to elder rune to gain access to the Living Library—the same place that was currently on lockdown because he had managed to get into a room he wasn't supposed to and had then "borrowed" a rune—it would look like he was going back for more of the same.

"Shit, it looks bad. Is there another way to get into Ziller's place without using the elder rune? Because if you're going to do what I think you're going to do, we are going to step into a world of pain."

"I could try to open a portal directly to the Living Library. However, with the upgraded defenses, that won't work...not without reinforcing the cast with the elder rune," he said. "I can bypass the Hellfire entirely, but to enter the Argosy Bookstore, I would need to use the rune."

"I doubt that was an accident," I said. "Ziller probably set it up that way."

"Most likely the Keepers were behind the fortified defenses," he said. "They don't have to go looking for me, even though I'm certain they will, eventually."

"It's an early-warning system," I said. "If you really want to access the Living Library, you need to use the elder rune, which will probably give them a heads up."

"It would seem so," Monty said. "I do have to applaud the ingenuity. It's a creative solution that resolves several problems at once. It deters me from using the elder rune a second time, while maintaining the integrity of the Living Library. It's quite elegant."

"Except it's not really a deterrent, is it? At least not to you."

"No, not much of one."

"So we have to assume there will be someone watching the Argosy."

"At the very least," he said. "Like I said, elegant."

"We don't need elegant, we need access," I said. "How about this Treadwell person Dex mentioned? Can he help us?"

"Not without a cost."

"Everything has a cost," I said. "If he can get us in without letting the Keepers know about it, it may be worth it."

"With Sebastian, the costs were always too high."

"If it means not facing a Keeper, can we pay this cost?"

"As I said, knowing Sebastian, the cost will be undesirable. Let's reserve that option as a last resort."

"I'm starting to feel that you don't like him," I said. "What's the history between you two?"

"I'll tell you on the way," Monty said, pulling on one of the sleeves of his jacket. "We need to pay the Argosy a visit to see if this alternative is even possible."

"Scout mission?"

"Surveillance would be the prudent course of action here," he said. "I have no intention of walking into a trap. Treadwell has never been known for his subtlety."

I knew that every time he pulled on his sleeve mid-conversation, he was either upset or nervous about a particular topic. Since he didn't seem any angrier than usual, it meant he really wanted to avoid the whole Treadwell topic of conversation.

Seeing as how I was a good friend, I couldn't possibly let him deal with this nervousness alone. It was my job as a friend—and even deeper, as his Aspis—to help him confront difficult dangers, even when those dangers were rooted in the memories of his past.

I did what any good friend would do: I pushed his buttons.

"So, this Sebastian," I said as we headed out of the space, "you two go back all the way to the Golden Circle?"

"Yes," Monty said as we stepped into the hallway outside. "I've known him my entire life."

"Long time," I said with a nod, trying to read between the lines. "How long...exactly?"

"Long enough that I'd rather not discuss it at the moment."

There was something he wasn't sharing. The fact that Dex could reach out to this Sebastian and get him to cooperate, when Monty couldn't, seemed important.

Monty turned to activate the defenses on the door as my hellhound bumped my leg with his shoulder. Getting tackled by an ogre was probably gentler than his not-so-subtle nudges.

<Stop bumping into me. You keep that up, I'm going to need a hip replacement.>

<I didn't bump into you. I was getting your attention.>

<By trying to knock my hip out of alignment?>

<If you ate more meat, my bumps wouldn't move you. You would be mighty, like me.>

<I'll work on it. Why do you need my attention? You're hungry?>

<I'm always hungry. I'm a growing hellhound. There is a dark smell outside.>

<A dark smell?>

<A dark smell that smells bad.>

<Is it getting closer?>

<No, it is not moving.>

<I'll tell Monty. Keep your nose on it. If it starts to get closer, let me know.>

"Peaches is smelling a dark smell," I said before I realized what I'd said. "Any chance you would have an idea what it could be?"

"A dark smell?" Monty asked, still focused on the door. "It has been my experience that smells do not possess hues or colors. Is this his classification of an energy signature? Is this smell getting closer?"

"Not yet, no."

"Then the best course of action would be to monitor the proximity of said smell," he said, finishing on the door. "We can't take action on a dark smell unless a dark being materializes to accompany that smell."

"I told him to keep his nose on it," I said. "If it changes, he'll let me know."

He nodded as we stepped away from the door and headed downstairs to the garage.

"If you had managed to master your transposition, you could have smelled whatever it is he's smelling," Monty said as we descended. "Your experience could have given us more insight to what kind of threat a dark smell presents."

"You expected me to master that skill on the first try?"

"You're bonded," he said. "It should be simple for you at this point—like breathing."

"I hardly think it's that easy," I said. "I'm pretty sure some training is involved. I'll ask Hades when I see him again."

"It could be a deficiency in your brainpower," he added. "Perhaps if you concentrate harder?"

"That's your solution? Concentrate harder?"

"I say it's worth a try."

"Considering you're not bonded to a hellhound," I said, "I'm going to file your suggestion under *things not to try* unless desperate."

"It makes the most logical sense."

"Tell you what: when my brain gets stronger, I'll get right on smelling like my hellhound," I said. "Until then, we're going to have to deal with dark smells."

"We will have to remain vigilant then. It's most likely Verity waiting for us to be vulnerable to strike."

"How about we don't give them the chance?"

"The logistics make it impossible, unless we remain enclosed in a secure location for the duration of the time we are being targeted."

"A vacation off-plane sounds like it could be a secure location," I suggested. "We could always visit Hades. I'm sure Elysium is excellent this time of year."

"I doubt that changing weather is a factor in the underworld," he said, "unless you factor in the impact a lake of lava and flame has on ideal vacationing weather."

"Elysium had perfect weather when we went there."

"Because it's not subject to atmospheric influence. I'm certain that is all Hades' doing. Elysium is designed to be a type of paradise, unlike the area Cerberus guards."

"I doubt Verity could follow us into Elysium. Would they?"

"Unlikely. We only managed it because Orethe was with us," he said. "I don't know how to travel to her home. I would imagine that, now that it's yours, there must be some way for you to access Elysium."

"Sounds like a perfect place to lay low."

"Orethe's home is still an unknown, however," he said. "We don't know what defenses it may or may not have. It would require a thorough investigation before using it as your getaway bungalow. Preferably with Hades' supervision."

"That and the fact that I don't know how to teleport," I said. "Maybe I can have Peaches plane-walk me there?"

"A viable option, but if it doesn't work, you could end up irrevocably lost between planes," he said. "Further testing is needed."

"I'm not liking the *irrevocably lost between planes* part," I said as we reached the Dark Goat. "Can we test this without risking getting lost forever?"

"Yes, I'll fit it into the schedule...right between dealing with Verity agents—who are trying to kill us, by the way—and evading discovery by the Keepers of the Arcana, who possess near or greater levels of Archmage power. This, all as we break into a book store that is most likely guarded," he said, getting into the passenger side as I held the suicide door open for my hellhound, Sprawly the Sprawlificent. "I'm sure if we juggle the times, we can fit in testing an unknown location in Hades for potentially deadly traps."

"No need to get snippy," I said, getting behind the wheel. "I was just asking if we can test the method of transport before going there."

"I am not snippy," he snapped. "I am merely pointing out that we have other priorities at the moment. Chief among them is staying alive."

"I'm totally behind *that* priority," I said, starting the engine of the Dark Goat. "Where is this Argosy Bookstore?"

"59th Street between Park and Lexington Avenues," he said, sitting back and closing his eyes. "It's the oldest book store in the city. Ziller chose it as a portal link decades ago. We run a risk using it, but it's the best chance we have at the moment."

"A risk? Why?"

"If you were a Keeper tasked with protecting elder runes, what would you be watching?" he asked. "Where would your focus be?"

I gave it thought for a moment listening to the engine. It settled into a throaty purr as I formed a response.

"Ingress and egress," I said. "All the entrances and exits that could possibly access the elder runes."

"Of which Argosy is one of the oldest," he said. "So old, it's rarely used."

"You're hoping it's only being watched, not guarded?"

"Precisely. I'm counting on its lack of use to buy us enough time to get into the Living Library without drawing attention to ourselves." He glanced behind us. "And, although it's difficult for your creature to blend in, I have a plan."

"This plan seems thin to nonexistent," I said. "I doubt the Keepers are stupid. They'll have someone watching the book store."

"I never said they were stupid, just lax," Monty said, as we pulled out of the Moscow garage. "I'm counting on a modicum of complacency."

"What if they are on their toes, especially after you borrowed that latest elder rune?"

"Let's burn that bridge when we get to it," he said. "I just hope we don't encounter any Arcanists on the way there."

"This is so going to hurt," I said as the Dark Goat roared out of the Moscow.

"I'm afraid you're correct in your assessment, but what is a little pain?" he said. "By now, pain is a firm and familiar companion in our lives. We must deal with this and find a way to overcome these obstacles. We can do this."

I didn't share his optimism.

EIGHT

We couldn't do this.

I drove uptown and stopped on Park Avenue—several blocks away from the bookstore, but still within its line of sight. Monty noticed the first Arcanist as we rolled to a stop.

"It would be best if we remained in the vehicle," Monty said, narrowing his eyes at the man standing outside the bookstore entrance. "The defensive runes on the vehicle can work to partially obscure our energy signatures from that Arcanist."

"You can't mask us if we step out of the Dark Goat?"

"The initial energy it would take to mask us would reveal our location," he said, still focused on the Arcanist. "That would defeat the purpose of the mask, don't you think?"

I nodded.

"See? This is what happens when you go around messing with elder runes," I said, glancing at the Arcanist. "It's getting so you can't even walk in the street without attracting attention."

Monty turned to face me with a raised eyebrow. I braced

myself, knowing he was getting ready to enter university-professor mode.

"Are you insinuating *I'm* the reason a mask would be ineffective?" he asked. "That somehow *I* am the cause of the inability to cast an effective mask on us?"

"You have been extra magey since you borrowed that elder rune," I said. "I noticed your signature had increased back at the Moscow. Even Olga noticed."

"It has increased somewhat, but I would attribute that more to the Restoring Palm than to the acquired knowledge of the elder rune," he explained, looking pensive. "The elder rune has not significantly bolstered my energy signature, which is curious, now that I think of it."

"You're saying the elder rune *isn't* the reason?" I countered. "I'm not the mage who borrowed some ancient rune that has everyone agitated. If it's not the elder rune, then what is it?"

He stared at me for a good three seconds. I knew it was coming. All he was missing was a lecture hall and a lectern.

"Let me enlighten you as to why we are currently facing this difficulty," he started, entering full-blown university professor mode. "*You* happen to be bonded to a hellhound."

"I'm aware," I said, motioning to the back seat, where the Sensei of Sprawl had conquered the backseat in a spectacular capturing of territory, stretching from door to door. "It's not like I can hide him. He doesn't shrink to pocket size, you know."

"That you know of. In all your years walking this earth, how many hellhounds have you encountered, before you were bonded?"

"Before? None. It's not like packs of hellhounds are out there roaming the streets."

"My point exactly."

I shook my head.

"What point?" I asked. "That I'm the one attached to an enormous hellhound?"

"You're the only person I know, outside of Hades, who is bound to a hellhound. That sort of thing tends to get noticed. The usual reactions are fear, and an acute inclination to destroy said hellhound."

"Peaches also happens to be the best hellhound I know."

"Yes, out of a vast pool of two hellhounds, the other being his sire, who guards the underworld, I'd say your sample size is a little on the minuscule side."

"Doesn't matter," I said. "Out of all the hellhounds I know, he's the best."

"Right, let's continue."

I immediately regretted pointing out my theory of the elder rune being the reason it was hard to mask us.

"Do we have to?"

"Out of the two of us, which one is currently marked by a goddess of Death and Destruction?" he asked, ignoring me. "A goddess of considerable power, I might add."

"Hey, Kali is also the goddess of creation," I countered. "She just has some bad PR."

"Bad PR?" he said. "You're saying she has an image problem? Not that she is authentically one of the most feared goddesses in any of the pantheons?"

"Definitely a PR issue," I said, with a nod. "Also, holding a severed head in all those images where she's wielding an arsenal isn't doing her any favors. Then she's stepping on some guy and it looks like she's gloating. That's going to upset some people."

"That *guy* is Shiva, her consort," he answered. "You recall —the one who tried to kill us?"

"My point exactly," I said. "If they're a couple, she could

have an image of them having a chat over coffee or something. Stepping on his head is a bad look."

"A bad look? That is your assessment of the imagery depicting her?"

"Well, if we're going into detail, what's with the arms?"

"The arms?"

"She has so many arms; it's overkill, if you ask me," I explained. "If she needs that many arms, would it kill her if one of them held a cake or a pie or something? She really should upgrade her look. Everybody loves cake. The red tongue sticking out isn't winning her any points, either. That's just creepy."

"Maybe you should bring that up the next time you meet her," he said, shaking his head slightly. "I'm sure she'd appreciate your constructive criticism."

"Pass," I said, shaking my head. "She doesn't seem big on feedback from those who thwart her five-thousand-year-old plans."

"Let's move on to another topic, then."

"How about we don't?"

There was no stopping him now.

He had entered full-blown professor mode. Only a major explosion of some kind could stop him at this point, and even then, I think he would only pause to explain the cause of the explosion and then continue.

"One of us is in possession of a necromantic seraphic siphon," he continued. "Would you like to guess who that would be?"

"At least my weapon doesn't go around wailing all the time," I said defensively. "Ebonsoul is a quiet weapon of death, as all weapons should be. You don't hear it sobbing all over the place."

"Your weapon is also part of a set in which a bloodthirsty psychotic goddess resides in a sword—the counterpart to your blade," he said. "I'm sensing a trend here with you and dangerous goddesses."

"I didn't know that when Ebonsoul was gifted to me there were major strings attached which would only get worse over time," I answered. "None of that was *my* doing. I also did not ask Orethe to make my weapon the Wikiblade of necromancy."

"You—also, as a result of your interaction with the earlier mentioned Death goddess—are currently immortal."

"Your point?" I said, irritated. "The correct term is *cursed alive*. I didn't ask for any of that."

"What about the dragon blood?"

"What dragon blood?"

"I distinctly recall the words, 'I can hear purple.' Does that ring any bells?"

"Not really, no," I said, focusing on some dust particles on the dash. "Are you sure that was me?"

"Those words were followed by, 'Purple is a pretty color. It smells so purple.' Then you started calling me...Trissy, at which point, I thought you had lost what little mind you had left. *That* dragon blood."

"Oh, *that* dragon blood," I said. "The transfusion with Rocky. It must've slipped my mind."

"I'm certain a particular enclave of dragons hasn't forgotten about our exploits with their kind," he said. "The fact that *your* blood has mingled with dragon blood makes you particularly interesting to them."

"Again, out of my control," I said. "I didn't tell Roque to cut himself with Ebonsoul and then slice my hand to join our blood. What the hell was he thinking? He was losing it, that's what it was."

"Be that as it may, your choices have consequences," he said, looking across the street at the Arcanist again. "Those consequences make *you* much harder to mask than a mage who has acquired an elder rune. At your current level, masking you is a near impossibility. Your energy signature, along with your blood, is a beacon. Dira didn't find *us* across an ocean because of me or an elder rune. She is hunting you."

"Thanks for the reminder."

"Of course," he said. "It's my pleasure to keep you aware of the threats we face and pose, *Aspis*."

I gave him a look that said: *You don't need to rub it in*.

"You may be right, but we *both* share the stormblood thanks to York, and that was the thing that really got Verity's attention. So no matter what you say, the Arcanist over there isn't looking for me. He's looking for *you*. That's my theory, and I'm sticking with it."

I turned to focus on the Arcanist, who was doing his best to blend into the background and failing.

The man was standing a few feet away from the entrance to the Argosy Bookstore, which, judging from the window lettering, occupied an entire six-story townhouse.

"That whole building is the bookstore?" I asked, somewhat surprised. "Six floors in the middle of the city?"

"Seven," Monty said. "The Argosy contains seven floors."

I counted the floors and then, just to make sure, I counted them again.

"I'm only seeing six," I said. "Is there a floor there I can't see?"

"Yes," he said. "Between the third and fourth, there is a secret floor which contains some of the rarest magical tomes ever housed outside of the Living Library."

I narrowed my eyes at the building and couldn't see any hint of the secret floor.

"The place must cost a fortune," I said, looking at the building again.

"It was founded a few years before the Great Depression

and is privately owned," he said. "The cost has never been an issue, due to the service the bookstore provides."

"Has it always been a passage to the Living Library?"

"Since its inception, there was an agreement to have a connecting passage to the Library," Monty said. "Some mages or scholars who would rather avoid the oversight associated with the Living Library would use the Argosy for their research."

"I see," I said. "That explains the Arcanist outside trying, unsuccessfully, to blend in."

The Arcanist kept looking at his phone and then looking up and around as if lost. There were a few flaws in his cover.

He was trying too hard to look lost, for one, scanning the area and looking up too often to really be paying attention to his phone.

The other tell was the suit. He clearly belonged to the mage couture group. It wasn't quite a Zegna, but I was sure it was a vintage Armani, with the shoes to match. Verity agents didn't have the wardrobe to dress that well, which left the upscale librarians as the major possibility.

"So we're going with *Arcanist*? Really?" I asked, doubtful. "Are you sure that's what they are called?"

"Rune Researcher doesn't seem to fit," Monty said, "and Assistant to the Keeper of the Arcana is a mouthful. Arcanist encapsulates their position and purpose."

"If you say so," I said. "Are you sure he's an Arcanist?"

"Judging from the energy signature, I would presume so," Monty said, still glancing at the man. "He's not a Verity agent —this person reads differently, stronger than the rank and file."

"Dresses differently, too," I said. "Verity agents never dress like that. This guy's suit looks tailor-made; most of the Verity wardrobes I've seen look off the rack."

"There appears to be only one of him," Monty said,

glancing around the area. "Verity would have had the area flooded with personnel by now if they suspected we would be here."

"True and Verity agents rarely travel solo," I said, looking at the man doing his best to stand nonchalantly near the entrance of the Argosy Bookstore. "You think there are more inside?"

"Hard to say, but I would assume so," Monty said. "He may be there just to report to the Keeper assigned this task."

"Do we know how many Keepers there are?"

"I was hoping to glean that information from Professor Ziller," Monty said. "But according to my uncle, even facing one Keeper is facing one Keeper too many."

"Would be good to know how many total, though," I said. "I have a feeling going after these runes may get all the Keepers riled up in a lethal sort of way."

"He may just be there as a deterrent," Monty said. "His presence is certainly curtailing *our* activity."

"Or he may be there to confront us himself," I said. "His signature feels strong. Can you tell how strong he is? Can you face him?"

"It's not a matter of if I *can* face him," Monty said, narrowing his eyes in the direction of the Arcanist. "It's a matter of if I *should*. He could be part of a tripwire force."

"That would be bad," I said, still focused on the Arcanist. "He would slow us down just enough for a Keeper to get here and smush us to paste."

"Colorful, but accurate," Monty said. "I have no intention to be rendered to paste—smushed or otherwise. We need to find another way in, or create a diversion to allow us access."

I was about to answer when a mountain of a man appeared next to the driver's side of the Dark Goat, blocking my view of, well, everything.

"Whoa," I said, reaching for Grim Whisper as I pulled

back from the window. Even Monty was startled, which was rare—I had never seen Monty look this surprised. He placed a hand on mine to prevent me from drawing my weapon. "What? Are you not seeing the mobile land mass that just appeared next to us?"

He quickly composed himself and stared at the giant next to us. It was impossible for someone so large to move so silently without alerting any of us. Even Peaches gave off a low rumble at the presence of the Large Man.

The Large Man tapped the window gently with a knuckle and made a motion for me to roll it down. I was certain he could probably lift the Dark Goat and take it, and us, with him if he really wanted to.

"My name is Ox," the large man said, his voice a deep gravelly bass. "Mr. Treadwell would like a word with you both."

Ox was dressed in the uber-maximum XL gray suit version of a mageiform. His white shirt was accented by a dark gray tie with ivory accents down its length. If Ox ever felt generous, he could donate his suit and have about a dozen standard-sized suits made from it.

It took me a moment to recognize the designer, because I was in mild shock from the amount of fabric that had been needed just to create the jacket, much less the shirt and pants. I realized he was wearing a Tom Ford, and wearing it well. I sensed the softly glowing runes before seeing the silver symbols in the fabric.

I stared up at him while he looked down at me with a smile. The smile wasn't threatening, but then again, people who created their own gravitational wells could afford to be friendly—at least, right before unleashing some world-ending power and obliterating you.

"Has Sebastian forgotten how to use a telephone?" Monty asked, peering up at Ox. "I'm certain he has my number."

"He said you'd say that," Ox replied. "He informed me to tell you that this requires an actual meeting, since a certain Dexter Montague made a point of asking."

"Of course he did," Monty said, his expression becoming dark.

"How did you do that?" I asked. "Appear without giving any warning?"

"I'm light on my feet," Ox said. "My apologies for the sudden appearance." He glanced over at the Argosy. "It would seem you are about to make a mistake. We would like to prevent that from happening. Would you be so kind as to follow me?"

"Follow you where?" I managed, once I found my voice. "How did you even find us? More importantly, how many herds of sheep did it take to make that one suit?"

Ox smiled at me.

"You have a keen eye," he said. "What you fail to see are the Keeper's several assistants, as well as the Arcanists masked inside the Argosy—which is your current destination, yes?"

"You are well informed," Monty said. "Where exactly would Sebastian like us to meet?"

"The White House," Ox said. "Do you know of it?"

"I do," Monty answered. "I take it he is back in the country, then."

"As of yesterday morning, yes," Ox said. "Made a special trip back for you."

"I'm flattered," Monty said dryly. "I'm certain that's my uncle's doing."

"You didn't tell me Sebastian worked with the President." I hissed under my breath. "Since when do we get involved with the government?"

"We don't," Monty said. "The White House is the current

Treadwell Headquarters located on Central Park West and 86th Street, not the presidential residence."

"Oh, *that* White House," I said, turning to the human wall standing next to us. "You plan on carrying us there, or should I drive?"

"Funny," Ox said with another smile. "Mr. Montague knows where it is. It should take you approximately twenty minutes to get there from here. Take Park Avenue to 86th and head west, crossing the park using the 85th Street traverse."

He knew the city.

"What if I wanted to stop for a cup of coffee on the way?"

"My associates behind you would be most displeased if you attempted to lead them on an unauthorized tour of the city."

"Your associates?" I asked, looking around. "What associates?"

The whine of powerful engines suddenly filled the air.

I turned and saw half a dozen black motorcycles glide in behind us in a V formation. They came to a stop several feet behind the Dark Goat with their engines running.

"*Those* associates," Ox said. "I request you don't make their life more difficult. We know this vehicle is nearly indestructible," he continued, tapping the top of the Dark Goat. "You, on the other hand, are not."

Seeing as how my curse wasn't common knowledge, it didn't surprise me that he thought I wasn't nearly indestructible. It was also clear he hadn't collected enough information on my hellhound who was—at least according to me—mostly indestructible.

I wasn't about to correct him, though.

"I'm guessing that's a no on the coffee?"

"Amenities will be provided at the meeting," Ox said.

"Please use the route I've provided. Deviation from it will result in a less-than-pleasant response."

Again, another smile. This one wasn't as friendly. He stepped away, nodded to the lead rider of the motorcade behind us, and then disappeared from sight.

The group of motorcycles waited for us to move.

NINE

It seemed we didn't have a choice.

"How did he do that?" I asked. "I didn't even sense a disturbance in the Force when he appeared next to us, trying to give me a heart attack, much less right now as he blinked out."

"His skill in the temporal discipline is quite high, as is his ability to mask," Monty said as he narrowed his eyes and gazed at the entrance of the Argosy. "He managed to keep from drawing the Arcanist's attention as he spoke to us. In addition, I would not be surprised if the riders behind us were enhanced in some way."

I glanced back at the motorcade and narrowed my eyes to see their enhancement and only saw…six motorcycles through squinty eyes. Not much enhancement that I could see.

"So you're saying I shouldn't try to lose them in traffic?"

"I doubt you could," Monty said. "These are Treadwell's people, which means they are elite riders. We are not losing them without actively trying to destroy their vehicles. Besides, it would be rude."

"Rude?" I said. "This whole *invitation* feels more like a

threat of violence than an invitation to a meeting. He would like a word? Who even speaks like that?"

"You need to work it backwards," Monty said. "Sebastian is only reaching out because of my uncle Dexter."

"Which means?"

"It means he would hardly pay us any attention if not for my uncle's request," Monty clarified. "Otherwise, we would hardly register on his radar. He occupies himself with other matters."

"How is my evading our escort rude, though?"

"If we try to lose this escort, it would reflect poorly on my uncle, not on Sebastian, who reached out to meet with us."

"By sending a moving mountain and half a dozen motorcycle assassins to escort us," I said. "Because nothing says, '*Welcome, let's be friends,*' like six riders sliding up from behind while a giant gently menaces you."

"Be that as it may, we would show poor form if we were to attempt to lose them or attack without provocation. My uncle would be displeased. Would you like to explain to him how you felt the need to detonate them to him?"

"No need to escalate that quickly," I said, shaking my head. "This isn't a scene from Mad Max. I just wanted to know if we could lose them without violence."

"To allow you a coffee stop?"

"Very few things are more important than coffee," I said. "For the proper functioning of the brain, there is no greater priority than javambrosia."

"Except tea, of course," he countered. "Let's go see what Sebastian wants. He may have some useful information for us regarding the runes."

"How would he even know about them?"

"Most mages know about them; they just don't entertain the thought of locating, much less using, them."

"Right," I said. "Only those *special* mages with a death wish actually want to find and use them?"

"I want to find them," he said. "Using them is another matter entirely. In any case, Sebastian has resources. He may be of assistance in locating them."

"He certainly has the hardware," I said, glancing in the rearview mirror at the half dozen motorcycles behind us. "Those bikes are Ducatti Superlegerra V4s. They're fast, but they're one nudge away from becoming carbon-fiber street art if I bump them with the larger mass that is the menace of the Dark Goat."

"I thought we had concluded violence was not a strategy in this instance."

"Just keeping the options open," I said. "They're pretty, but all that carbon fiber is no match for the Dark Goat's steel. You know, just in case they get twitchy."

"All of those motorcycles are runed," Monty said, glancing behind us. "I doubt it's Cecil's handiwork, but I would imagine that they are runed to withstand most conventional damage. I don't intend on unleashing orbs of destruction at them. Do you plan on using your magic missile?"

"Not at the moment," I said. "That would probably attract too much attention."

"Agreed. Let's keep the very expensive motorcycles and their riders intact, and head over to Sebastian without incident," Monty said, still glancing behind us. "Try not to speed on the way there."

As I pulled away from the sidewalk and headed uptown on Park Avenue, our motorcade kept pace right behind us. I took stock of the situation and several thoughts came to me at once.

"I've been thinking—"

"Are you ill?"

"Oh, hilarious, mage humor," I said. "Why is it that most mages lack an *actual* sense of humor?"

"I have a fully developed sense of humor," Monty said, to my disbelief. "It just happens to be elevated beyond most. What you would find humorous would barely register for me, and vice versa."

"That, and the fact that you're English, makes me doubt you have *any* kind of humor," I said. "Each one individually—mages and the English—aren't known for their senses of humor, but an English mage? I think anything that passes for humor with you must be elevated beyond this dimension."

"I disagree," he said, raising a finger. "For example, I find the confluence of events we currently find ourselves in the midst of quite humorous."

"You...what?" I asked, confused. "You find us being chased by Verity, for a death sentence, mind you, as well as being gently menaced by this Treadwell character into a meet, humorous?"

"Well, there's much more to it than that. Don't forget your standing issue with Kali; being her Marked One is no small threat."

"You find all this humorous?"

"In a very profound sense, yes," he said, after giving it some thought. "You yourself have accused me of taking myself too seriously, but there is a deep humor here, don't you think?"

"No. No, I don't think," I snapped. "There's nothing humorous about any of these situations. I don't even understand how you can find anything remotely humorous about any of this."

"That's because you're taking yourself too seriously."

"Because the situation we're in is serious!" I said, raising my voice. "Are you not seeing that?"

"It reminds me of something Master Yat used to say during my training."

I took a deep breath and let it out slowly before I spoke.

"What did he say?" I asked. "Life is too short to take seriously? Or something else very zen-like as he *thwapped* you with his staff?"

"No, this was back during the war, when I was significantly younger and took everything much too seriously, including myself."

"What did he say?"

"Life is but a heartbeat of time: too short not to laugh, too long not to smile."

"Typical Yat. That makes absolutely no sense," I said. "And for the record, I have not witnessed you ever laughing or even breaking into a large enough smile to remove the scowl from your face."

"It's a state of being," he said, with a scowl. "I'm smiling even now...on the inside."

"I'll keep that in mind," I said. "I'll have to rethink my opinion of you...maybe even give you a new title: Mage Montague, Master of Mirth. That work for you?"

"Absolutely not," he snapped. "There will be no titles bestowed upon my person, not now, not ever."

"Right," I said slowly. "I can totally feel that humorous side shining through. Wow, how did I ever miss it?"

"Titles have a way of bringing out the worst in people," he said. "Apologies. I have seen how they can transform personalities, and not for the better."

"Got it, no titles...ever."

"Thank you," he said. "There are a few things I need to share with you about Sebastian, things you should know."

"Before we get into that—I've been thinking, and I have a serious question."

"Which is?"

"What are you going to do with them?"

"You may need to clarify. Do with what?"

"The elder runes? What are you going to do if you find them?"

"*When* I find them," he corrected. "I don't understand the question."

"What is your intention? If you use them, everyone will be after us, but just the fact that you are looking for them is going to bring us major heat. This sounds totally lose-lose. What are you going to do if—when—you find them?"

"Safeguard them, I suppose," he said, his voice pensive. "Make them accessible to other mages seeking the knowledge."

"Is that such a good idea?" I asked, concerned. "Don't you think some knowledge should be kept secret?"

"When something like these elder runes is forbidden, it creates—especially within mages—a covetous desire to acquire the knowledge," he said. "It has the opposite effect of keeping them hidden."

"Not just in mages: it's human nature, wanting what you can't have," I agreed. "But aren't these runes hidden because they're too dangerous?"

"Too dangerous for whom?" he scoffed. "Those who determine things need to be hidden from others usually fail to apply those same restrictions to themselves."

"I'm all for transparency especially, if it's the non-lethal kind," I said. "These runes sound like they come with baggage—deadly baggage."

"Baggage I intend to unveil," he said. "Why did the elders create these runes? It wasn't to keep them hidden away. I intend to make them accessible...within reason, of course."

"Of course," I said, with a nod as we crossed the park on 85th Street. "How, exactly? Without blowing up the city, preferably."

"I have a plan, but first, we must locate them."

We arrived at The White House, under the twenty minutes predicted by Ox. I parked in front of the building. The motorcade of ninjas behind us came to a stop and waited for us to exit the vehicle.

I understood the name right away. The entire building was made up of white brick and stone, taking up the entire block from 86th to 87th Streets with a great view of Central Park.

"This is their HQ?" I asked, gazing up at the building. "Pretty nice location."

"Only the top three floors," Monty said. "Most of the time, Sebastian is abroad, engaged in what he calls *business*. The Treadwell Supernatural Directive operates out of this address, but is a global organization."

"So, business mogul and mage?"

"He tends to focus on the business aspects, predominantly."

"But he is a mage."

"Yes, he is a mage."

"Impressive," I said, glancing at the motorcade behind us. "What exactly are they waiting for?"

"To deter us from trying to escape would be my best guess," Monty said. "By keeping the cycles ready, we can't speed off."

"Smart," I said with a nod. "One we could probably shake off, but six? That's a recipe for disaster, one I would like to avoid today."

"A wise course of action," Monty said, unstrapping his seatbelt. "About Sebastian—"

"You wanted to tell me something?"

"He's a mage, but not the typical sort," Monty said. "He has a tendency to move in unsavory circles."

"Unsavory circles?"

"As I said, he has resources," Monty continued. "Most of them are of the illicit kind."

"Are you saying he's a dark mage?"

"Nothing of the sort," Monty said, opening the door and stepping out of the Dark Goat. "He is what would be considered a criminal."

"A criminal?" I asked as I opened the door for Sensei Sprawl. "What kind of criminal?"

"He fashions himself a gentleman criminal," Monty said, heading to the entrance as the motorcade behind us turned off their motorcycles and waited in silence. "It doesn't change the fact that he skirts laws, and most of the time bends them to the breaking point."

"Why?"

"Why what?"

"Why does he bend laws?" I asked. "And more specifically, which laws is he breaking? Is he some kind of cold-blooded murderer?"

"No, he has only ever acted in violence to preserve the lives of his people," Monty assured me. "Violence is—and has always been—a last resort for him."

"So why is he a criminal?" I asked. "I'm not seeing it here. He cheats on his taxes?"

We stopped and waited at the entrance as the doorman opened the door for us. I felt a gentle wave of energy run over me after we crossed the rune-covered threshold.

"Runic scan?" I continued. "He takes his security seriously."

Monty nodded.

"Sophisticated," I said. "What does it scan for?"

"Weaponry, most likely," Monty said as we approached the elevator. "Among other things, I'm sure."

"You wanted to warn me he was a criminal?"

Monty gave me a look that said the lobby of the White House was not the place to have this conversation.

"There's more, but it will become apparent soon enough."

"I'm not a big fan of surprises, especially when I'm walking into a building after being summoned," I said, lowering my voice. "Are we going to have to fight our way out of here?"

"Unlikely," Monty said, glancing to our side as a woman approached. "We will pick this up later. We have an escort."

Peaches rumbled by my side as the woman stopped near us at the elevator. She was wearing a black Zegna business suit tailored to fit her perfectly. The skirt she wore was offset by the Condora Louboutins, which added at least three inches to her height.

I noticed the softly glowing runes in the fabric as she stepped closer. Her black hair was cut in a short bob which partially hid one side of her face.

"Montague and Strong," she said with a nod, placing her hand on a panel next to the elevator door. "My name is Tiger. It is a pleasure to meet you both."

"Tiger?" I said. "Does that mean, Rabbit, Dragon, Snake, and the rest are upstairs?"

She turned to face me and gave me a penetrating look of approval.

"Ox did say you were sharp," she answered. "Most of them are upstairs. Others are out on assignment, but should return within the week, if it goes well."

"I was right?"

She nodded.

"Right about what exactly?" Monty asked.

"Your associate here," she said with a glance my way, "correctly surmised that each of the Treadwell Twelve have taken a moniker from the Chinese Zodiac."

"No real names, I'm guessing?" I said. "Helps to keep things simple."

"None, except for Sebastian," she said as the elevator doors opened with a whisper. "I'm sure you're sharp enough to guess which name would be his, if he did pick one. If you'll join me, he is waiting for you upstairs."

"Not like we have much of a choice," I said as we stepped in behind her. "He did want to have a *word*."

A faint smile crossed her lips as she nodded.

"He can be quite persuasive—when the mood strikes."

TEN

We reached the top floor of The White House.

The elevator opened into a reception area large enough to have its own zip code, complete with a massive black steel desk sporting legs that had probably been tank hedgehogs in a prior life.

The barricade of a desk sat on the polished gray marble and faced the elevator. I noticed the defensive runes etched into the marble as we crossed the floor to the receptionist.

Behind the desk was a woman who looked about as friendly as a fist to the face—if the fist was wrapped in a spike-covered iron glove. She was dressed in a suit similar to Tiger's, giving her a similar appearance. Instead of fancy dress Louboutins, she was wearing steel-toed Buckle Dune boots, giving fashion an edge of lethality. Her head was shaved on one side, and she grew out her hair, which was a bright white, and long on the opposite side.

"Rabbit," Tiger said with a nod. "He's expecting us."

Rabbit narrowed her eyes at us, her gaze hard as granite. It visibly softened at the sight of my hellhound.

"A hellhound?" she said, glancing at me after gazing at Peaches. "My kind of spirit animal. You must be Strong."

"Guilty as charged," I said, rubbing my hellhound's head. "A pleasure to meet you."

"Only because you don't know us...yet," she said with a smile, then grew serious as she looked at Tiger. "Brace yourself. He's in a mood."

"Wonderful," Tiger said with a small sigh. "Have the others arrived?"

"I wouldn't be sitting here behind the Great Wall if they had," Rabbit snapped. "Snake, Horse, and Goat are still in the field. Rooster, Dog, Monkey, and Pig are on special assignment; they aren't due back for weeks."

"And Rat?" Tiger asked. "Is he still in deep cover?"

"No," she said, thumbing at the door behind her. "He's in there with Sebastian. Good luck."

Tiger released a small groan as she headed to the large door behind Rabbit. She placed her hand on the surface of the door, and it flared a dull orange as symbols bloomed to life with white energy.

The door clicked open a second later with a low hiss.

Tiger led us beyond the door into a large office.

"That leaves Dragon," I said under my breath to Monty. "Sebastian—if he uses a code name—would be the Dragon."

"Correct," said Tiger without looking back. "Whatever you do, however, do not refer to him as Dragon. The name has some uncomfortable memories for him, which he doesn't appreciate."

"Not a huge fan of dragons myself," I said. "They've always been a little heavy on the megalomania for me to be comfortable."

Tiger gave me a sidelong look and smiled.

"I like you," she said, keeping her voice low. "You may even survive this meeting."

"Dragon? Fitting, actually," Monty said as we followed Tiger in. "He always was a bit self-important."

The office dwarfed the reception area by orders of magnitude, making the space outside the door seem like a closet compared to the enormous space of the office.

One side of the office, the area where we stood, was furnished in antiques which I had no doubt were authentic. As we approached the sleek white marble desk, the space became more minimalist and modern.

"Is that a Nougat Desk?" I asked, as we crossed the gray marble floor that had been continued from the reception area. "With extras, it seems."

I saw that the runes that had been inscribed into the floor had continued on the surface of the desk. It made me realize that the desk, while a decorative element, probably doubled as some kind of protection.

On the desk I could see several monitors attached in a stacked configuration on one side. On the other side rested two phones, with a notebook and assorted papers placed neatly in the center of the desk.

The entire room was lined with windows that let in the natural light, bathing the office in a warm glow. The room became more sparse the closer we got to the desk. In front of the desk, I saw three comfortable black chairs, one of them occupied by a thin young man.

It took a moment for my brain to register that these were the Kennedy Cabinet chairs.

Along either side of the office, under the very large bookcases that lined both walls, all of which were filled with books, I noticed the sofas as we crossed the space. It was a pair of Wharton Esherick Important sofas, on either side of us—each worth a small fortune. Behind the Nougat desk, probably in a bout of practicality, sat an Eames Executive chair.

I slowed my pace as I took in the decor. Whoever Sebastian was, one thing was clear, he had extravagant taste in furniture.

"Whatever you do," I said under my breath to Monty, "don't let Roxanne visit this office. She may get ideas for more furniture we can't use without her authorization."

"Duly noted," Monty said, his expression serious as he focused forward. "Let's not keep our host waiting."

I turned to focus on the person at the other end of the office.

Standing behind the Nougat Desk, and looking out of one of the windows, was a tall man with his back turned to us.

He was dressed in a black Zegna bespoke mageiform. I could sense his energy signature and realized he posed a serious threat should he decide we needed to leave his office using another, more immediate method, like the windows.

His salt-and-pepper hair was cut short and neat, finishing off the business-magnate look. He wore a pair of dark-rimmed glasses with lenses that shimmered with power.

"Thank you for coming," Sebastian said as we drew closer. "That will be all, Rat. See that the task is carried out to your satisfaction. Report when you see a change."

"Yes, sir," the thin young man sitting in front of the desk answered. "It'll be a day or so before I know anything."

"Very well. Dismissed."

Rat, who was dressed in motorcycle leathers similar to the ones worn by our motorcade, stood up, glanced our way, and nodded to Sebastian, before leaving the office through a side door close to the desk.

"Rabbit?" Sebastian said.

A voice came over a speaker somewhere on the desk.

"Yes?"

I noticed the lack of formality in her response.

"Please have Ox join us," Sebastian said. "This pertains directly to his responsibilities."

"Will do," Rabbit said. "He should be up in ten."

"Thank you," Sebastian said, and then turned to face us. "Welcome."

I nearly stumbled and fell on my face as I looked at him.

Sebastian smiled.

"I gather from your response that my esteemed cousin neglected to mention our connection."

It was like looking at Monty—if Monty had gotten a haircut, become the CEO of a multinational corporation, and lost his constant scowl.

"You're related?" I asked, still stunned. "How?"

"We're distant cousins," Monty said. "I do have other uncles besides my uncle Dexter. Sebastian is a distant relation from the Treadwell branch of the family. Hello, Sebastian."

"You didn't think that was an important piece of information to share?"

"I figured you would put it together eventually," Monty answered. "Why else would my uncle call him personally?"

"Tristan, Simon," Sebastian said, gesturing to the chairs in front of the desk. "Please, sit."

Tiger stepped to the side and sat on one of the Wharton sofas. We sat in the Kennedy Cabinet chairs as Sebastian sat behind his desk. I was still stunned as Sebastian smiled in my direction again.

"Thanks," I said. "You two look so much alike."

"Montague genes are quite strong," Sebastian answered. "Would you like anything to drink? I can offer you some of the best Earl Grey and Death Wish you have ever had the opportunity to taste."

"How?" I asked. "How did you know?"

"The greatest currency in the world is—"

"Information," Monty finished, turning to me. "Sebastian is an information broker."

"Data broker," Sebastian corrected. "We must stay modern. Coffee? Tea?"

Monty nodded.

"I could always use a good cup of coffee," I said. "Are you sure it's Death Wish?"

"Absolutely certain," he said. "I'll make sure Robu sends it up. Rabbit," he raised his voice slightly, "please have Ox inform the kitchen we need one Earl Grey steeped to perfection, an extra strong mug of Death Wish—wait, make that two—and a large bowl of pastrami from Ezra's, along with... Tiger, anything?"

"Nothing for me, thanks," Tiger said, pulling out her phone. "If you'll excuse me, I have to take this."

"Of course," Sebastian said, and then focused on us. "Uncle Dexter tells me you are intent on recovering the lost runes. Is this true?"

"Yes," Monty said. "I was instructed to do so by the Caretaker."

Sebastian leaned back in his chair and stared at Monty.

"What were his words exactly, Tristan?"

Monty returned the stare.

"He explained that the elder runes are power I need to harness," Monty said, after a brief pause. "I reminded him they were lost."

"Not lost—hidden," Sebastian answered. "They have never been lost."

"A sentiment he expressed, using the same words," Monty said. "Then he said I needed to find them and harness them, before it's too late."

"Before it's too late?" Sebastian asked. "Too late for what?"

"In a manner typical of beings at his power level, he

neglected to inform me what he meant," Monty replied. "Only that I should harness their power."

"Do you know where the elder runes are?" I asked "I mean, being a data broker and all, you must have an idea."

"I do," Sebastian said, looking at me, "Have an idea, that is."

"How bad is it?" Monty asked.

"You are not going to like it," Sebastian said. "There is a reason why they haven't been recovered."

I was about to say something, when the side door that Rat had used opened.

ELEVEN

A member of the kitchen staff entered the office, placing a large tray on a small table next to the desk. On the floor, he placed a large titanium bowl filled with pastrami for my ever-ravenous hellhound.

Sebastian took one of the mugs of Death Wish and took a long pull. He closed his eyes and savored the taste for several seconds before nodding his approval.

"Felix, please inform Robu that the coffee is sheer perfection," Sebastian said. "I can assume the same for the tea."

Felix gave Sebastian a short bow.

"I will, Mr. Treadwell," Felix said, with a small smile. "Do you need anything else?"

"Not at the moment," Sebastian said, after taking another pull from his mug and motioning for Monty and me to drink. "Express my deepest thanks to Robu. If we need anything more, I'll have Ox inform the kitchen."

"Very well, Mr. Treadwell."

Felix left the office through the same door he had entered.

I looked down at my barely contained hellhound, who had targeted the bowl of pastrami and had begun to drool.

<Can I go eat now? That meat is for me. Can I eat it now?>

<Hold on a second. Let's not be rude.>

<It would be rude not to eat it. This is meat from the place. It smells so good and I'm so starving.>

<You haven't starved one second in your life.>

"Simon," Sebastian began, getting my attention and pulling me out of my conversation with my hellhound. "You don't mind if I call you Simon, do you?"

"Not at all," I said, looking up at Sebastian before giving Peaches a stern look that said, *Do not pounce on the meat.* "As long as you don't mind me calling you Sebastian."

"Sebastian is fine," Sebastian said, with a smile and a nod. "I don't know much about hellhounds, the information on them being scarce. However, I do know that a large amount of hellhound drool on a waxed marble floor presents a hazard to anyone walking over the area, wouldn't you agree?"

"I would," I said. "Give me a moment."

<Hey, boy. Go eat, but do not inhale it all at once. Make it last at least a few seconds. Show some decorum.>

<Decorum means I should starve?>

<Decorum means to behave the right way. We are visiting this office. You should behave properly.>

<I always behave properly. I am a growing hellhound and I must eat. Not eating would be bad decorum.>

There was no arguing with hellhound logic.

<Go for it, and do not make a mess.>

<I never make a mess...when it comes to meat from the place.>

He padded over to the titanium bowl and began, to his credit, to slowly inhale the pastrami. That lasted all of three seconds before the full-blown black-hole action took over. He devoured the entire bowl moments later. He padded back next to me, turned in a circle a few times and plopped down by me.

The snores followed a few seconds after that.

"Extraordinary," Sebastian said. "Is it true he is still a puppy?"

"As far as I can tell, yes," I said. "He didn't come with a manual, so this is learning as we go."

"Fascinating," Sebastian answered. "I'd be interested in learning more about him—with your approval, of course. I'll make sure he is amply fed in the process."

"Sure. It would probably help me learn more about him, too," I said. "I have to warn you, though: he can eat."

"So I see," Sebastian said. "That will be a conversation for another day. Today, let's discuss the elder runes. Tristan?"

"Yes?" Monty said, putting down his tea cup. "You have questions."

"As you well know, I'm a pragmatist," Sebastian said, standing and moving to the nearby window. "There is a high probability that, without my assistance, this mission of yours is doomed to failure."

"Which is why our uncle called you."

"My initial reaction was to refuse. In fact, I did refuse, at first," he said. "The risks are considerable, even if these runes are not blood runes like the one you currently possess. It's still dangerous."

"Risks for whom?" Monty asked. "Are you joining us?"

"I'm afraid not," Sebastian said. "However, my absence doesn't preclude the risks to the Directive. Helping you locate and obtain elder runes will have considerable blowback."

"Bad for business?" Monty asked.

"Actually, no," Sebastian admitted. "Bad for the *operation* of business. Rest assured, there would be several parties interested in getting hold of an elder rune...or the mage wielding one."

"That sounds like a not-so-subtle threat," I said.

"A warning," Sebastian replied, taking another pull from

his mug. "I have no desire to be the center of attention because of your actions."

"What changed your mind?" Monty asked. "You usually have a policy of non-involvement."

"True, but Uncle Dexter can be quite persuasive," he said. "That, and I have no wish to be visited by his consort."

"He threatened you with the Morrigan?" I asked, trying to hide a smile by taking my mug of coffee. My brain exploded with javambrosia goodness as I took a long pull. "That sounds just like Dex."

"Threatened is a strong word," Sebastian said as he turned, a small smile on his lips. "He strongly urged I get involved, Tristan being family and all."

"*Distant* family," Monty added. "We're barely related."

"Semantics," Sebastian said. "The Treadwells and the Montagues may as well be one. I agree, we've had our difficulties in the past—"

"If by difficulties, you mean the Treadwells have a loose association with the laws, magical or otherwise, then yes, we've had difficulties."

Sebastian smiled.

"You know I've never done well with authority figures or their rules," Sebastian said. "Not even in the Golden Circle during our studies."

"I recall you nearly getting expelled several times, and almost banished from this plane at least twice."

"Those were misunderstandings."

"Of course they were," Monty said before taking another sip from his cup. His expression told me he had heard this song and dance before. "Uncle Dexter saved you both of those times."

"For which I'm eternally grateful."

"So, Dex strongly urged you to help Monty, and then he

threatened you with the Morrigan?" I said. "You must like to live dangerously."

"Initially, when I refused, he may have made some comments about her paying the Treadwell offices a visit," he said, "just to see how the organization is run. I think he's getting worse with age."

I let out a short laugh.

"Dexter is a crafty and dangerous old man."

"You don't know the half of it, trust me," Sebastian said with a short laugh of his own, before becoming serious. "My assistance is conditional, however. He allowed me that much."

"What are your conditions?" Monty asked, his expression becoming darker than usual. "What do you want?"

"You misunderstand me," Sebastian said. "I only have one condition."

Monty raised an eyebrow, but said nothing.

"What's the cost?" I asked. "I don't think Monty is going to give you the elder rune." I glanced at Monty. "Can you give him the elder rune?"

"He knows I can't," Monty said. "Even if I show it to him, there would be a component missing. It's not like the rune of sealing. The elder runes we are going after are major runes. There are failsafes in place."

"True," Sebastian agreed. "There are only five major runes. Once learned, the process of imparting the information to another can prove fatal without the proper precautions. These are not blood runes, which are easily acquired and used."

"Excuse me?" I said, looking at Monty. "You didn't say anything about this being fatal."

"Imparting the information, not *acquiring* the information," Monty clarified. "The major runes contain a failsafe to prevent dissemination of the information contained within each rune."

"Once you learn the rune, you can't share it, ever?"

"No, not ever," Monty said. "You recall the safeguard on the book that rendered it blank when you attempted to read the pages?"

"I do," I said with a wince, remembering the blast that had sent me across a room. "After I tried to read it, the pages became blank. Albert said we'd need an Archmage to read it."

Monty nodded.

"It's a similar process with the major elder runes, only more complicated," Monty said. "I can obtain the information, but in order to share it with another mage, I'd need a Keeper to facilitate the process."

"Why do I get the feeling that the Keepers won't be excited to help you share the information?"

"Quite right," Sebastian said. "There is another way, though."

"One that doesn't require a Keeper?" I asked. "How?"

"Tristan would have to be stronger," Sebastian said, looking at Monty as he walked over to one of the other windows that faced the Park. "He'd have to shift to become an Archmage."

"You know I'm several shifts and centuries away from that," Monty said. "Even if I could accelerate the process—which I can't—it would very likely cause irreparable damage to my mind."

"True," Sebastian said, glancing at Tiger, who sat silently watching our conversation. "The room please, Tiger."

She nodded and stood, leaving the room a few seconds later.

He turned to us when she was out of the room. With a short gesture, I felt the familiar sensation of being in a sphere of silence, except this one felt as large as the entire office.

"The rune of seals you currently possess, is one of the seven minor blood runes," Sebastian said. "Powerful in their own right, but that power pales in comparison to the five major runes."

"How did you know?" I asked.

"It is in the best interest of my organization to know these things," Sebastian said. "Also, you three are about as subtle as a thermonuclear explosion. How Verity hadn't hunted you down and detained you before your little display at the Cloisters escapes me."

"We can do subtle," I said defensively. "In fact, we're doing subtle right now."

Sebastian shook his head and smiled.

"You can't possibly be this delusional," he said. "How have you managed to live this long?"

"Escaping certain death is my special skill," I said. "It's a gift, really."

"Your energy signature broadcasts your location like a beacon," he said. "Especially with that Mark of Kali on you. Tristan's little show of force at St. Johns was noticed to the extent that I was contacted."

"You were contacted?" I asked. "Why would anyone contact *you* because of something Monty did?"

"Because my headstrong cousin managed to get the attention of certain individuals better left undisturbed," he answered, giving Monty a glance. "Individuals of considerable power who would be eager to obtain the elder runes. Continuing on your present path will only get you more attention."

"Are you suggesting I should desist from this mission?" Monty asked.

Sebastian shook his head.

"Despite my reservations, if the Caretaker placed you on this path, you must follow it until its end," he said. "You aren't strong enough to wield, much less harness, the power of one major rune. If you attempted all five at your current level of power, it would utterly destroy you."

"I'm aware of my limitations," Monty answered. "Are you implying *you* are strong enough?"

"Far from it," Sebastian said. "I think, in this matter, your power surpasses mine, Tristan. At least, your willingness to embrace the risks exceeds my own."

"I'm aware of the risks."

"I don't think you are—not yet, at least," he said. "Allow me to propose the condition to my assistance."

"Please do," Monty said. "I would be curious to know the nature of your *condition*, Sebastian."

"I am prepared to provide Ox, Tiger, and Rat," he said. "They will assist you in this mission, until such a point that the rune, or runes, you acquire are safeguarded, or your demise. Whichever happens first."

"Thanks for the vote of confidence," I said.

"As I said, I'm a pragmatist. Even with my assistance, the odds of your success are slim to none."

"I thought there were twelve of you?" I said. "Why only Ox, Tiger, and Rat?"

He gave me a look of approval.

"Tiger is my second, and is an expert at strategy and logistics. Ox is a null with an emphasis on teleportation, and Rat is an expert in surveillance as well as an elite tracker," he answered. "They will do everything in their power to help you succeed. The rest of the Directive is otherwise engaged, myself included."

"You're missing the party?"

"Sadly, other matters require my presence abroad," he said with a nod. "Or else I would seriously consider joining you on this adventure, if only to confront a Keeper."

"You *want* to confront a Keeper?" I asked. "Isn't that dangerous?"

"I didn't say it was prudent," Sebastian said. "Isn't that what you were risking by attempting to gain entry to the Argosy? Without my assistance, mind you."

"Yes, but—"

"The only way to gauge one's true strength and power is to face a stronger enemy," Sebastian answered. "A Keeper would be an ideal test."

"Basically, you're insane," I said. "Fighting a Keeper would be suicide, according to Dexter."

"I'm not insane, Simon, merely driven," he said, staring at me. "In any case, the Caretaker didn't task me, he tasked Tristan. As for my condition, it is a simple one."

"Things are rarely simple with you, Sebastian," Monty said. "What is your condition?"

"The first rune you must acquire is Mu, or also known as the rune of wood," he said. "The Arcanists at the Argosy belong to Keeper Evergreen. Each of the five runes must be acquired in a specific sequence. Mu is the first, and unlocks the access to the second."

"What is the second?" I asked. "Why can't we skip the order?"

"For now, let's focus on the first," he said. "To attempt to skip the order would alert more than one Keeper. That is not a risk you want to take. Even collectively, standing against more than one Keeper would be unwise."

"Understood," Monty said. "Your condition."

"Once you acquire the first rune, or rather if you acquire the first rune—"

"*When* I acquire it," Monty said. "What is your proposal?"

"Since you can't wield it, the rune must be safeguarded from abuse," he said. "You must allow it to be transferred to a secure location."

"Isn't it in a secure location now?" I asked. "I mean, it's hidden."

"If it were secure, the Caretaker wouldn't have asked Tristan to find and harness its power," Sebastian said. "It means they are being sought out. If you can secure the first one, you can delay the recovery of the other four."

"A secure location?" Monty asked. "Which secure location? Let me guess, somewhere in the Treadwell vaults?"

"Absolutely not," Sebastian said. "Whoever possesses that rune becomes a target. My business thrives on my being able to blend into the shadows. That rune would act like a beacon on me and the Directive."

"Who do you suggest, then?"

"My suggestion, which was agreed to, was placing the rune with uncle Dexter," Sebastian said. "Anyone after it would think twice before confronting him and the Morrigan to retrieve it."

Monty rubbed his chin for a few seconds before nodding.

"That is actually a sound suggestion," Monty said. "He agreed to this?"

"You know him," Sebastian answered. "He actually looked pleased at the prospect of Keepers and their mages coming after him."

"That sounds like him," I said, shaking my head. "Where is the first rune?"

"The Living Library, but not where you think," he said. "Even Ziller would have trouble getting to it. It was placed there without his knowledge."

"How is that even possible?" Monty asked. "Ziller knows everything about the Living Library."

"Did he know you had borrowed the minor rune?" Sebastian asked. "He didn't, at least not until he was informed by LD. As powerful as Ziller is, there are things hidden in the Library, even from him. This rune is in an interstitial location within the Living Library created by one of Evergreen's second in command."

I remained silent for a few seconds, awed at the depth of Sebastian's knowledge of events. He knew things few could possibly know.

"And you know this how?" I asked. "How did you know about LD?"

"My discipline allows me to glean hidden information," Sebastian answered, tapping his glasses. "I can see where others are blind."

"Regina," Monty said. "She told you."

Sebastian's expression darkened.

"Who's Regina?" I asked. "Is she part of the Directive?"

"She was," Monty answered. "Long ago, she helped create it—with Sebastian. She is a skilled mage, who also happens to be a sociopath."

"That's a bit harsh," Sebastian said. "Regina has...issues."

"Sociopathic issues," Monty said. "Can her information be trusted?"

"Absolutely," he said. "I vetted and confirmed its veracity myself. She may be many things, but she is one of the best at getting information, although she may have inadvertently reduced the number of Arcanists on guard upon her exit from the Argosy."

"You're *still* smitten," Monty said. "After everything she did?"

"It's complicated."

"She's dangerous, Sebastian. You know this."

"You're one to speak," Sebastian scoffed. "How is Doctor Death doing these days—oh, pardon me, I meant Roxanne."

It was Monty's turn to look upset.

"She's fine," Monty said brusquely. "Would you like me to send her your regards?"

"Don't you dare," Sebastian answered, pointing a finger at Monty. "I'm serious. In any case, Regina provided invaluable information. Information you will need to get inside."

"No more Arcanists killed," Monty said, his voice hard. "Those at the Argosy are only there to secure the entrance. They don't need to sacrifice their lives."

"They know the risks," Sebastian said, his voice equally unforgiving. "Every mage does."

"No more deaths at the Argosy," Monty said. "I'm sure your team is skilled enough to pull this off without collateral damage. Or are you telling me they aren't?"

"They are the best at what they do," Sebastian said. "It will be a zero-kill op."

"Thank you," Monty said. "I appreciate it."

"The security will be heightened now," Sebastian said. "I will honor your request, but I will not sacrifice my team for your principles."

"I would imagine that your team is so skilled that they would never be put in that situation."

Sebastian shook his head and smiled.

"The world is more nuanced than you think, Tristan," he said. "That was always your problem—you always chose the difficult over the expedient. We can expect more patrols at the Argosy now."

"That would explain the Arcanists situated at the Argosy," Monty said. "They are preventing entry to the Living Library and access to the first rune."

"You'll need the minor elder rune to access the location," Sebastian said. "I'm sure that's not a coincidence. I would assume it's a trap."

"By keying it to an elder rune, it ensures a way of knowing who is accessing the location," Monty said. "Efficient and effective."

Sebastian nodded.

"The group at the bookstore is the smallest contingent of Evergreen's people," Sebastian said. "The Argosy hasn't been used for decades, but they are taking no chances. The other, more familiar entrances to the Living Library are considerably more protected."

"Does Ziller know about this?" Monty asked. "Does he know that this access to the Library is currently under surveillance?"

"Does it matter?" Sebastian said. "Evergreen feels one of the major runes may be in danger of discovery. He is acting within his jurisdiction. Do not deceive yourself; they know you acquired a minor rune. Why they haven't acted directly against you is still a mystery to me."

"Maybe they're waiting for Monty to try for a major rune," I said. "Then they'll pounce on him."

"It's not like them," Sebastian said, shaking his head. "Even the acquisition of a minor rune should have prompted them to act, unless there is more at play here."

I heard a soft knock at the door.

"That will be Ox," Sebastian continued. "He will help you prepare for this evening."

"This evening?" I asked. "We're doing this tonight?"

"Would you prefer we wait a few days, or perhaps weeks?" Sebastian asked. "I'm sure you can send a message to Verity, asking them for a reprieve from your current death sentence."

"On second thought, the sooner we do this the better."

"In any case, the access to the Living Library is prevented at the Argosy," Monty said. "We don't even know how many are inside. The variables are too great to attempt a breach of their defenses."

"Not for me," Sebastian said. "You will gain entry tonight."

TWELVE

We arrived at the location near the Argosy bookstore around midnight.

Sebastian remained at the White House, but had sent Ox, Tiger, and Rat as promised. We were standing on the corner of 59th and Park Avenue—Ox was currently masking all of our energy signatures, which made sense, since he was a null.

It explained how he could move without being sensed: he had the ability to completely shut down his energy signature. The fact that he could do that for the entire group only spoke to how much power he possessed.

The bookstore was closed for the night, but the lights on the top floor were on. I closed my eyes and was about to expand my senses to get a feel for how many Arcanists were on site, when a large finger tapped me on the forehead.

My eyes flew open in surprise as I stumbled back a step.

"Don't do that," Ox said, towering over me. "You want to let them know we're coming?"

"No," I said, composing myself. "I was just going to—"

"Don't," Ox said, shaking his head. "You'll set them off,

and then we'll have to fight for our lives." He glanced down at Peaches. "Can he run in stealth mode?"

"He's not a submarine or a fighter jet," I snapped, annoyed at my rookie mistake, but more annoyed at being called out for it. "He can be quiet when he needs to be."

"That would be good," Rat said next to me in a quiet voice. "We will need the element of surprise to gain entry."

"Tiger, what's the plan?" Ox asked as he cracked his neck. "Boss wants us to keep the building intact *and* evade detection—we need to be ghosts."

"Both of those conditions are diametrically opposed to your usual method of operation," she said, focused on the Argosy. "Cover me and give me a moment."

She kept focusing on the bookstore as her eyes glazed over. Her irises faded, leaving only the sclera of her eyes visible. A violet glow spilled from her eyes as she turned her head.

"Rat," she started, "you and your riders will split into two groups. The first group will split, approaching from the front and back of the bookstore—the other will maintain situational awareness on a three-block radius, in case they call for reinforcements."

"Will three blocks be enough?" Rat asked. "These aren't amateurs we're facing."

"We will have approximately twenty minutes from point of contact to either reach the top floor and open the portal to the Living Library, or exit the building if it goes sideways."

"Wait, the top floor?" I asked. "Why the top floor?"

"The access point you need is on the top floor," she said. "Did you think it would be easy, and be waiting for us on the ground floor?"

"Of course it's on the top floor," I said, gazing in the direction of the bookstore. "What happens after twenty minutes?"

"We'll have to deal with a Keeper or one of his seconds, which is almost as bad," she said. "We don't want to meet either, at least not yet."

"Agreed," Monty said. "Where do you want us?"

"Tristan, Simon, his hellhound, and I will join the group approaching from the rear," she said. "Ox will disable the Arcanists at the front of the bookstore." She gave Ox a pointed look. "I repeat: we need them disabled, not deceased."

"I know what disabled means," Ox said, mocking offense. "I do have a capacity for restraint."

"I only have one word for you," Tiger replied. "Peru."

"Hey, not fair," Ox said, raising a hand. "How was I supposed to know those ruins were rigged to explode?"

Rat smiled and then grew serious.

"My riders will create the initial distraction, but that won't last longer than ten to fifteen seconds," Rat said, "which means I won't be able to pull the front guard from their posts."

"I can work with fifteen seconds," Ox said. "Twenty would be better."

"I'll try, but no promises," Rat answered. "Once you hear them, move into position."

Rat stepped back into the shadows and disappeared.

"Ox, you head out in ten seconds and approach the entrance," Tiger said once Rat had gone. "We will make our way to the rear."

Ox nodded and cracked his neck.

"Is this no-kill policy strict?" he asked. "Or do I have self-defense latitude?"

"This part of the mission is zero kill," she said. "These Arcanists are to be treated as non-combatants. If that changes later on, we can reevaluate that position. For now, zero kill."

"Clear," Ox said. "Broken and bruised it is."

Her eyes reverted to normal as he nodded and silently slipped into the shadows.

"I don't think I'm ever going to get used to that," I said, glancing around for Ox. "Can all of you do that?"

"Can your hellhound really be silent?" Tiger asked, ignoring my question. She looked at Peaches, then at me. "It's imperative we don't alert the perimeter guards."

"He can be ultra quiet if he needs to be," I said. "Give me a second."

"You have one minute before we have to move."

"Plenty of time," I said, crouching down and grabbing my hellhound's massive head.

<Hey, boy. I need you to be extra quiet when we go to the bookstore.>

<Bookstore? Do you need to read?>

<Not exactly. That bookstore will lead us to the Living Library. We need to go there to get a rune.>

<Will this rune help you make meat?>

<What? No. It's not for making meat. It's for Monty. He needs to find it.>

<Is it lost?>

<Not lost, hidden.>

<Who hid it? Are they going to make meat?>

<Meat is not the important thing here.>

I felt the frustration creep into my thoughts.

<Meat is always the most important thing. Meat is life.>

I needed to use hellhound logic.

<If you can be super quiet while we go into that building, I'll make sure Monty makes you extra meat.>

<I can do that. Then, later, can we go to the place?>

The depths of his stomach were truly staggering.

<When we get back, we'll go see Ezra and get you a nice bowl of your favorite meat.>

<For my favorite meat from the place, I can be very quiet.>

"He understands," I said to Tiger. "He'll be quiet."

"You can really communicate with him?"

"Yes—as long as the conversation involves meat somewhere, he pays attention."

"Thirty seconds," she said, looking at her watch. "How intelligent is he?"

"Off the charts, actually," I said, rubbing my hellhound's head. "Also depends on his size."

"His size?"

"His conversational ability grows as he does," I said. "He dumbs it down so I can understand him."

"I see," she said, nodding. "We need to move...now."

We raced across the street, a group of shadows in the night.

THIRTEEN

One minute later, I heard motorcycles around the front of the bookstore, followed by loud voices. Immediately after, I could feel the energy surges of casts being used.

This lasted for a few seconds before it became silent again. Tiger placed her hand on the rear door and gestured. The door opened with a whisper as Rat's team slid into position behind us and guarded the exit.

Rat materialized a moment later and gave us a quick nod.

Tiger returned the nod and led the way inside, leaving Rat and his group outside.

We stood still in the darkness, allowing our eyes to adjust to the low light. I looked down and saw my hellhound's softly glowing eyes.

"Is that part of your bond?" Tiger looked at me and asked as we moved forward. "Interesting. I didn't notice it before."

"What?" I asked as we moved quickly upstairs and stopped on the second floor. "Is what part of the bond?"

"Your eyes," she said, turning her head and holding up a fist as we froze in place. "Patrol."

An Arcanist traveled across the floor, stepping between a

row of shelves. He was about to turn the corner and step right into our little group. I let my hand drift to Grim Whisper, but Tiger shook her head, pointed to her eyes and then pointed across the floor.

I saw Ox slide out from the shelves and shadow the Arcanist. Before the latter could turn the corner, Ox struck him in the side of the neck. The Arcanist crumpled into Ox's arms a second later, leaving the big man to carry him to a corner and lower him quietly, out of sight.

"Zero kill means no fatalities," Tiger said, turning to me, her expression angry. "What were you planning to do?"

"Persuaders," I said, tapping Grim Whisper. "Non-lethal."

"So you shoot him, and then?"

"He loses control of his bodily functions...all of them."

"Sounds disgustingly effective, and loud," she said.

"It persuades them to stop attacking."

"I can only imagine," she said. "Is this persuading a silent event, or would he be moaning all over the floor in distress?"

"It's not silent," I answered, keeping my voice low. "It neutralizes the ability to cast by scrambling neurons. The side effect is the loss of bodily functions."

"So the target becomes a moaning alarm as we alert the floor, if not the entire building, to our presence?" she asked. "Is this your idea of subtle?"

"You said zero kill," I shot back. "This is a non-lethal option."

"This mission doesn't feel challenging enough for you?"

"More than," I said. "I just thought it would be better if I—"

"Let us handle the guards," she said, cutting me off. "Keep your weapon holstered at all times. Understood?"

I nodded.

She led us to the next stairwell as Ox faded back into the shadows. I didn't know how he was moving from floor to floor, but I figured it was some kind of advanced teleportation.

The next two floors were uneventful as Ox incapacitated the guards ahead of us, probably fearing I would shoot someone and alert the entire building.

We kept climbing in silence. At the foot of the staircase leading to the fifth floor, Tiger held up a fist and stopped us from moving again.

"Don't bother hiding," a voice with a slight accent said from above us. "I can sense you. Why not come up so we can converse and put this foolish mission to rest?"

"What the hell is H&H doing here?" Tiger muttered as she patted one of her pockets, pulling out a pair of thick latex gloves. "This is going to get complicated."

"H&H?"

"They're a pair of mages, and contract killers," she said. "You just heard Henri. If he's here, Hemlock is close by. Whatever you do, don't let her touch you."

"Hemlock?" Monty said. "She's a venomancer?"

Tiger nodded.

"Nasty piece of work," she said. "She's the more dangerous of the two. Henri is a basic mage at best, but he's fast and can phase shift. He uses a poisoned blade, which makes him a problem in close quarters. Hemlock can exude a toxin from her skin and direct a blast of that toxin at her targets."

"No skin contact, understood," Monty said. "Can his phase shift be neutralized?"

"Not to my knowledge," she said. "Our best chance was Ox, and he's either dead or unconscious."

"That's how he knows we're down here?"

She nodded.

"If he can sense us, Ox is down," Tiger said more to herself than Monty and me. "Don't underestimate him—he looks like an old university professor, but he's dangerous. Let me do the talking."

We climbed the stairs to the fifth floor to a small welcoming committee. Three men stood in the middle of a small open area with a desk.

Their energy signatures told me they were mages—each individually less strong than Monty—but there were three of them. At first, I thought they were Arcanists, but they were dressed differently. The one in the center, who I assumed was Henri, wore casual clothing.

He wore a dark brown tweed jacket over a patterned vest, dark tie, and tan shirt ensemble, finished off with a pair of loose-fitting khakis and comfortable loafers. The other two, one on each side, were dressed in variations of the same theme.

It was a trio of dangerous university professors.

I even noticed the elbow pads on the jackets. Henri smiled as he saw us. I glanced to the side and saw Ox sitting on the ground, semi-conscious and rubbing his head. Next to him were two unconscious Arcanists.

"Henri," Tiger said, her voice tight with anger as she took in the scene. "What are you doing here? Shouldn't you be doing research in some dusty library somewhere?"

"I would love nothing more, trust me," he said. "Alas, our services have been requested."

"Where's Hemlock?"

"Upstairs," he said. "She is unhappy."

"She's toxic, in more ways than one. Is she ever happy?" Tiger answered. "Who sent you?"

"Tiger, Tiger," Henri said with a slight shake of his head and a wag of his finger. "We are professionals. You know we do not divulge clients."

"Bullshit. Are you forgetting who you're talking to?" she asked. "I know you only work for six figures and above. The question is, who has the deep pockets and the interest in sending you here to intercept us?"

"I think the real question is: what are Treadwell's Stray Dogs doing here, ma cherie?" Henri asked, pointing at Tiger. "Why are *you* here with them?"

"Working," she said. "Henri, as a professional courtesy, I'm going to advise you to leave. I appreciate you not killing Ox, which is the only reason we're speaking at this moment, but I'd hate to have to retire you. It's not personal—this is business."

"For me as well," Henri answered, glancing at Ox. "He is very good. I could not snuff out such talent, but you must stop now. My instructions are clear."

"What instructions?" she asked, taking a step away from me. "Who contracted you?"

Henri gave Tiger a hard stare.

"Verity," Henri answered after a few seconds. "I am sorry, but your evening ends here. They were very specific. If you surrender Mage Montague and his associate, you can go."

Tiger smiled and shook her head.

"Don't lie to a liar," she said. "You're here to clean all of us."

He nodded slowly.

"I am afraid they are too dangerous to be allowed to continue. This floor is sealed," he said, materializing a silver blade coated in dark green energy. "On the next floor"—he pointed up with the poisoned blade—"Hemlock is waiting, blocking the portal to the Living Library. You do not want to face her."

"I'll take my chances," she said. "I never liked you, but I respected your work ethic. Walk away."

"I cannot," he said. "Verity thinks Mage Montague has gone dark and is after more power at the Living Library. He has been classified as a dark mage, threat level—black."

Monty raised an eyebrow. "They are paying a handsome sum to make sure he never reaches the Living Library...at least, not alive."

Tiger glanced at Monty who had stepped to the side, giving himself some space as Peaches let out a low rumble next to me.

"Shit," Tiger said under her breath. "Strong, please disregard what I said earlier about your holster."

"Got it."

"I'll let Hemlock know you tried your best," Tiger said and unleashed a blast of energy from her eyes at Henri.

FOURTEEN

Henri pivoted his body and disappeared, reappearing next to Tiger, who ducked the moment she sensed him.

She narrowly avoided a slash from his blade aimed at her neck as he disappeared again. The other two mages formed dark red orbs of energy and unleashed them in our direction.

I dove to the side, sliding on the floor and landing in between the shelves of books. Monty formed a shield and deflected one of the orbs into one of the mages, knocking him back into the wall with force. He slid to the ground unconscious.

Henri reappeared and confronted Tiger, who stood still this time. Now, I understood the reason for the thick latex gloves: as Henri attacked, she deflected his strikes using her sheathed hands.

I didn't know if she couldn't form orbs or not, but this seemed like a dangerous fight for her. Henri only had to cut her once. She had to be flawless in every deflection. One mistake, one mistimed block and he would get past her defenses. The energy on the blade was a deep, dark green with tinges of black. Everything about that blade said *death*.

Tiger was keeping Henri busy, but I could see she was losing this fight. He had started using his ability to attack from off angles—lunging forward before vanishing, only to reappear behind Tiger or to her side, and then striking. Each time, she dodged and evaded his attack, but he was getting closer.

The second mage attempted to attack Monty, unleashing another red orb at him. Monty batted it away and slammed the mage with a beam of violet energy. The mage fell to his knees, immobilized as the beam of energy enveloped him. A right cross from Monty incapacitated the mage where he knelt.

We needed to stop Henri before he cut Tiger.

<*Hey, boy. Can you follow the man with the blade when he goes in-between?*>

Peaches stared fixedly at Henri and Tiger.

<*I can see him.*>

<*I have an idea that might hurt. I'm going to distract him and you grab his arm which holds the blade. Once you have him, don't let go.*>

<*Can I remove his arm?*>

<*Not yet, no. Just grab him and hold him. No chewing. He deals with a poisoned weapon. I have no idea if the poison is inside his body, too.*>

<*That would be bad.*>

<*Which is why you just hold him, but no chewing. Got it?*>

<*Hold, no chewing.*>

<*Excellent. I'm going to get his attention. Stay close.*>

He rumbled in response as I headed for the door leading to the next level above. I figured Henri's main goal was to stop us from getting to the portal leading to the Living Library.

I saw the orange glowing runic failsafes when I got to the stairs. I had no idea how to disable them, but that wasn't the plan. Henri didn't know if I could disable them, which meant he would have to act to stop me.

I knew if I tried to cross the runic seals on the stairs, it would probably be a lethal experiment—but I wasn't going to cross them. I was going to *look* like I was going to cross them.

I approached the stairs and felt the energy shift.

<*Get ready, boy. He's coming.*>

I glanced over to where Tiger and Henri had been fighting, and saw Tiger now standing alone with a look of horror on her face.

"Strong, no!" she yelled. "Get back!"

I felt the surge of energy to my side and moved to dodge the strike. I noticed a few things in that split second: my hellhound was nowhere to be seen, and Henri was much faster than I anticipated.

He buried the blade in my side, to the hilt, before disappearing again. I hit the floor with a groan as waves of pain rushed from the wound to the rest of my body.

When he reappeared again, my hellhound had attached himself to his arm. He tried to drop the blade into his other hand, but before he could pull off the switch, Peaches blinked out again, taking Henri with him.

The poisoned blade fell to the floor.

Tiger picked up the blade and ran to my side.

"You didn't tell me your hellhound could plane-walk," she said, moving to the desk and finding a first-aid kit. "He's almost as fast as Henri."

"He's fast, just not fast enough," I said with a groan as I shifted position. "This is not fun."

"Serves you right for volunteering to be a target," Monty said, looking down at me. "You knew you couldn't disable the failsafes."

"*He* didn't know that," I said. "Ow—can't you do some of your finger-wiggles to make this hurt less?"

"I could," he said. "But then, how would you learn the lesson here?"

"Lesson? What lesson? This is only pain."

Tiger knelt down next to me removing bandages from the first-aid kit. Her movements were urgent but controlled. She knew how to keep herself focused in emergency situations.

"We're not going to be able to get you help in time." She turned to Tristan, her face tight with fear. "Can't you do something? He's been stabbed and poisoned."

"Of course," Monty said, forming a large sausage. "I'm sure this will prove adequate for the time being."

Tiger stared at Monty, her mouth dropping open for a few seconds.

"Have you completely lost your mind?" she asked, raising her voice. "Simon is dying! What am I supposed to do with that?"

"You? Nothing," Monty said, turning to me. "You did inform your creature not to kill him?"

"I did, but he's not going to be happy Henri stabbed me," I said, looking down at the rapidly closing wound as my body flushed with heat, the curse working overtime. "He might express his anger at him a bit."

"As long as he doesn't kill him, expressing his displeasure is understandable," Monty said. "We will need Henri to undo those seals on the stairs. In addition, there are some questions I'd like to ask."

Tiger stood staring at the two of us.

"You're both insane," she said, shaking her head. "Henri took your hellhound who knows where, and you're here creating sausages?"

"Henri didn't take him anywhere," I said, wincing as she pressed on my side with a large bandage. "I'm okay, really."

"You are not okay," she snapped. "You must be delirious from the poison."

"No, really," I said, holding her hand before she did more damage than good. "See? Good as new."

She looked at the wound which was now gone. I had been healing faster lately. The burning sensation rushed through my body—I was sure it was the poison coursing through my system.

The heat ratcheted up to inferno for a half-a-minute, making me dizzy as I tried to sit up. I leaned against a bookshelf as the feeling passed.

Tiger looked at the wound site in awe.

"How are you not dead?" she asked. "The wound was fatal, and Henri's poison is a mixture Hemlock uses. You should be in paralyzed agony right now, heading to your death. What are you?"

"I'm complicated," I said. "We don't have the time to get into it right now."

She turned to Monty, who shrugged.

"He's right," Monty said. "It's involved, and we have a portal to reach. Verity's involvement complicates things."

I felt another surge of energy.

"Incoming," I said, waving her away. "You may want to move back."

Tiger stepped away from me as my hellhound blinked back in with an unconscious Henri.

"How did Verity know you would be here?" she asked, staring at me. "We took precautions to make sure we were under their radar."

"Simon, this is no time for a rest," Monty said, heading over to the unconscious Henri as he tossed me the sausage. "Give this to your creature while I wake up our would-be assassin."

I slid over to where my hellhound sat.

I handed Peaches the large sausage—which in true hellhound style he proceeded to inhale before dropping into a sprawl that took up more space than I thought possible.

<What happened? How did he get past you?>

<He is very fast, but I did catch him.>

<After he stabbed me. You couldn't stop him before he buried his blade in my side?>

<No, he was too fast. I showed him I was unhappy he hurt you.>

<How exactly?>

<I shook him until his head hit the floor, and then I shook him some more. You said no chewing. I did not chew.>

<So you gave him a concussion?>

<But he is still together. I did not rip off his arms or legs.>

<There is that. You did great, boy. Slow down and enjoy your meat.>

He did not slow down, and the sausage proceeded to disappear into the black hole that was his stomach.

I got unsteadily to my feet and joined Monty.

Tiger trailed behind me, still giving me careful glances. Considering I should've been agonizing on the floor and—according to her—headed to my death, I could understand the looks.

Somehow, going into detail about how my body dealt with injuries, and now poison, felt like something I needed to keep to myself. I knew Monty had put it together the moment he formed a sausage instead of rushing to my side and trying to heal me.

It was a calculated risk.

I knew the curse could deal with my getting stabbed. I had a good idea it could deal with the poison, too, but there had been a chance the poison would be too fast-acting for the curse to stop before it killed me.

Monty gestured over Henri, and a few seconds later Henri came to.

"My god, my head," he said, holding his head with a groan.

His expression shifted to one of terror as he saw Peaches laying down a few feet away. He slid back and away from my hellhound. "Keep that monster away from me."

"That monster has a name. It's Peaches," Monty said. "Now, I just fed him an appetizer, but what he really enjoys is flesh, particularly that of a recent victim."

Peaches took that moment to stare at the commotion Henri was making. I saw my hellhound's eyes flare a brighter red for a few seconds before he let out a low growl.

Henri shook his head and I turned away to hide my smile. Monty was milking this for all it was worth. Tiger just stared hard at Henri.

"No," Henri said, extending a hand and sliding back even farther. "Keep him away. What do you want?"

"How did Verity know we would be here?" Monty asked. "We were masked."

"Tracker," Henri said, never taking his eyes off my hellhound. "They've been following him." Henri pointed at me. "His energy signature is distinct enough to follow you."

Monty followed Henri's finger with his gaze.

"You're saying he has a runic trail they can follow?" Monty asked, pointing at me. "Even with Ox's masking?"

Henri nodded, still looking at Peaches.

"Are you going to feed me to it?"

"That would depend on your next answers," Monty deadpanned as he glanced over at Peaches. "He's never quite satiated." Monty turned back and gave Henri the once over. "You're just about the right size for a meal. He does get peckish at this time of night."

"What do you want?" Henri answered. "Ask."

"Tell Hemlock to stand down," Tiger said, "and tell us the name of the tracker."

"I don't know the name of the tracker," Henri said, panic

entering his voice. "We never met. I got messages from a private number telling us your movements."

"Call Hemlock. Tell her to stand down."

"She's not going to like it," Henri said, pulling out a phone. "Verity paid us half our fee. The other half is contingent upon delivery."

"Call her," Tiger said, extending a hand. "I'll explain it to her."

Henri pressed a button and handed the phone to Tiger, as the call connected to Hemlock.

"Why are you calling me, Henri?" a husky female voice answered. "Have they arrived?"

"Hello, Hemlock," Tiger said, her voice soft. "You have a choice to make."

"Tiger." Hemlock said the name like a curse. "What are the *Stray Dogs* doing here?"

"Working, just like you," Tiger replied. "But unlike you, I'm not about to lose my partner."

"How do I know you haven't killed him?" Hemlock said. "For all I know, he's lying there in a pool of his own blood."

"I'm not that vicious," Tiger said. "He's still alive…for now."

"You'll forgive me if I don't believe you," Hemlock said. "Your reputation precedes you. Proof of life."

Tiger held the phone in front of Henri.

"I'm fine," Henri said with a quick glance at Peaches. "Stand down, dear, if you'd like me to remain that way."

"Shit," Hemlock said. "Verity is going to lose their collective minds if we renege on this mission."

"I'll call Sebastian," Tiger said. "He will match the delivery fee and help you disappear, *if* you stand down."

"And if I don't?" Hemlock asked after a brief pause. "What if I think I can make the delivery?"

Tiger smiled.

"We retire Henri first—painfully," Tiger said. "Then, once you realize you've made a fatal error, I'll make sure to retire you as well. It's your call. Walk away and live to kill another day, or die in a bookstore tonight."

Another pause.

"You guarantee Sebastian will cover the delivery fee?"

"I'll make the call and have it wired over the moment you vacate the premises," Tiger said. "I'll hold onto Henri here a little longer to make sure you don't have a sudden change of heart. Don't take it personally. It's not that I don't trust you, it's just—"

"Business," Hemlock finished. "Shame. I was looking forward to facing you tonight."

"Hemlock," Tiger said, her voice hard, "the day you face me will be the last day you're breathing."

Hemlock laughed.

"That's the Tiger I expected," she said with a short laugh before growing serious. "If you hurt him, I will come after you, Tiger. Stray Dogs or not, no one will save you."

"I've never needed saving," Tiger said. "I don't intend to start now."

"Fine, I'll agree to your deal on the condition Sebastian covers the delivery fee and provides egress out of the country."

"Done," Tiger said. "I'll make arrangements the moment you leave the building."

A few seconds later, I felt a spike of energy above us.

Ox stood up with a groan and headed our way.

"She's gone," he said, looking down at Henri. "That was an impressive tactic you and your friends used. Underhanded and dirty, but effective."

"Apologies," Henri said. "We had to plan for each of you being on site. We could not neutralize a null head-on. Subterfuge was the only choice."

"It worked…this time," Ox said, then turned to Tiger. "Am I taking them back?"

Tiger handed the phone back to Henri and pulled out her own.

"Yes," she said with a curt nod. "I'll stay here until Tristan and Strong get through the portal. Rat will keep watch. We're still on the clock."

"Right, I got the gist of the conversation," Ox said. "The boss will cover the delivery fee and an extended vacation for H&H. Anything else?"

"One more thing," Tiger said, holding up a finger to Ox as she drew closer to Henri. "As professionals, I will concede that you and your partner are a credible threat. That being said, if you two ever feel the need to cut your lives short, you come after the Stray Dogs. I will introduce you to such fear and pain, it will make being fed to a hellhound feel like mercy. Do we understand each other?"

Henri nodded mutely.

"Good," Tiger continued and focused on Ox. "Tell Sebastian we have a Verity tracker on us—a good one. He needs to get Rabbit on this. She can flush him out and throw him off, if need be."

"I'll let him know," Ox said, gazing at the ceiling. "You going to be good? Probably still some Arcanists up there."

"Nothing we can't handle," she said. "By the time the Keepers send backup, these three will be at the Living Library and I'll be at HQ."

Ox nodded and assembled the two unconscious librarians next to Henri, leaving the Arcanists where they lay.

"Watch your six," Ox said.

"Always," Tiger answered. "Get out of here."

Ox gestured and disappeared along with Henri and his two assistants.

"I better let Sebastian know the situation," she said. "He will not be pleased about Verity."

"Will he take action?" Monty asked. "Engaging them can be problematic for his desire to remain anonymous."

"There are some things he's willing to tolerate," Tiger said, pressing a button on her phone. "Rogue operators attempting to retire those he's watching is not one of them."

FIFTEEN

"Ox is incoming with H&H," Tiger said into her phone. "He will give you the details, but Verity is on the board. They have a tracker on Strong."

"On Strong?" Sebastian said. "Not Tristan?"

"They're tracking Strong," she said. "You'll need to call SuNaTran. I don't think they're leaving the same way they got here."

"Arrangements have been made," Sebastian answered. "That vehicle creates a...particular area of effect. It can't be left on the streets untended."

"Not if you want people to walk around this neighborhood without running for their lives in fear," she said, giving me a look. "What was Cecil thinking with the runes on that thing?"

"It's one of his pet projects, I assume," Sebastian answered. "Are you sure about the tracker?"

"Absolutely," she said. "They're following Strong. Tristan is too hard to pinpoint Strong may as well be walking around with a neon arrow pointing at his head. He's easier for them."

"It's to be expected," Sebastian said after a moment.

"Even Ox's masking skill would be challenged by his particular energy signature. Tell me of H&H."

"I convinced them to stand down from the completion of their mission."

"Which was?"

"Delivery of Tristan and Strong to Verity—for a fee, of course."

"Are they both still alive?"

"Yes. I did say I *convinced* them," Tiger said. "They are *both* alive."

"Good. You have been known to convince adversaries into the afterlife," Sebastian said. "I was just making certain that reparations were not needed. Am I to assume we are covering the delivery fee?"

"Yes," Tiger said. "Verity paid half on inception, half on delivery."

"We'll have to cover the entire thing to ensure Verity takes no further action against them," he said. "Even with the funds returned, H&H will need to go on an extended hiatus until this situation is resolved."

"I told them they could resolve that with you," Tiger said. "I hear the Aleutian Islands are excellent this time of year."

"The Aleutians? Your heart gives cold a new definition," he said. "I'll find a suitable location that's off radar."

"This is why *you're* the nice one," she said. "I'll make sure Tristan and Strong get to the portal and then head back."

"See that you do," Sebastian said. "Time is of the essence; the Keepers will soon know of your presence. By the time that happens, you need to be off-site."

"You need to find out who hired H&H and who this tracker is," she said. "Someone inside Verity really dislikes these two."

"It will be dealt with as soon as I return," Sebastian said.

"In the meantime, Rabbit will be tasked with locating and neutralizing the tracker on Strong."

"Good," she said. "I don't appreciate being followed."

"Understood. We'll converse when I return. Oh, one more thing—is Tristan within earshot?"

"I am," Monty said.

"Once you use the minor rune to open the door, you will alert the Keeper and his people," Sebastian said. "You must enter the portal immediately."

"I had no intention of waiting for them to arrive," Monty said, picking up on something in Sebastian's voice. "What's wrong? This warning is unlike you."

"I hate relying on rumors, but it's all we have at the moment," Sebastian admitted. "It appears Arch Keeper Evergreen has gone missing. This has been unsubstantiated, but there seems to be unrest in Evergreen's House. Do I need to stress how important this is if true?"

"No," Monty said. "If the Wood Rune unlocks the other four, Evergreen would be the pivotal Keeper to target. Through him, access to the other runes is attained."

"Precisely," Sebastian said, his voice grim. "I do not need to express how catastrophic it would be if the wrong people got hold of those runes."

"Who is his second?"

"Seconds," Sebastian corrected. "Every Keeper has two seconds—one of their faction and one belonging to the opposing faction of another Keeper—to balance the power of the Keepers."

"Who are these seconds?"

"Arcanist Patrick Tellus and Arcanist Myrtle Pine," Sebastian said. "According to my information, Tellus is the one who may be susceptible to betrayal. Pine was close to Evergreen even before becoming his student; she studied under him her entire life. But I've learned not to rule out anything until I have the truth."

"Do you have more information on Tellus?"

"It's scant," Sebastian said. "He was placed with Evergreen by the Keeper of the Earth Rune, Keeper Gault."

"Would Gault seek to undermine Evergreen?" Monty asked, managing to keep the names straight. "Does he have any animosity towards Evergreen?"

"The Keepers understand the law of balance," Sebastian said. "That being said, toppling a Keeper is not unheard of. If such an event occurs, a new Arch Keeper is chosen immediately."

"Toppling?" I asked. "They've killed each other?"

"Nothing so final as that," Sebastian said. "It's enough to make them lose face or make them appear incompetent. For example, if a certain minor rune were to be acquired by an inquisitive mage, it would make Evergreen look weak."

"Which would give Gault an opportunity to move against him in a play for power," Monty said. "Can any of the five become Arch Keeper?"

"Yes, and the position rotates every fifty years," Sebastian said. "Next in line would be the Keeper of the Fire Rune—Keeper Ustrina."

"Do you know when the next rotation is due?"

"Evergreen recently acquired the mantle of Arch Keeper."

"Which means Gault would have to wait close to a century before taking the mantle," Monty said. "What do you know about him?"

"Precious little," Sebastian said. "Keepers are reclusive and rarely leave their spheres of influence. I'll see if I can find out more."

"One last question: is there a conferring of power or abilities on the Arch Keeper?" Monty asked. "Some special dispensation?"

"The Arch Keeper determines the path of the Keepers as whole for the fifty years of their term," Sebastian replied. "They are tasked with maintaining the balance in the magical world on this plane while they lead the group."

"That sounds like a major responsibilty," I said. "I can't imagine anyone would actively look for more responsibilty; it sounds like a massive headache."

"There is one more thing."

"Which is?" Monty asked.

"The Arch Keeper has access to all five of the runes and their power during their tenure as Arch Keeper," Sebastian added. "If a Keeper were particularly ambitious, I would imagine that much power would provide considerable incentive. That's as much as I was able to uncover on short notice."

"It would seem Gault has other plans besides maintaining the balance," Monty said after a brief pause. "Anything more you can learn about Gault or any of the other Keepers would prove beneficial."

"Understood. In the meantime, I'll make sure to handle Verity's fee and arrange egress for H&H. Do not linger in the bookstore. Get them to the portal, Tiger."

"Will do," she said and ended the call, before looking at her watch. "We should move."

We headed across the floor to the opposite side where the stairwell waited. A knot of concern made a fist in my gut. If one Keeper with an elder rune was a major threat, what kind of threat would he be with all five elder runes?

"Do you think your borrowing the minor elder rune set this all in motion?" I asked. "Sounds like there is more going on than we know."

"Much more, apparently. It would seem my actions, unbeknownst to me, have had far-reaching repercussions," Monty said. "It's quite possible my acquisition of the rune of sealing created the opening for Gault."

"How could you even know that would happen?" I asked, still wondering about the world of Keepers. "This is a riddle, wrapped in a mystery, inside an enigma."

"Aptly stated," Monty said. "The British Bulldog would be proud. We, however, find ourselves in the midst of this riddle, and we somehow must unravel it."

"That sounds like taking a fatal action," I said as we cautiously approached the next staircase going up. "I have a bad track record with stepping into extensive plans and screwing them up. Ask Kali."

"Kali?" Tiger asked. "*The* Kali?"

"Yes. She and I have some history, most of it painful...for me."

"We will have to confront this, but we must be prudent," Monty said. "We can't face a Keeper, according to my uncle."

"We probably could. It's the surviving part that would be tough."

"Sebastian has proven more resourceful than I gave him credit for," Monty said after a moment of silence. "He is playing a long game with the two assassins."

"I'm surprised he's going to cover the *entire* fee," I said. "He didn't even ask how much it was."

"Money isn't an issue for the Directive," Tiger said. "We'll fold it into operating costs."

"Why cover the entire fee, though?" I asked. "Why not just give H&H the other half and send them on their way?"

"Makes life easier for us," she said as we walked. "It allows Verity to save face and puts H&H in our debt. Wins all around."

"In your debt?" I asked, incredulous. "You're thinking of using *their* services?"

"This is a different world from the one you may know or be accustomed to," she said. "We don't go around eliminating everyone who stands against us. Today's enemy could be tomorrow's ally."

"The enemy of my enemy is my friend?"

"Close enough," she said with a nod. "H&H may prove useful in the future. It helps to have them owe us their lives—if only in the long term. At the very least, it removes them from the board."

"And in the short term?"

"Better to have them far away, so as to curtail any complications."

"Far away, like the Aleutian Islands?"

"Well, there's always the Svalbard Islands, but I don't think they'd like Norway," she said with a wicked smile. "They make the Aleutian Islands feel like a tropical retreat."

"You really are cold," I said. "Remind me to never ask you for vacation destinations."

"That's probably wise."

"It's a practical measure," Monty said as we headed to the end of the floor. "It will make them difficult to locate and prevent an easy return to this country."

"Good to see someone understands my rationale," Tiger said. "It also sends a message."

"A message?" I asked. "What message?"

"You don't cross the Directive without consequences," she said. "I gave Henri a chance to walk away. He didn't take it. This option was his next best outcome."

"What if he had refused this option?"

"We would have left them for Verity to deal with," she answered. "I hear they don't take failure well."

"They don't," I said, remembering how Edith dealt with Ines. "It's usually a fatal reaction."

Tiger nodded as Peaches nudged into my leg, nearly knocking me down. I gently attempted to shove him back and found myself pushing off him.

"Do hellhounds really eat human flesh?" Tiger asked, glancing at Peaches as we headed to the last stairwell with Monty in the lead. "That sounds like it would be problematic for upkeep."

We paused at the foot of the steps.

"I have no idea," Monty said as we looked up the stairwell. "Henri seemed to have had a traumatic experience; I merely capitalized on it."

"You lied?" she asked. "He was scared to within an inch of his life."

"I prefer to call it a creative extrapolation of the facts," Monty answered. "He does eat flesh, it's just not human flesh. I skewed the facts somewhat to create the desired outcome."

I shook my head with a smile, before a thought hit me.

That last sentence was how Monty was operating lately. It was effective, but it was also dangerous, especially now that we were dealing with the elder runes.

I had to keep an eye on him to make sure that the skewing of facts in this case didn't lead to him being corrupted by the elder runes while he was trying to create the desired outcome.

We climbed the last stairwell.

SIXTEEN

"If I know Hemlock," Tiger said as we reached the top of the stairs, "the Arcanists on this floor should be neutralized."

"She killed them?" I asked. "That is low."

Tiger gave me a look that said, *Get a grip*.

"Strong, you need to get out more," Tiger said, looking around the floor for the Arcanists. "Hemlock, like Henri, is a professional. If the job didn't call for killing everyone in the building, she didn't kill them."

"*You're* the one who said 'neutralize,'" I said. "*Contract killer* and *neutralize* in the same sentence translates to dead bodies in my mind. I'm just surprised by the honorable code of conduct. Usually it's cutthroat behavior...literally."

"Not if they're not the designated targets," she said. "They should be around here somewhere."

After some searching, Tiger pointed to a group of bodies lying out of sight between the shelves along the far wall. I counted five Arcanists, all unconscious.

"She took them out alone?" I asked surprised. "All five?"

"She is a venomancer," Monty said, looking at the unconscious mages. "To incapacitate this group without killing them speaks to her skill. This is not a person to take lightly."

"Her toxin is very effective," Tiger said, looking at the Arcanists. "She can vary the lethality of the poison, making it an efficient neutralizing agent."

"Even water, which we need for life, can be deadly in too large a dose," Monty added with a slight nod. "That she can vary the lethality of her poison makes her a serious threat."

"It's what makes her so dangerous." Tiger looked down at the Arcanists again, nudging one with her boot. He didn't even stir. "One moment you're standing guard, and the next, you're falling on the floor unconscious."

"And you were willing to face her alone?"

She nodded her expression hard.

"I've encountered H&H in the past," she said. "They *are* dangerous, but have vulnerabilities, particularly Hemlock."

"They care for each other," Monty said after a moment. "It creates a leverage point. This is why you let her know Henri's life would be forfeit if she didn't comply."

"Exactly," Tiger said, looking around. "I don't pretend to understand their relationship, but I have seen them take unnecessary, even potentially fatal, risks to protect each other. Effective assassins can't have connections—they become liabilities."

"The assassins, or the connections?" I asked.

"Both," she said, looking at her watch. "We're on the clock. Tristan, can you find this portal?"

Monty narrowed his eyes and he took in the room.

"It's been some time since I used this entrance to the Living Library, and I don't know if it's been altered recently," he said. "Professor Ziller may have hidden it further or removed it entirely."

"Well, if it's still here, I suggest you find it fast, because in approximately six minutes, we're going to get a visit from Evergreen or one of his seconds," she said, looking around. "I, for one, do not intend to be here when that happens."

Monty closed his eyes and focused.

"What happened to seeing us through the portal?" I asked, as Monty channeled his inner mage. "Wasn't the job to see us through to this special location in the Living Library?"

She turned to give me a look.

"I never said I would see you *through* the portal," she said, her voice tight as she glanced around the space again. "I said I would see you *to* the portal. There's a world of difference there."

"Sounds like CYA semantics to me," I said. "That, and fear. Are you scared?"

"Only someone monumentally ignorant or unfathomably oblivious would live in this world without a healthy dose of fear," she said. "Which are you?"

"I belong to the *thrust into this world without any warning* group," I said. "So, you're scared."

Her gaze hardened as she took a breath. I could tell she was doing a mental ten-count to prevent herself from shredding me, or some other violent response.

"I don't know you, and more importantly, you don't know me," she said in a calm measured tone which let me know she was about a heartbeat away from unleashing the pain and agony on me. "Sebastian requested I do this, and in deference to his leadership, I'm here doing my job to the best of my ability. However, I will not be insulted."

"I wasn't trying to insult—"

"I'm not finished," she said, cutting me off. "I do not base my actions on fear. I never have and never will. It's irrational, and that means it's stupid—and worse, deadly. Reacting out of fear is one of the fastest ways to get yourself and your team retired. Do you know how I've managed to survive so long in *my* world?"

"You know when to disengage."

She nodded.

"Precisely," she said with a semi-surprised look, and extended an arm outward in a sweeping motion. "We are currently on the floor that contains the portal. For all intents and purposes, I saw you *to* the portal. Technically, my job is now done."

"I was just saying that—"

"Don't," she said, raising a finger. "Taking you through the portal was never part of the job description, and if it were, I wouldn't be the one standing here."

"It's over there," Monty said, opening his eyes and moving fast to one side of floor. He stood in front of a blank wall. "It's here."

Tiger looked at the wall and then looked at Monty. She tapped the wall and then looked at Monty again.

"Are you sure?" she asked. "Because I'm not sensing anything besides a brick wall. A very solid brick wall, I might add."

"I'm certain," Monty said. "Please give Sebastian my regards upon your return. Thank you for your assistance in getting us this far."

"I need to at least *see* the portal," she said. "If something goes wrong—not that I'm doubting your ability to sense this wall—but if we have to come back and remove your dismembered bodies, the first question Sebastian will ask is: Did you actually see the portal?"

Monty nodded and gestured, moving his hands in a figure-eight pattern in front of the wall. The plain brick wall transformed into a large, solid, rune-covered wooden door. The orange runes on its surface pulsed with latent energy as Tiger drew close and made to touch the door with a hand.

Monty shot out a hand faster than I could track and grabbed her by the wrist before she made contact.

"That...would be a bad idea," Monty said, releasing her hand slowly. "These runes are designed to eliminate anyone who touches the door. It would explain why it's so well hidden."

Tiger retracted her hand and cautiously took a few steps back.

"Thank you," she said. "Death by door would be a foolish way to go."

"I would have to agree," Monty said. "This door should take us where we need to go."

"I've seen the portal." She looked down at her watch. "You have four minutes. If I were you, I'd get scarce right about now."

"As soon as you exit the premises, I'll begin our exit as well," Monty said with a small smile. "It's been a pleasure."

Tiger smiled back and I felt like I had missed what was so amusing.

"Never hurts to try, right?" she said, still smiling and cocking her head to one side. "Hope to see you both soon...alive."

Monty nodded as she disappeared.

"What was that?" I asked. "What was she trying? Were you flirting with her, and if so, do I need to remind you how dangerous an angry Roxanne can be to your health?"

"I'd say about as dangerous as an ancient vampire intent on visiting bodily harm on any of your dates."

"Ouch. It was *one* date and I saw that smile," I said. "Are you sure you weren't flirting?"

"I do not flirt," Monty said, turning to the door again, the smile gone, his face a mask of focus. "Do you recall which rune Sebastian instructed me to use to access the location we need?"

"Yes," I said after giving it some thought. "He said you needed to use the minor elder rune you know. The rune of sealing."

"Why that rune, specifically?"

"I figure that, since it's one of the elder runes it leads to the others—the major runes?"

"That logic is flawed," he said, still studying the runes on the door. "Using an elder rune of sealing to access a prohibited area in the Living Library is the equivalent of using a hammer to kill an ant. Inelegant and inefficient."

"Then why suggest that rune?"

"That is a good question," Monty said. "But I think that information came from another source, not from Sebastian. The answer lies in this group of symbols."

I turned to the door and looked at the runes.

"That's the key, isn't it?"

Monty nodded.

"The unlocking is embedded in these symbols," he said. "They are the key."

"Was Sebastian lying about you needing the elder rune?"

"Not necessarily," Monty said, stepping closer to the door. "I do need to use the elder rune, just not in the way he imagined."

"Are you saying Tiger wanted to see you use the elder rune?"

"I'm fairly certain she was instructed to wait until I opened the portal before returning to their base of operations."

"Why?" I asked. "And if those were her instructions, why leave so quickly?"

"She wasn't lying about our window rapidly closing," he said. "What she did was the equivalent of a nudge to see if I would take the bait. She couldn't risk waiting any longer and neither can we."

"She doesn't know what the rune looks like," I said as it dawned on me. "This was a move to get a look at the rune in action."

"She was waiting for me to use the rune," he said as he focused on the runes on the door. "I would imagine her ability would give her some kind of photographic memory."

"How could that help her?" I asked. "Can she even *use* the rune?"

"Probably not, but Sebastian could—if he knew the *entire* rune, which he doesn't," Monty said, glancing at me. "I'm more than willing to answer any of your questions later, but if she's correct in her time estimate, we have a narrow window in which to open this door."

I stepped back and waved him on.

"Do your mage-wiggling," I said. "I'll keep an eye out for any threats."

"Thank you," he said. "From what I can see, I only have one opportunity to try this sequence. I'd like to get it right."

"What happens if you get it wrong?"

"Seeing as how *I'm* not cursed by Kali, if I get it wrong, this will be the last time we will have a conversation. The Argosy will cease to exist."

"Cease to exist?" I asked. "As in explode?"

"Cease to exist as in be completely unraveled from reality and rendered into particles."

"Does that involve a violent explosion? How much unraveling are we talking about, exactly?"

"Implosion, and significantly violent," Monty said, rubbing his chin. "There seems to be enough latent power contained in these symbols to undo the entire block, if not more. The failsafes are quite intriguing, as is the trigger."

"Monty?"

"Yes?"

"I understand that you're channeling your inner Spock,

finding this intriguing and all," I said. "Can I make one small suggestion?"

"Does it have to do with the runes on this particular door?" he asked, pointing at the door without looking at me. "Or is this going to be some sage wisdom from your months of deep mage study at the Magical University of Inexperience?"

"Oh, mage humor," I deadpanned. "I see what you did there."

Now I was really scared.

If Monty was unleashing the mage humor, there was a good chance he was in over his head, which meant death was close. Closer than I felt comfortable admitting.

"One question first," I continued. "Then, I'll leave you alone to figure this out."

"That would be welcome. What is your question?"

"Can you read these runes?" I asked, glancing at the pulsing runes on the door. "Really read them?"

"I can surmise the meaning," he said. "These runes have elements of the elder rune I know."

"Surmise?" I asked as my blood chilled. "You're going to...guess?"

"Yes, but it's an *educated* guess," he said with a straight face. "That makes all the difference. Do I need to remind you that time is of the essence?"

"No, I'm aware."

"Is your suggestion related to these runes?"

"Only indirectly, I think," I said. "Do *not* get the sequence wrong."

"I would say that's rather direct, but I will take your suggestion under advisement."

"I'd rather not be undone tonight, if it's not too much trouble."

"I'll do my best to get it right," he said with a short nod. "Now, if I could focus on the door?"

"All yours," I said, moving back. "I'm just going to back up a little, though."

"If it makes you feel better," he said, glancing at me. "By all means, back up."

Peaches padded over to where I stood and sat next to me—he, too, was focused on the door and I wondered if he knew what Monty was doing.

<Monty is going to open that door, but we can't distract him.>

<We? I never distract him. I think he doesn't want you to distract him.>

<I'm not a distraction. I'm an essential facilitator of focus.>

<Sometimes, you talk when I'm starving and need to eat.>

<I'm just warning you to eat slowly—it's probably bad for you to inhale everything so fast. What's your point?>

<I am a hellhound. When it's time to eat, I eat. I don't talk. Doing anything else is a distraction. The angry man needs to open the door right now. If you talk, you are being a distraction.>

I was about to respond when I realized he was right.

Being schooled by hellhound logic stung.

<You're right. Let's move back a little more.>

Once we were several feet away, Monty nodded and focused on the door again. I could see the sweat forming on his forehead. He didn't look nervous—at least not on the outside.

Being a mage, I knew he was a master of understatement. That included how much danger and devastation we were facing. This time, though, one mistake could disintegrate the entire building if not the entire block.

Starting with us.

If I asked him for the details of how this would happen, he'd say something like: This sequence has been arranged to coincide with the fluctuation of ambient energy around us. Therefore, triggering the failsafes would initiate a collapsing cascade effect that would unravel all of the matter in proximity to this door, beginning with the matter that makes up our bodies.

Which would be his mage way of saying we're dead. He would then continue with: *This would result in a catastrophic chain of events, beginning with our demise and ending with the complete annihilation of this portal and this edifice, including but not limited to all of the valuable books contained within the Argosy Bookstore... That,* or some other magey answer like it that downplayed the absolute destruction that would occur if he messed up the sequence.

I started feeling the energy buildup about twenty seconds later.

At first, I thought it was just the fear of what Monty was about to do. We had been in tight spots before, but I had never felt this kind of dread, not even when I knew one mistake made by either of us could mean the end.

This was different, somehow—deeper and overwhelming, like a massive weight had fallen on me and was pressing me down into the floor.

It was the feeling of impending death. The sensation hovered around the stairwell for close to a minute before moving again.

It was heading our way.

"I...I don't mean to distract you," I said, looking toward the stairwell, "but—"

"I feel it as well," he said, still focused on the door. "Would you prefer I deal with the incoming presence of death, or open this door so we can escape?"

"Just checking. You should continue," I said quickly, still focused on the stairwell. "As fast you can without blowing us to bits would be a bonus."

"It would be easier to do that if you weren't speaking to me."

I nodded to myself in response and Peaches gave off a high-pitched whine.

"These runes are ancient," Monty said to himself. "Ziller couldn't have possibly altered them into this configuration. They predate...Fascinating. These are *protorunes*, but the sequence is all wrong. It's... Of course... Ingenious."

"I'm...I'm really glad you find all this so fascinating," I said, the words becoming difficult as the overwhelming sense of terror gripped me by the throat and slowly forced the air out of me. "Monty...you need to hurry."

Monty moved his hands in several rapid gestures. The runes flared orange for several seconds before the door swung open. I turned at the sound of the door opening behind me—and that's when I heard the footsteps on the stairs and froze in place.

The terror that gripped my body was beyond explanation. Every neuron in my brain was telling me to run; but why bother? I was going to die where I stood.

Accept it. Accept death. Embrace the end. To fight against it would be futile. There was no point.

"If you walk through that door, you'll be walking to your death," a voice said from the bottom of the stairs. "Don't be in such a rush to die. We should speak first."

The energy signature coming from the stairs nearly drove me to my knees. My body felt like it weighed a few tons, and all I wanted to do was lay down and let death claim me. I staggered where I stood, as the waves of energy washed over me.

"Inside," Monty said, raising his voice as he grabbed my arm. With a low growl, Peaches reacted better than I did. He rumbled and gripped my other arm in his jaws and tugged on me, pulling me to the doorway. Monty, with a vise grip around my arm dragged us in as I stood frozen in place, looking at the stairwell. "Now!"

We tumbled inside and as the door slammed shut behind us, I caught a glimpse of a man reaching the top of the stairs.

SEVENTEEN

"Who the hell was that?" I nearly screamed, getting to my feet. "What the hell was that?"

Monty who appeared as shaken as I was, was rapidly tracing runes in the air and securing the door. When he was done, he leaned on the door and let out a long breath.

We stood in an empty stone room. The only feature that stood out was the door we had just used. Everything else was bare stone. As I looked closer, I saw that every surface of the small room was covered in soft violet runes.

"Do you know where we are?" I asked, taking in the empty room. "This isn't the Living Library."

"Not that I can recall, no. I've never seen a room like this in the Library—but the Library is vast. We could be in the Living Library, just an area I'm not familiar with."

"That fear..." I said with a shudder. "That wasn't normal fear, Monty. I've felt normal fear, and what I felt in the Argosy was *not* normal fear."

"I've felt that fear before," he said. "It felt like a much stronger version of Niall, the pavormancer."

"It felt like the void passage—except on steroids—mixed with Dex's insane test to get into his School of Battle Magic."

He nodded and took another long breath.

A sudden wave of nausea hit me, and my body seriously considered ejecting the contents of my stomach all over the floor. I took another breath and focused, breathing through the wave of nausea until my stomach calmed down.

I looked down at my shaking hands and forced myself to take a few more deep breaths. Peaches stood protectively near me, but I could tell even he had been affected by the fear that had filled the bookstore.

He focused on the door, standing in *shred and maim* mode as a low, long rumble escaped from him. I crouched down and got close to my hellhound.

I hugged him around the neck—more for me than for him. After a minute or two, I was able to get myself slightly under control. My breathing had returned to mostly normal and my heartbeat wasn't doing a world-record breaking hundred-meter dash.

The fear remained.

It was less intense, but I knew it was there, just under the surface, waiting to freeze me in place at any moment.

"Whoever that was, let's not meet him again," I said, forcing the slight tremble in my voice to disappear. "Do we even know who it was?

Monty shook his head.

"I doubt that was Evergreen," Monty said, taking a short pause between his words. "The energy signature was powerful, but I would expect an Arch Keeper to be even stronger than that."

"Stronger?" I asked in disbelief. "But if that wasn't Evergreen, then who was—?"

"*That* was Arcanist Tellus," a voice said from behind us. "My second. I could sense the betrayal from here."

Startled, Monty and I turned at the sound of the voice. My hand flew to Grim Whisper. It took half a second for me to realize how futile that was.

Bullets—entropy or persuader rounds—weren't going do anything in the weight class we were currently moving around in. I was going to need major firepower, maybe entropy bombs, just to be on safe side.

An older man stepped into view. He was dressed in a loose-fitting, tan linen shirt and dark slacks. He was completely bald, but wore an impressive beard which was more salt than pepper.

"Arch Keeper Evergreen?" Monty said with a slight nod of his head as he composed himself. "Well met; you honor us."

"Evergreen," the old man said, waving Monty's words away. "I have no use for the title, at least not in this place."

Even though the Keeper had to be centuries—maybe even millennia—old, his voice sounded like that of a man in his late forties, early fifties at most. He stood there for a few seconds and gazed at us.

My body was still reacting to the fear blast from Tellus. My brain was stuck in a vicious cycle of wanting to shoot everything in sight, run for it, or curl into a ball on the ground.

"You're safe for now," Evergreen said, his voice calm as he rested a hand on my shoulder. "Be at peace."

Instantly, a sense of peace and tranquility descended over me. Any fear I felt...vanished and became a distant memory.

"There you go," he said. "That should feel better."

I nodded.

"Much," I said with a long sigh, composing myself. "What...what was that? The fear?"

"An activation of the sympathetic nervous system," Monty said, sounding more like himself now. "Our minds and bodies were stressed to levels beyond comprehension.

That is the fear casting of a pavormancer of exceptional power."

"I feel like I've been run over by a truck," I said, as a headache gripped the base of my neck. A sudden exhaustion came over me. "I couldn't think about anything else but running away or fighting for my life."

"You have experienced a fraction of Tellus's power," Evergreen said, his voice grim. "That you both survived means his fear is well-founded. You pose a threat to him and his master."

"Survived?" I asked. "Not feeling like much of a survivor at the moment."

"Where are we?" Monty asked. "This is not the Living Library."

"You are correct," Evergreen said. "Welcome to the interstitial—a space between here and there."

"The interstitial?" I asked. "That sounds like when Peaches goes in-between."

"Similar, but not exactly," Evergreen said. "This would be closer to when you count one and two. This is the and."

I could tell we were entering magespeak territory, because even though I understood the words he was using, the way he was using them was beginning to melt my brain.

"Can you explain that again? In English this time?"

Evergreen smiled and nodded. The next second, he clapped his hands twice. I winced as the sound of a small thunderclap threatened to deafen me twice.

"Did you hear that?" Evergreen asked. "The space between the claps?"

"How could I not? You wanted me to listen for the space between your attempts to deafen me?" I asked, rubbing my ears. "A little warning next time might be nice."

"This place is the sound between the two thunderclaps,"

he said, as if I knew what that meant. "When you count one and two, we are standing in the *and* of that sentence."

"Does time flow here?" Monty asked, looking around, clearly understanding what Evergreen was referring to—another sign we had entered magespeak territory. "Is this location in stasis?"

"No," Evergreen said, shaking his head. "Time is slowed here, but it's not static. It's moving slowly, but it's still moving. Let's not tarry; we don't have much time."

"What do you mean?" I asked even more confused. "You just said time is slowed here. Why don't we have much time?"

"Tellus knows where you are headed," Evergreen said, slashing an arm through the air and opening a portal. "He will try to follow you."

"Can he?" I asked, suddenly not looking forward to being scared shitless again. "I'd rather not go through that fear fest again."

"He can't follow quickly enough to make a difference. Now, quickly," he said, pointing to the portal, "through here."

We stepped through the portal and found ourselves in a comfortable sitting room. Several large sofas were spread out around the floor. Large bay windows gave us a fantastic view of a lake and a deep forest on either side of the lake.

I could hear the birds outside, and on the lake, flocks of geese landed and took off again. I saw several deer run through the trees as the sunlight reflected off the water.

"Where are we?" I asked, amazed by the view. "This could be a perfect vacation spot."

"This is still the interstitial, but I prefer this over an empty stone room," Evergreen said, moving over to one of the bookcases that filled the walls of the room. "Like the Living Library, this place exists slightly adjacent to the flow of time. It's"—he saw my eyes begin to glaze over—"a safe space for now. Tellus won't be able to locate you here."

"Thank you," I said. "I don't suppose you can go back there and blast Tellus to subatomic particles?"

"Tellus is the least of your concerns—and to answer your question, no, I won't go back and blast him to particles."

"Is there a reason you can't?" I asked, slightly upset. "It would make our lives much easier."

"I didn't say can't, I said *won't*," Evergreen answered, moving to one of the windows to take in the view. "If I did, your already precarious situation would become untenable. I need you alive."

"And your blasting Tellus would get us killed?"

"My blasting Tellus would force Gault to take direct action," he said. "He would move against Ustrina and accelerate the imbalance."

"You can't help us?"

"You don't need my help," Evergreen said. "You do need to be pointed in the right direction, but you don't need me to accompany you."

I looked at Monty.

"Could you explain the situation to the Keeper please?" I asked. "Maybe he can buff up your abilities and make you a temporary Keeper?"

Monty remained silent and stared at the Keeper. I could tell he was processing the information and had questions.

"How long have you been influencing events?" Monty asked. "How long?"

"Since you decided it was prudent to unleash not one, but two entropic vortices in your city," Evergreen said with a gesture and materialized a large mug of hot chocolate. "I must say it was quite impressive, if not entirely foolhardy."

"You saw that?" I asked.

"Yes," he said. "It helped form my decision."

"Your decision?" Monty asked. "Your decision about what?"

"You," Evergreen, said. "Specifically, the two of you."

"Excuse me?" I said. "What about the two of us?"

"Gault is looking to activate the elder runes out of sequence," Evergreen said. "In order to do this, he needs to remove me."

"Remove you," I said slowly. "You mean kill you?"

"No, though I don't put it past him to try," Evergreen said. "No, he needs to remove my ability to manipulate the other five runes."

"Is that even possible?" Monty asked. "I thought each rune was interrelated, with yours being the first and giving access to the others."

"For the most part that is true so long as I am Arch Keeper," Evergreen said. "If he manages to become Arch Keeper—"

"Oh no," I said, seeing the situation. "His rune becomes the gateway rune. He can have access to all the others through his rune."

"Yes," Evergreen answered. "That would be catastrophic."

"What does he want? Power?"

"He wants the end."

"The end?" I asked. "The end of what?"

"Everything," Evergreen said. "Gault is a nihilist. He is of the mind that we have wielded power for too long. It is time to let go and undo everything. He wants to usher in an age of entropy."

"Entropy?" I said. "But that would destroy…"

"Everything," Monty said. "It would become the ultimate form of—"

"Chaos," Evergreen said. "That is his goal—Chaos."

A cold fist gripped my chest.

EIGHTEEN

"Is it possible Gault is an agent of Chaos?" I asked.

"I honestly don't know," Evergreen said after taking a sip from his mug, "but he has unleashed his disciple, Tellus, to usurp the first rune."

"That is why you chose us," Monty said. "You want us to face Tellus."

"I'm afraid so," Evergreen said, turning to us. "Unfortunately, you are currently outmatched in power."

"And he can't use your rune?"

Evergreen looked at me and took another pull from his mug. The aroma of chocolate filled the room as he stared at me. It was one of those looks I saw occasionally on beings of power, that said: *Do you realize how easy it would be to remove you from existence?*

"No, it would destroy him if he tried."

"Why Monty?" I asked, pushing the envelope of near death experiences as I became upset. "Why not pick Dexter? You do know Monty has an uncle who is off-the-charts powerful, right?"

"I am aware."

"Then why pick Monty if he isn't strong enough?" I asked. "This sounds like you're setting him up to fail, or worse—to be obliterated by this Tellus."

"Simon, perhaps you should temper the questions with some prudence?" Monty said, glancing at me. "We *are* speaking to an Arch Keeper."

"An Arch Keeper who sees a problem, but won't face it himself, is all I'm seeing," I snapped. "Why don't *you* deal with Gault?"

"I am dealing with Gault," he said. "You are my solution."

"This feels like deflecting. You yourself said we are outmatched," I said, letting the anger rise in my voice. "What are we supposed to do against a Keeper and his minions?"

"Even a splinter can cause enough discomfort to create an advantage," he said. "Don't you agree?"

"I agree that this solution feels suicidal."

"What do you think should be done with the first elder rune, Simon?" Evergreen asked taking me off-guard. "Should it remain hidden, or lost, as some have chosen to call it?"

"Can you hide it so well no one will ever find it?"

"I think you know the answer to that question," he said. "Power draws both good and evil to itself. I could, perhaps, hide it for some time, but eventually it will be discovered."

"Then why not give it to someone who can use it to stop Gault and Tellus?"

"You tell me," Evergreen said. "Why not give it to Dexter? He can certainly use it. I did extend the offer to him. What do you think he said?"

"No," Monty said. "My uncle turned you down in no uncertain terms."

"In his typical colorful way," Evergreen said with a small chuckle. "When the Caretaker approached him, he used some very descriptive language about the placement of said elder rune. I always did enjoy Dexter's frankness."

"Why would he turn it down?" I asked, suppressing a smile and imagining Dex telling the Caretaker where he could put said rune. "He knows we're in danger if Gault gets it. Everything is in danger if Gault gets it, and he turns it down?"

"Because there is such a thing as too much power," Monty said. "He turned it down because he knew the danger of one person wielding that much power."

Evergreen nodded.

"The more power one possesses, the more circumspect one must be," Evergreen said. "An outright battle between Keepers cannot be allowed to occur. The collateral damage would be unimaginable, not only on this plane, but on several planes."

"Gault knows this, doesn't he?"

"He does, and he's counting on the Keepers' reluctance to engage him directly," Evergreen answered. "By the time they react, it will be too late. He will have made his move."

"And be in possession of three runes," Monty said. "Can the Keepers be warned? Can you convey the gravity of the situation to them?"

"Each Keeper is a faction unto itself," Evergreen said, shaking his head. "Cooperation is not our strong suit. If even two of us joined forces—"

"The balance would be upset," Monty finished. "Collaboration is too risky. Even for the greater good."

"Even for the greater good," Evergreen echoed. "The steps I'm taking are unprecedented. Involving you would never be suspected."

"Except by Gault," I said. "He's playing by a different set of rules. The Keepers are playing checkers, and he's out there playing 4D chess."

"Agreed," he said. "Which is why I have taken steps."

"What about the other Keepers?" I asked. "Not Ustrina, the other two. They each wield a rune, and you, the Arch Keeper, have access to all five. That's not enough power for one person to stop Gault?"

"As I mentioned earlier, they will not join forces—not even with me," Evergreen said. "The isolation is a method of protection."

"It's a disaster is what it is," I said. "This whole thing has serious flaws all over the place. Absolute power corrupts—"

"Absolutely," Evergreen finished. "I'm aware, and have seen this play out many times among the Keepers."

"Yet no failsafe was put in place?" I asked in disbelief. "How was this allowed to happen?"

"Keepers are neither infallible nor gods," Evergreen said. "We can and do make mistakes. That being said, we have lived long enough not to be enticed by the lures of power. A failsafe was not needed."

I stared at him for a few seconds.

This was the answer of someone who believed their own hype. This was the reason I hated dealing with gods—they ended up living and existing in echo chambers of their own making.

The Keepers weren't gods, exactly, but they were so far removed from normal humans in the scope of power, that they forgot the basics. Give someone access to enough power, and sooner or later they were going to try to use it selfishly.

"Seems like Gault was absent when that class was being taught," I said. "You'd think living a long time would make some people understand that thirsting for power always ends badly."

"As I said, Keepers are not infallible," Evergreen said. "This is also not being forced on you. The Caretaker made a suggestion—to find and harness the power of the runes. He never said you should wield it yourselves. You are also free to decline this quest."

"What happens if we decline?"

"Tellus will locate the first elder rune eventually, using it to displace me," he said. "This will give him access to Ustrina and her rune. Together with Gault, Ustrina will be neutralized. Gault will obtain three of the five runes and either force the other two Keepers into compliance, or kill them. With three runes, he will be too powerful to stop."

"What happens if he gets all five? Isn't there some group or body or organization created to stop this abuse from happening? Someone to stop the abuse of magical abilities on this plane?"

"Of course," Evergreen said with a small smile. "They are called the Keepers of the Arcana."

"So, basically we're screwed," I said. "There's no one to watch the watchers?"

"If you rise high enough, there is always only one person or one group tasked with keeping the order," Evergreen said. "The Keepers are that group. It is who we are and why we exist. To answer your question, no, there is no one else we can turn to if Gault gets hold of three runes. With all five, it would be the end."

"Well, shit," I said. "What are we supposed to do? What *can* we possibly do against a Keeper?"

"I have a solution," Evergreen said. "It's risky, but it can work—precisely because you aren't strong enough to wield the rune. Would you like to hear it?"

"Not really, no," I said. "I'm sure it's going to involve pain and agony, but do we have a choice?"

"Always," he said. "The real question is: are you prepared to live with the consequences of your choices?"

"Not if it means the destruction of everything," I said with a short sigh. "I'm in. Monty?"

"I will not be party to the annihilation of reality," he said. "If I can prevent Gault from unleashing entropy on this plane of existence, I will do everything within my power to stop him from doing so."

Peaches rumbled by my leg and nudged me.

"Even my hellhound is in," I said. "What's your solution?"

NINETEEN

"This is suicide," I said when I heard the solution. "We are going to die, and I mean really die. All of us."

"There is a chance," Evergreen said. "It becomes a certainty if no action is taken."

"So, try the solution, and we have a chance of being blasted from existence—or refuse, and definitely be turned to dust?"

"Succinctly put, and yes," Evergreen replied. "What is your answer?"

"Do you really have to ask?"

"Of course. You have free will," he said. "I will not force you to risk your lives. You must do so willingly."

"My will isn't feeling particularly free these days," I said. "I can't believe this is your contingency plan. In fact, my will hasn't felt free since I stepped into this world."

"That is a matter of perception, Simon," Evergreen said. "You have always had free will, and you have exercised it. Officer Ramirez didn't force you to take the case that would cross your path with Mage Montague, did he?"

It didn't surprise me that Evergreen knew about my first

meeting with Monty. That he brought it up at this particular moment did.

"No, he didn't."

"If you analyze every step you have taken to reach this present moment, you will discover that it has all been a product of you exercising your free will," he said. "At each moment, you had a choice to make—as you do now. Each choice will lead you down a different path."

"Is this solution reversible?" I asked. "Or are we going to be stuck like this forever?"

"Forever is a long time," Evergreen said. "Undoing what I would have to do will depend on the both of you. Once you are strong enough, you will be able to undo what I must do with the rune."

"And in the meantime?" Monty asked. "This solution will jeopardize our lives significantly."

"How do you feel about the hidden runes, Tristan?" Evergreen asked. "What do you feel should be done with them? Should the knowledge be disseminated freely among all mages?"

"That sounds like a bad idea," I said. "If you share it freely with all mages, that power can be abused."

"Is this your position, Mage Montague?" Evergreen asked. "Should they remain lost?"

"No," Monty said. "I believe the knowledge should be accessible to those who would not abuse it."

"And how would you determine those who would use the knowledge for good, as opposed to those who would not?" Evergreen asked. "Can you read the intention of the heart?"

"I cannot," Monty said, after a moment of reflection. "What I do know is that making this knowledge forbidden primarily attracts those who would use it for selfish gain. If I can prevent that, I will."

"What do you think, Simon?" Evergreen asked, looking at me. "Is Tristan right?"

"I'm not a mage."

Evergreen laughed.

"I think it's time to put that excuse to rest...permanently," he said, his voice becoming hard. "Answer the question."

"It's not an excuse—I don't think I'm qualified to answer a question about some ancient rune that has incredible power. That is way out of my league."

"In your previous life as an operator," Evergreen said, throwing me off again, "how did you feel about dealing with classified information?"

"We don't discuss my previous life."

"And we won't," Evergreen assured me. "We are discussing how you feel about classified information."

"If it's classified to keep the world safe, it should remain classified," I said, my expression as hard as his voice. "If it's too dangerous to share, then it should be kept hidden."

"Who determines the level of danger?" Evergreen asked. "Who sets the classification of too dangerous? Who decides who needs to know when something is need-to-know?"

"Now you know one of the reasons why I'm no longer an operator," I said. "It's usually those who would abuse the information that want to keep it secret. It gives them an unfair advantage which they leverage for profit or more power. That still doesn't mean it should be shared."

"Then you disagree with Mage Montague?" Evergreen said. "You believe dangerous, classified information should remain hidden, even if it could benefit those who learn of it?"

"It's been my experience that that sort of information is rarely beneficial to any but a small group," I said, looking at Monty. "I think the lost runes should stay lost or hidden, but we all know that's not going to happen, or else the Caretaker wouldn't have told Monty to 'look for them and harness their energy.' I trust Monty. If anyone is going to make sure they're not abused, it's him."

"This dichotomy between the two of you is why I chose you," Evergreen said. "You each hold opposing views, but can see past them for the greater good."

"The greater good is going to get us killed."

"It sometimes requires sacrifice, yes," Evergreen agreed. "For unto whomsoever much is given, of him shall much be required."

"No need to get biblical," I said. "I understand the argument and what you are trying to do. I may not agree with all of it, but my entire life has shifted into areas I no longer agree with as par for the course. We can start with the fact that I don't agree with a premature death."

"Which you feel will be the result of your partaking in this?"

"Like Monty said, your solution will make our lives hell," I said. "We may disagree on the principle, but that won't matter. Everyone will be after us if we agree to this solution."

"You are both being hunted by Verity. Simon, you have successors after you." Evergreen looked down at Peaches before turning back to me. "The moment this magnificent creature reaches maturity and attains a battle form, you and he become an immediate threat to all of the organized bodies in this plane. They will hunt you both down."

"What?" I asked, surprised. "What are you talking about?"

He turned to Monty.

"Tristan, you currently possess a minor elder rune, a blood rune. Gault has marked you for elimination to prevent you from acquiring more," Evergreen said, ignoring me. "He cannot allow you to obtain any of the major elder runes."

"This is why Tellus was at the bookstore," Monty said pensively. "He was tasked with our removal."

"And still is," Evergreen said. "In fact, I would say the only way out for either of you *is* my solution. I would not be putting you in any more jeopardy than you currently find yourselves in."

"Have you ever done anything like this before?" I asked, a little nervous. "It's not that I don't trust you, but this doesn't seem like the normal method of rune sharing. Monty didn't do this for the minor rune." I glanced at Monty. "Did you?"

"No. To my knowledge, what the Keeper is proposing has never been done—at least not in this manner," Monty said. "The theory is sound, but I would have never thought it possible to convey the rune in this manner, and with these particular failsafes."

"That's the entire point—neither would the Keepers," Evergreen said. "Especially not Gault."

"We would in effect be hiding in plain sight," Monty continued. "How is this possible?"

"This is possible because of both the bond you share and my level of power," Evergreen said. "I would not recommend anyone below an Archmage attempting this transfer of information, and even then, it would be risky."

"I see the risk we are facing," I said. "Where's the risk to you? What risk are you taking?"

"Simon," Monty hissed while shaking his head. "He's a Keeper."

"Who's asking us to risk our lives," I said. "I think it's a fair question. Don't you?"

"I think he doesn't owe us an explanation," Monty snapped. "He's trying to save not just our lives, but the entire plane."

"Not good enough," I said, as the anger broiled under the surface. "Every time we are on these missions, *we* are the ones on the front lines, risking everything. For once, I'd like to know if someone else is going to be risking just as much as we are."

"Will knowing change anything?"

"Probably not," I said. "But I still want to know. If I'm heading to my death, I want to do it with my eyes open."

"It is a reasonable question," Evergreen said, raising a hand at Monty to prevent him from speaking. "If we do this, I estimate that I will be vulnerable for a period of one year, before my power begins to return. From that moment, I won't be at full power for a full century, until the shift of the next Arch Keeper."

"No," Monty said, realizing a lot more than I did in that moment. "They will kill you. Gault will capitalize on your weakness and move in to destroy you."

"It's a risk I'm prepared to take," Evergreen said, looking at me. "I'm not entirely defenseless, but I will have to remain in hiding for some time. Does that answer your question, Simon?"

"Are you *sure* this is the only way?"

"It is the only way to impart the rune and to have you both survive, yes," Evergreen answered. "Any other method would kill you both at your current power levels. It would take a little longer with you, Simon, due to Kali's curse upon you, but I can guarantee your death would be inevitable. Even Kali's power has limits."

I didn't know what concerned me more—that I was agreeing to a procedure that was possibly stronger than Kali's curse on my body, which meant it had the power to negate it and kill me, or that Evergreen even knew the details about my curse. It wasn't surprising, it just made me uncomfortable. What else did he know about me?

"Are we all in agreement?" Evergreen asked, putting down his mug after one last sip. "Are there any further questions?"

"One more," I said, holding up a finger. "Does this solution of yours have any unexpected side effects?"

"Side effects? Such as?"

"I don't know...Monty becomes an ultimate mage? Or I can wield energy of mass destruction?" I said. "You know, side effects that have *positive* outcomes."

"Well, there is the distinct possibility of an increase in power, but—"

"Now we're talking," I said, giving Monty a glance. "Wait a minute, though—you said 'but.' Why did you say *but*?"

"I wouldn't want to bore you with any of the other aspects," Evergreen said, looking out of the window again. "There may be some negative effects."

"Negative effects?" I asked, concerned. "What negative effects?"

"The cost," Monty added. "There is always a cost."

"Yes. Are you certain you want to know?" Evergreen asked. "This is all speculation, mind you. I've never tried this before."

"Tell us," I said. "What is the cost?"

"There is a distinct possibility of an increase in power for Mage Montague," Evergreen said, looking at Monty, "but power comes at a cost, even when it is imparted this way. There is always a cost to power—it is an immutable law."

"What is the cost?" I pressed, stepping past concerned and sliding into scared now. "What's going to happen to him?"

"Not just him," Evergreen said. "This is a shared cast. Both of you will be affected. With Tristan, the outcome is somewhat predictable—his being a mage and all—but with you, I truly don't know. I have never encountered a being with so many diverse bonds all at once."

"That doesn't sound good," I said. "You don't even have an educated guess?"

"It could be a myriad of effects," he said. "It could amplify your current abilities, or it could shatter your psyche and drive you insane. I have no way of gauging an unknown quantity. I'm sorry."

I could tell he was hedging and didn't want to share what he thought would happen.

"If you had to guess," I pressed. "I mean, you've been around a long time. I'm sure you've seen something close to, if not exactly the same as my condition. What do *you* think will happen?"

Evergreen's expression became hard and sad simultaneously.

"Kali's curse will try to keep you alive," he started. "At first, it will succeed."

"That doesn't sound so bad."

"Over time—and this could be days or centuries, I really don't know—you will transform into a dark immortal due to the increase in power."

"Why would the increase transform me into a dark anything?" I asked, remembering the whole argument about power not being good or evil. "Power doesn't have a morality. Why should I go dark? I could always be a light immortal."

"You know why," he said, his voice tinged with sadness and certainty. "Power corrupts, and absolute power—"

"Corrupts absolutely," I finished. "Is that just me, or is Monty going dark, too?"

"You do recall the part where I said this was all speculation?" he said. "I don't know." He glanced at Monty. "Mage Montague has hovered near the edge of darkness for some time now, but has not succumbed to its allure."

"I will never go dark," Monty said. "It holds no allure for me."

"If he remains steadfast and resists the darkness, you will have an opportunity to overcome any transformation into a dark immortal," Evergreen said. "If he fails to resist the temptation, then your journey into darkness will be easier."

"But not certain?" I asked. "There's still a chance I can resist the darkness?"

Evergreen nodded with a small smile.

"There is always a choice, Simon," he replied. "If that moment comes, you will face the hardest choice of your life."

"I guess we'll burn that bridge when we get to it, then," I said. "Monty? You see another option?"

"None that are tenable, no. We will have to see this to the end and face the consequences as they arise."

Evergreen nodded.

"Then we are in agreement," he said. "Once we begin the imparting, there is no turning back. Are you both completely certain?"

Monty and I both gave him short nods. Peaches let out a rumble and chuffed as he stepped closer to me.

"Very well," Evergreen continued. "Please produce your spiritual weapons. I must interlace the rune into the fabric of your very being. This requires they be part of the process."

"Does this mean Ebonsoul will get even more powerful?"

Evergreen smiled as he rolled up his sleeves and narrowed his eyes at me.

"More powerful than a siphoning necrotic seraph?" Evergreen asked. "Do you expect to face off against gods in the near future?"

"No, not really, but when I woke up this morning, I didn't expect to be part of an elder rune transfer either," I said. "I just want to know if there are going to be any changes to my weapon."

"This will be similar to your acquisition of the stormblood cast," Evergreen said, his voice serious. "The difference will be in the scale of power."

"Similar to the stormblood cast? That sounds painful," I said with a wince, remembering the agony of what York did to us. "Why does that sound painful?"

"If you both survive—" Evergreen started.

"If we both survive?" I asked, raising my voice slightly. "What do you mean, if we both survive?"

"Am I not being clear?" Evergreen asked. "There are always risks in doing the untried. You *both* must survive for this transfer to be successful. If only one of you survives the initial process, the flow of power will attempt to fill the vacuum created by either of your deaths."

"The overload would obliterate the survivor," Monty said with a nod. "That makes sense. The energy would try to restore the balance, but we would not be up to the task and will perish."

"Precisely so," Evergreen said. "As I was saying, if you both survive—"

"I'm not comfortable with any sentence that contains both obliterate and perish, when I'm the subject," I said, shaking my head. "Can't you just tattoo the rune on Monty or something similar?"

"Only if I want to kill him," Evergreen said. "Ready?"

"As ready as I can be," I said after a pause. "Let's do it."

TWENTY

I was not ready.

Evergreen stood between Monty and me. He called to Peaches and made sure my hellhound sat next to me. Monty held the Wailers in his hands, and I held Ebonsoul.

I smiled as the thought of Monty and the Wailers made me think of some renegade reggae band led by an English mage. *Maybe in another life.*

Evergreen stood in the center and took a deep breath. As he let it out, power flooded the room. It wasn't just power, though—it was pure energy, the essence of power, and the promise of creation and destruction, all combined.

The presence of that much power stole my breath away. My eyes began to tear up as it wrapped itself around me. The next thought that surfaced was that each time something like this had happened, there had never been a pain-free solution. I really hoped this time would be different.

"Mage Montague, you will be the repository of the rune," Evergreen said, his voice thunderous as he spoke. "You are the mage and you will bear the burden of holding the magic."

For a moment, I breathed out a breath of relief. If Monty bore the burden of the magic, that wouldn't leave much for me to worry about. I really hoped that translated into the burden of the pain, too.

I hoped wrong.

"Simon Strong, you are the *Aspis*, the shield warrior and the catalyst," Evergreen continued. "You will bear the burden of causality. The activation of the rune will rest with you."

The pressure of the power around us increased. It was immense. I could barely withstand it, but if it maintained at this level, I could get through this without any major agony.

I should've known better.

Evergreen began to glow.

Not his hands, but his entire body, became golden with hints of orange energy flaring around him. It was like staring at a human sun. After a few seconds, the glow was so intense I had to look away. He extended his arms, resting one hand on my shoulder and one on Monty's.

When he spoke, the pressure of the power on my body was too much. I couldn't make out the words, but the pain was unmistakable.

Agony shot through my body, rooting me in place. Golden energy blazed from Evergreen and traveled down his arms into each of us. He was still whispering something, but the words were lost to me. I could see his lips moving, but there was no sound.

The golden energy, which seemed innocent at first glance, covered my entire body. For a few seconds, it was just energy and power. The next second, it took on an entirely new feeling.

Any thoughts I had about this being a pain-free experience evaporated in that moment. Transcendent, brain-melting, body-destroying heat enveloped me.

I tried to step away, but found myself immobile. Evergreen's grip was a vise of power I couldn't break.

The golden energy became hotter as I wondered if this is what it felt like to be thrown into the center of the sun, or tossed into the open mouth of an active volcano.

And still, the heat increased.

I started screaming then, using a fist to strike at Evergreen's hand in an effort to dislodge him. Nothing worked. He squeezed even harder and I felt my legs go weak.

My knees buckled and I saw Monty go down on his knees. I followed a moment later, and still the heat increased. At this point, death would have been a welcome relief—anything to stop the pain, the agony, and the pure white-hot destruction of my being.

Only Peaches seemed unaffected. He sat there focused on me, his eyes getting brighter by the second. The runes along his flank flared to life, the red symbols bright in my eyes.

He raised his head and unleashed a long howl. This was followed by a deep low rumble. As Evergreen continued, tremors rocked the room we stood in. Twin beams of energy shot out from Peaches' eyes, up into the ceiling and beyond it. His baleful glare was almost as bright as the energy coming off of Evergreen.

I sensed it before it happened. Energy began to fill my hellhound as he took a breath. The energy around us began, impossibly, to increase. Peaches sank his legs into the floor, creating a crater where he stood. He lowered his massive head for a moment and then looked up, his eyes a brilliant red as he stared at me.

I knew what was coming next.

He unleashed a world-shattering bark.

I had been exposed to his barks in the past. Each time, they were sonic blasts of enormous destructive power. This time was different.

This wasn't just a sonic blast of power.

This was energy.

Golden light shot forward from my hellhound's eyes and landed on Evergreen, who didn't even flinch. He nodded and said something—at least I thought he said something. His lips moved, but I was in no condition to understand what he was saying.

The golden light intensified, blinding me to everything except the agony.

That's when Peaches barked again and undid Evergreen's world.

I floated in darkness with no sense of time. The pain was gone. In fact, everything was gone. I was alone, floating in nothingness.

I tried to expand my senses, but picked up nothing.

Is this how it ends? I guess I didn't survive the transfer.

You survived.

This doesn't feel like I survived. Where am I? Who are you?

No one of consequence. Now, if you're done lounging around, you have a Keeper to stop.

No need to be sarcastic about it. How am I—?"

Heads up.

A bright light slammed into me from the side.

When I could see again, we were in the small, stone room again. I was on the floor and everything hurt.

"He's awake," Evergreen said, looking down at me. "Welcome back, Simon. I thought we lost you there for a moment. Your hellhound was concerned."

Peaches dropped his head and slapped me across the face with his tongue. Judging from the drool on my shirt, he had been at it for a while.

<*Where did you go? I couldn't follow you.*>

<*Hey, boy. You can stop with the slobber bath. I'm better now, thanks.*>

I attempted to push him away and only succeeded in pushing myself back. I really needed to put him on a diet.

<*I'm your bondmate. Where you go, I go. Where were you?*>

<*I don't...I don't know. It was dark and I wasn't in pain—that much I remember.*>

<*Are you in pain now?*>

<*Yes, everything hurts.*>

He padded closer to unleash another tongue lashing.

<*But I'm feeling much better now! Your saliva really does heal. Thank you. I'm feeling so much better.*>

<*You can't do that again. I lost you. Wherever you go...I go.*>

<*I won't do that again, boy.*>

I rubbed his massive head and flanks, as I stood unsteadily.

"What happened to the lakeside retreat?" I asked, looking around. "How did we end up here?"

"I'm afraid my diminished ability will not allow for us to remain in the interstices for long," Evergreen said, looking over his shoulder. "Even now, Tellus is closing in on our location."

"Can we stop him?" I asked, looking at a worn-out Monty. "Was the transfer successful?"

"Yes," Evergreen said as he gestured. "But you two are in no condition to face him. Even at your full strength, he will prove to be formidable. I will slow him down."

Evergreen suddenly looked like an old man. His movements were slower, but his eyes were still sharp.

"Your power is diminished," I said. "How can you?"

"Diminished doesn't mean powerless," Evergreen said, forming a large portal. Through it, I could see the Randy Rump—specifically, the door to the back room. "If it were Gault after you, this would be a fatal exercise. Tellus will prove challenging, but I should be able to buy you enough time to recover."

"Are you sure?" I asked. "How much power did you give up with the rune?"

Monty narrowed his eyes at Evergreen.

"You're dying," he said, lowering his voice. "What did you do?"

"What was needed," Evergreen said curtly. "This was the only way."

"Sacrificing yourself was the only way?" I asked incredulously, turning to Monty. "We need to give it back, Monty. Give it back to him."

Evergreen let out a short laugh which became a series of coughs. He was looking more frail by the second.

"Neither of you are strong enough to give back what I placed in you, individually or together," Evergreen said once the coughing stopped. "This was my choice, and the best way to stop Gault."

"What did you do?" Monty asked, this time concerned. "You didn't just impart the elder rune." Monty looked down at his body. "This...this feels like more."

"It should," Evergreen said. "In time, you will need what I have given you. I only hope it's enough."

"You can't do this," I said, angry he had done this without telling us. "Tellus will kill you."

"When you've lived as long as I have, you learn a few things," he said, his voice suddenly filled with conviction and strength. "Tellus will try to eliminate me, but he will fail. I may be old, but I'm not dead yet. You three need to get going."

I could see we weren't going to change his mind. He had made his peace and his choice; nothing we said would change that. I realized I was angry not at Evergreen, but at the situation that put him in this position, that he felt he had to sacrifice his life to make sure we would survive to stop Gault.

"But the Keepers? If you're gone, won't that throw everything out of balance?" I asked, still trying to find a solution that didn't involve Evergreen dying. "Haven't we just given Gault everything he wanted?"

"Only if Tellus gets the elder rune from you," he said, pointing to the portal. "This is more complicated than we have time to explain. Understand that the Keepers are more than just bearers of the elder runes. Once you manage to stop Tellus, ask Dexter all of your questions. He will have most of the answers you seek."

"And if we don't stop him?"

"Dead men don't need answers."

A cold chill came over me as I looked through the portal again.

"The Rump?" I asked, incredulous. "Jimmy is going to lose his mind if we destroy his place...again."

"That room will temporarily hide you from Tellus until you recover from the transference," Evergreen said. "You cannot engage him there, but you can use the place to prepare."

"Can we stop him?" I asked. "He's Gault's disciple."

"And my second," Evergreen answered. "I know him. His arrogance is his greatest weakness. You can stop him."

"He will view us as inferior," Monty said. "We can use that."

"We *are* inferior to his power," I said. "You felt his energy signature. We are in deep sh—"

"You will have to be creative," Evergreen continued, cutting me off. "His fear attack will be ineffective on you now, but that doesn't mean he lacks other methods of attack. Use his pride to your advantage."

"I'm not seeing how creativity is going to help us," I said. "What we need are runic nukes, weapons of massive destruction."

"You need to use what only you two possess," he said.

"You both have faced formidable foes. Together, you possess all the weapons you need to stop him, but you *must* work together, or he will destroy you both. Do you understand?"

"No," I said, shaking my head. "Not that that's stopped me in the past."

"That's the spirit," Evergreen said, with a smile. "Now, on with the three of you."

We turned to face the portal.

"Mage Montague?"

Monty turned as we headed to the portal.

"I know," Monty said, his voice somber as he stared at Evergreen. "We can't use the elder rune."

"To attempt to do so would destroy you both and give the rune to Gault," Evergreen said with a nod. "You're not strong enough—yet. However, your other abilities will be enhanced. I've seen to that."

"I don't think that will be enough," Monty said. "As Simon said, I felt his energy signature at the Argosy. His power is beyond me."

"Alone, yes," Evergreen admitted. "You must utilize the skills you and Simon share. I apologize that I cannot help you further, but know I have placed my full trust in you three."

Evergreen crouched down and rubbed my hellhound's massive head. Peaches rumbled in response and for a split second it seemed like he was speaking to Evergreen the way he spoke to me.

After a moment, Evergreen laughed and whispered something in Peaches' ear. My hellhound let out a soft bark and moved closer to my side.

Evergreen nodded.

"Will we see you again?" I asked. "At the very least, to return what's yours?"

"No need. It's my gift to you both," he said, with a small

smile. "I have every confidence that you will use what I gave you wisely."

"But—"

"Time to go."

With a wave of his hand, the portal raced to where we stood, and Evergreen vanished.

TWENTY-ONE

The next moment, we were standing in the Randy Rump surrounded by a very surprised group of patrons. Tables and chairs were upended as people scattered away from us in a hurry.

Jimmy the Butcher raced to where we stood with Grohn in tow. Well, Jimmy raced—Grohn lumbered.

"You're not supposed to be able to do that in here," Jimmy said as he drew close, looking from Monty to me. "What's going on?"

"We need the back room," I said, heading to the large door. "You better close early tonight, just to be on the safe side."

"How much destruction is coming our way?" Jimmy said, giving Grohn a look before turning to him. "Montague Protocol."

"Yes, Mr. Jim," Grohn said, with a solemn nod. "Good evening, patrons. We will be closing early tonight."

His voice reverberated throughout the restaurant, causing everyone in the Randy Rump to turn in his direction as one.

Grohn stepped away from us and pressed a button behind

one of the large counters. Red lights turned on in various locations throughout the Rump. Several runes lit up with orange energy and began pulsing in a regular pattern.

"It is time to say goodnight," Grohn said in his loud but calm voice. "All meals will be credited to your accounts and your next meal will be complimentary. Thank you for visiting the Randy Rump. Please use all the exits. Goodnight."

"That is a good system," I said, as people filed out of the Rump. "It helps to have a trollgre make the announcement."

"I noticed you called it the Montague Protocol?" Monty asked. I could tell from the tone in his voice he wasn't thrilled about the name. "Any reason why?"

Jimmy coughed into his hand before answering.

"Well, you were the one who runed the Randy Rump," Jimmy said. "I thought it was a good idea to name our defensive protocol after the mage responsible for keeping us safe."

"Don't forget he's also the mage that reduced this place to rubble a few times," I added. "I think it's a perfect name."

Monty glared at me.

The patrons moved quickly and quietly, vacating their seats and tables. No one raised a fuss or argument—not that anyone would be reckless enough to argue with a trollgre. Grohn nodded to the people as they left; some even thanked him for the evening.

"We intend to avoid any and all destruction to your establishment, James," Monty said. "We only need the back room for a few moments to recover and prepare. Trust me when I say this was not our choice."

"You two look like hell," Jimmy said as we stood before the door. "I'll bring food and something to drink. Then we can discuss."

Jimmy left us and headed to the kitchen. I noticed that Grohn had taken up a position at the front door and was continuing to interact with the patrons as they left.

Monty was focused on the door, pressing the runes in sequence. After a few seconds, the door swung open. Monty headed in and removed his jacket, placing it carefully on a chair, then gestured and formed a violet-and-blue circle on the floor opposite the door.

Jimmy entered the room with several plates on a rolling table cart. He moved quietly and efficiently, putting the food on the table. On the lower level of the cart, I saw two large bowls of pastrami for my hellhound; an enormous salad waited for Monty, while a plate of Wagyu beef with a side of jasmine rice, baked potatoes, and sautéed mushrooms called my name.

Monty sat at the table and placed the napkin Jimmy provided on his lap. He took a long drink of water and proceeded to devour his salad. It was the first time I had ever seen Monty eat with urgency.

He gave me a look and pointed to my plate.

"You will need energy for what is coming," he said, pointing at me with his fork. "We cannot rest on decorum; eat, and recover. James, please brew a large pot of Death Wish for Simon. I'll have my usual."

Jimmy nodded.

"Earl Grey is steeping and a fresh pot of Death Wish is always brewing," Jimmy said. "It's a favorite with most of the regulars. How bad is it?"

"I am hoping you won't have to find out," Monty said. "We're currently being pursued by a formidable foe."

"Your energy signatures are off the charts," Jimmy said. "All three of you. Will you be able to stay off the radar in here?"

"For a short time, yes," Monty said as I took my seat and proceeded to imitate my hellhound and devour my food. "Our altered signatures will take some time to adjust. I should be able to create a mask in time, provided we survive our encounter."

Jimmy's expression hardened.

"Do you want me to call the Council?" he asked. "They can help."

"Not in this matter," Monty said. "I'm afraid they would only be victims. No, we will not shed blood needlessly. The tea and coffee should suffice with my utmost gratitude, James, and then please vacate the premises, along with Grohn."

"Are you sure?" Jimmy asked, glancing back at the door. "Grohn can be pretty handy in a fight. We both are."

"You are both essential to the maintenance of this neutral location," Monty said. "The city can't afford to lose it. Please exit as soon as possible."

"Understood," Jimmy said. "Be right back."

Jimmy left the back room a few seconds later, taking the cart with him.

"Are you sure we can't use his help?" I asked in between inhalations of my food. "Grohn looks tough enough to face a group of mages on his own."

"No, we will be calling on other assistance this evening: a group strong enough to withstand the onslaught we will be facing."

"I know we know some crazy people with questionable ideas about what it means to have fun," I said, "but who is crazy enough to join us in this fight willingly?"

He gestured and a white symbol floated from his fingers. It hung suspended in the air for a few seconds before vanishing from sight.

"What was that?" I asked. "How did you do that in here? I thought this room was supposed to be able to suppress your casting?"

"It was," Monty said. "As for what that was, that was a call to our reinforcements."

"I hope that was a call for reinforcements for at least a few thousand mages," I said. "I have a feeling Tellus isn't going to come at us alone."

"He has a ready-made army at his disposal," Monty said. "Keepers don't have minions; they don't need them. Each Keeper has two seconds and a large group of followers, but not enough to comprise an army of mages."

"How large a group are we talking about?"

"If other high-level mages can serve as an example, I would hazard a guess of one to two hundred at most. That's hardly an army."

"One to two hundred mages is hardly a cakewalk," I said, shaking my head. "This is impossible. We can't deal with Tellus *and* his group. Just us three? No way is that happening. We need to call in backup."

"The major concern would be Tellus," Monty assured me. "The rest of the group will be substantially more than two hundred."

"How?" I asked. "Where is Tellus going to get an army?"

"You know how," Monty said. "They have been after us for some time now."

"You're kidding me. Verity?"

"Indeed," he said with a short nod. "Those assassins at the bookstore were not a coincidence. Verity is involved somehow, and I imagine they are eager to neutralize the perceived threat we pose to the balance of magic on this plane."

"They do have the manpower to create a small army," I said. "I thought after Edith's electrifying exit, they'd back off for a while."

"Tellus probably made them an offer they couldn't refuse," Monty said. "He knows Verity would prefer us to stop breathing, and on this point, they are in alignment of purpose."

"Until he gets the elder rune for Gault," I said. "Then the

mask drops, and Gault unleashes the pain on everyone, Verity included."

Monty nodded.

"They are operating under a false premise—that Tellus is an ally."

"Tellus probably told them he could take us out," I said. "I doubt we can convince them to change their minds about us. They don't even know how dangerous he is."

"Neither do we," Monty said. "We must approach this entire situation with caution. The politics of Keepers seem to be several layers deep, played out over centuries. We are out of our depth here."

"Welcome to my world."

"That being said, I agree with your assessment regarding backup."

"Finally, now we're talking," I said, with a sense of relief. "We can start with Dex and the Morrigan."

"No, for obvious reasons," Monty said. "You *were* paying attention to the fact that the Caretaker offered the elder rune to my uncle before us, yes?"

"Okay, fine. Call in the Dark Council—all of it," I said. "We can at least slow down Verity with overwhelming numbers while we deal with Tellus."

"That, I'm afraid, is not an option," Monty answered. "Your vampire would not risk her position or people during the restructuring, especially not for me...or even you."

"So, we're not going to call the Dark Council?"

"They wouldn't answer even if I did," he said. "Not after our last interaction with Tartarus and Cerberus."

"True," I said, with a nod. "They might still be pissed about that."

"I have no doubt," he said. "No, I haven't called any of the Councils. This is a group designed to deal with a magical threat."

"Tell me you didn't call the NYTF," I said with a groan. "All they're going to be is target practice. Ramirez would kill me if you got him and his people killed."

"Think. Who would be perfectly equipped to deal with a Keeper's second, his mages, and Verity?" Monty asked. "A group fearless enough to face overwhelming odds, death, destruction, and still revel in the opportunity to do so?"

It took a few seconds before it dawned on me.

"You didn't," I said, my voice laced with concern. "Tell me you didn't call *them*."

"That would depend on who you consider *them* to be."

"The last time I dealt with one of them, I was flying out of a hole in the wall she improvised as an exit from Haven," I protested. "Then she told me I needed a more manly battle cry. They are insane."

"Who better to face off against Tellus and Verity?"

"How did you pull this off?" I asked, surprised. "I thought they worked exclusively for Hades?"

"I made some arrangements at Hades' request during your last visit to Haven," Monty said. "He insisted that we have access to their assistance and to several locations within his domain whenever we needed it...within reason."

"That's just it: there is no reasoning with them," I said, amazed that he would call probably the scariest black-ops team on the planet. "They are a force of nature. You can't control them—you just unleash them and stay out of their way."

"Sounds like them," Monty said before returning to his salad. "I'd suggest finishing your meal. We have a long night ahead of us."

"You really called them?"

"I did," he said. "It would be madness to attempt this on our own with an untested rune and whatever power Evergreen gave us. My power is inadequate, and your level of power is negligible in relation to the foe we face. We need help."

"Thanks for the vote of confidence," I said. "My power isn't exactly negligible, you know."

"True. If we ever need to bring a plane down mid-flight—"

"Hey, that was Dex, not me," I snapped. "He was the one that wanted to have an orb lesson in a plane—not exactly the swiftest of ideas. Still, I've gotten better with my magic missile. Are you saying that won't do anything?"

"In comparison to a Keeper's second? You may as well attack with magic pillows for all the damage you would do," he said, shaking his head. "Don't take it personally; I'm not much more advanced than you."

"Thanks for trying to make me feel better," I said. "The Montague Method of morale boosting still needs serious work, but let's be honest, there's no way you and I are even close when it comes to power levels, not even with the Stormblood."

"True," he said after a pause. "I *am* significantly beyond your level, but it won't matter to Tellus. He is beyond us both."

"Which is why you called them for help."

"Yes. At the very least, they can deal with the groups of mages so we can focus on Tellus," he said. "In that regard, they will be instrumental to our efforts."

"I don't know if I would call them *help*, exactly," I said, looking around the back room. "We can't have this confrontation anywhere near the Rump. It would become the Randy Rump Crater by the time they're done."

"Agreed. We need to stack the odds in our favor," Monty said. "Remember what Evergreen said about Tellus and his weakness?"

"He's arrogant; we need to exploit his pride."

"He will be under the impression that we don't pose a threat."

"Do we?"

"Not much of one, no, not when you compare raw power against power. He outclasses us by several orders of magnitude," he said. "Since we can't change the disparity in power—"

"We change the battlefield," I said. "That's very Sun Tzu of you. Where are we meeting our imminent demise?"

"They will be here shortly. From there, we will entice Tellus and Verity off-plane," Monty said. "We will use my uncle's entrance location to the School of Battle Magic to access a battlefield of our choosing."

I shuddered at the memory of Dex's vetting process.

"You can access that place?" I asked. "I thought Dex would have something like that under some kind of lockdown."

"I was able to reverse-engineer the activation runes," Monty said with a small smile. "I am, after all, my uncle's nephew."

"You're going to be your uncle's deceased nephew if you break the School of Battle Magic."

"We won't actually be going to the school. We will be creating a gateway to the location," Monty said, "a location where we can even the odds somewhat."

"Where, exactly?"

"The antithesis to Elysium," Monty said. "We will be entering a domain of misery, torment, and agony."

"Wait a minute, this sounds like Hades' neighborhood," I said. "Does he know we're paying him a visit?"

"We aren't paying *him* a visit," Monty said. "Not specifically. We are using a small portion of his domain to preserve the balance of an entire plane."

"Right, because nothing could go wrong with that," I said.

"I'm sure he won't mind us crashing his domain uninvited to take on Tellus in some mage battle royale."

"To preserve the balance of the plane," Monty repeated. "Even Hades would be affected by the entropy Gault would unleash."

"All I'm saying is that you're going to explain it to him, not me," I said. "What's to stop Tellus from tearing this location apart?"

"The initial gateway is vulnerable, which is why we are using the runes of the back room, but not even Tellus can destroy this domain."

"This domain have a name?"

"The simplest way to think of it...is Hell," Monty said. "In that place, we can negate many of Tellus' abilities."

"That's the upside. What's the downside?"

"Many of our abilities will be lessened as well," he said. "Our only advantage will be the elder rune."

"Evergreen said we couldn't use that," I reminded him. "He said it would kill us."

"I don't intend to use it," Monty said. "I intend to tap into its power to stop Tellus."

"That sounds very much like using it," I said. "You plan on using it without using it?"

"Exactly. It's still risky, but not as risky as trying to use the rune outright," he answered. "I've been able to harness the power of the minor elder rune in a similar way."

"A minor rune isn't the same as a major rune," I said. "Do you have a better option?"

"No," he said with a small shake of his head. "I'm open to suggestions if you have one?"

"I'm fresh out of ideas on how to use life-ending runes, sorry."

"Then we will have to make do with what we have."

"Tellus is going to follow us into Hell?" I asked in disbelief. "Why would he follow us into a place where his abilities are diminished?"

"I'm counting on his arrogance and his desire for the rune we now possess," Monty said. "We must keep his focus on me. He must believe I possess the entire rune and act accordingly."

"He's going to read your signature about two seconds in," I said. "Then he's going to know you aren't strong enough to wield it."

"Which means we will be easy prey," he said. "He will consider it only too easy to dispatch me and remove the rune for Gault. Then he will come for you."

"And what am I doing while all this is going on?" I asked, "I mean, besides running for my life in hell?"

"Evergreen said we need to work together," Monty said. "You will do what you do best—push his buttons until he makes a mistake. It seems to be one of your particular gifts."

"So, what you're saying is, I'm going to die first. Thanks," I said. "How many of them are coming? Do you know?"

"I told them not to overdo it," he said. "I would imagine Vi, along with Maul, Braun, and Nan should suffice."

I stared at him with barely controlled shock.

"You're serious?" I asked. "You called in the four horsemen—horsewomen—horsevalkyries of the apocalypse?"

"They're valkyries; they live for the apocalypse. Literally," Monty said. "Their group is significantly larger, but I thought that, while we engage Tellus off-plane, they could deal with Verity and any mages Tellus brings with him." He looked at my plate and pointed to it with his fork. "You really should finish. You're going to need all the energy you can muster."

I looked down at my plate, my appetite gone.

"This is feeling like the last meal of a death-row inmate," I said, putting down my fork. "What happens if we don't stop him? What happens if we fail?"

"Somehow, I don't think we will be around to have that conversation," he said. "If we fail, we will be the first casualties, followed by the valkyries, and then the rest of this plane. We should adopt their attitude regarding battle and death."

"Live for the moment of a glorious death in battle?"

"Not exactly," Monty said as he finished his salad and stepped over to the circle he had created. "Face death without fear, and if we must perish, we will do so with honor."

"So now we are samurai. Wonderful," I said, pushing my plate away. "I'm all for the living and dying with honor—mostly the living part—but I'm not planning on checking out tonight."

"Good," Monty said and sat in the circle. "We shall not flag nor fail. We shall go on to the end."

"We shall never surrender," I said with a nod. "The British Bulldog would approve."

"Agreed," Monty said, closing his eyes. "They will be here shortly. Try not to antagonize the valkyries before a battle. I hear it's ill advised."

I nodded and checked my ammunition as I prepped Grim Whisper.

I didn't realize he had that kind of contact with them, but it didn't surprise me. He was right, though; they were the one group designed for the battle we were about to face.

He had called the Midnight Echelon.

Specifically, he had summoned the Nightwing.

TWENTY-TWO

Jimmy stepped quietly into the back room holding two mugs as I reassembled Grim Whisper. I had no illusions about how effective it would be, even with entropy rounds.

If we were facing only Verity—regular run-of-the-mill psychomages bent on world domination and destruction—I would consider Grim Whisper a serious threat to them.

Tellus had changed that.

It seemed the world had run out of regular mages and had instead sent us megalomaniac super mages. It meant Grim Whisper would most likely remain holstered for the duration. Tonight, I had a feeling Monty and his abilities would be the weapons we needed.

I only hoped those were enough.

"You have guests," Jimmy said, causing me to look in his direction. "Dangerous-looking guests. They asked to speak to you, Tristan. All except one." He turned to me. "That one, the scariest of the group, asked specifically for you, Simon."

Monty opened his eyes and slowly stood, taking the cup from Jimmy's hand.

"Please have them join us here," Monty said. "Once they

are all inside, please secure the door and exit the Randy Rump. I'd like to prevent any collateral damage, if at all possible."

Jimmy stepped over to where I stood.

"That smells perfect," I said, as he stepped closer. "Extra Death Wish?"

"Always," Jimmy said, placing the large mug of Death Wish on the table. "Don't drink it all at once."

"Thanks," I said, with a nod, grabbing the mug and inhaling the aroma of rich, strong coffee. "I appreciate it."

For a second, I considered not using my flask of javambrosia, but since it was possible Tellus was going to shred us tonight, and this would be the last time I tasted something so amazing, I figured enhanced coffee was the way to go. I took out the flask and poured an ample dose of javambrosia into my mug.

The first sip was beyond words as my taste buds informed me that this was, by far, the most amazing mug of coffee I had ever tasted.

Jimmy gave me a head shake and turned as Monty approached the table.

"Is the Randy Rump going to be here when I come back?" Jimmy asked. I figured it was a valid question given our history. "Or will I be coming back to a blasted landscape of destruction that used to be the Randy Rump?"

"I will do everything in my power to preserve the integrity of your establishment," Monty said, his voice serious. "If it is damaged, and we manage to survive the night—"

"Whoa, what do you mean, if you *manage to survive* the night?" Jimmy asked, cutting Monty off. "If it's that bad, I'm staying."

"No, you aren't," Monty said, his voice full of finality. "You will escort our guests here to the back room. Then you will seal the door from the outside. I will do the same from within. Once the door is secure, you and Grohn will get as far as possible from here, as fast as possible. Do we understand each other?"

Jimmy stared at Monty, his gaze hard, but Monty wasn't leaving any room for argument. After a few moments, Jimmy turned away.

"Understood," Jimmy said, extending a hand, which Monty took. "If this is the last time we speak, I want to say thank you and it's been an honor."

"For me as well," Monty said. "Try not to worry too much about the Randy Rump. There are provisions in place to restore it, should it be damaged or obliterated."

Jimmy stepped over to where I stood and extended a hand. I took it, regretting it the moment I did, as he nearly crushed the bones in my hand to dust.

"Even if the Rump doesn't survive the night, I'd really appreciate it if you three did," he said and pulled my hand in for a bro-hug, nearly squeezing all of the air from my lungs. "Take care of yourself, Simon. It's been an honor."

I didn't trust my voice to respond, so I nodded back and squeezed his hand tighter. He crouched down and patted Peaches on the head.

"You take care of them," he said to my hellhound. "Make sure they get to see the dawn."

Peaches rumbled and nuzzled his hand with his ginormous head. Jimmy placed his forehead against Peaches' head for a few seconds and then stood.

"I'll bring them right in," Jimmy said, as he left the back room. "Be right back."

About a minute later, Jimmy was leading four members of the Midnight Echelon into the back room. I paused as they entered, not because they were fearsome to behold—they were—but because I had never seen them like this.

I paused because, for the first time, as they entered the

room with expressions of anticipation, I understood what it meant to face death willingly.

In their faces, I saw individuals who had accepted their mortality and embraced this opportunity to stare into the endless darkness. A huge part of me felt honored to fight by their side; the other, not-so-huge part of me was trying to run for the door, screaming in fear.

I raised the mug I held as Jimmy headed to the door. He gave us all a nod and closed the large Buloke door, sealing us in.

"Is our enemy in sight?" Vi asked, looking from Monty to me. "Will he come to us?"

"Yes," Monty said, stepping to the table. "Tellus' energy signature was evident in the space Evergreen had created. He is getting closer. The moment we expose our signatures, he will know where we are."

"Excellent," Nan said as she approached me, giving me a once-over. "This is a good night to die."

"Hello, Nan," I said, looking up into her face and returning the look. "You're looking menacing tonight."

"You've grown stronger. Good," she said with a smile and a clap on my shoulder. "Have you improved your battle cry?"

"Haven't had a chance to work on it," I said. "I figured I would get plenty of chances tonight."

She laughed and clapped me on the back this time. It felt like getting hit with a sledgehammer—a very large sledgehammer. I looked around and noticed she was suspiciously weapon-free. They all were. I wondered if it was the effect of the back room.

She must have read my expression, because she gave me a smile and a nod.

"Stormchaser will have his fill of blood," she said. "I am honored to stand with you in battle tonight."

"Mage Montague," Vi said, "Hades has instructed us to do

battle on your behalf. For that, we are grateful. Who is this enemy that would require our presence?"

"Tellus, a second to Arch Keeper Evergreen," Monty said. "Are you familiar with the Keepers?"

Vi smiled first, followed by Maul and Braun, who both glanced at each other and nodded. Nan's smile had never left her face. It was in this second that I became convinced that these valkyries were out of their minds.

"I am familiar," she said. "We all are. Will a Keeper be on the field of battle this evening?"

"I truly hope not," Monty said. "Tellus will be bringing mages and Verity to deal with us."

"Deal with you?" Vi asked. "He does not seek your life?"

"He does, but first he will want something we have recently acquired."

"Which is?"

"I think it would be better to show you."

Monty closed his eyes and took a deep breath. He focused his energy signature and let out the breath. The next second, he was glowing like Evergreen, just not as brightly as the Arch Keeper had.

Still, it was amazing to look at. After a few seconds, the brightness forced me to look away. A few moments after that, the brightness dimmed to nothing.

The four valkyries fixed their gazes on Monty, their looks a mixture of awe and acceptance.

"You possess an elder rune," Vi said. "But it is not complete. Where is the rest of it?"

Monty looked at me and pointed.

"Simon has the other part."

"Don't expect me to suddenly go golden," I said. "I don't do glowing. That's a mage thing."

All four valkyries narrowed their eyes at me, and after a few moments Vi nodded.

"It is as you say," Vi said, turning to Monty. "The other part of the elder rune is held by Strong. Only Arch Keeper Evergreen could have done this without killing you both. Why did he do it?"

"Keeper Gault wants this rune," Monty said. "If he gets it, it will upset the balance and bring about—"

"Entropy," Vi finished. "This must not be allowed to happen."

"That's the plan," I said. "Face off and stop Tellus from getting this rune to Gault. Oh, and survive."

"Tell me how this will be done," Vi said, looking at Monty. "What is our role in this plan?"

"Using the runes in this room, I will create a gateway," Monty said, pointing to the walls. "They possess enough latent energy to create a stable passage to where we need to go."

"A gateway to where?" Vi asked. "Can you harness the energy of this room safely?"

"I can," Monty said. "At least long enough to attract Tellus."

"Using these runes will create a significant energy signature," she said, looking around the room. "It will attract more than just Tellus. It will attract *everyone and everything*."

Monty nodded as I realized what she had just said.

"Tellus is actively looking for us," Monty said. "He and Verity will come first. By the time anyone else is aware of the gateway, we should be off this plane."

"And where, exactly?"

"Gehenna."

Silence descended on the room.

All four of the valkyries' expressions darkened for a few seconds.

"Are you certain, mage?" Vi asked, staring at Monty hard. "You can do this?"

"I'm reasonably certain I can, yes," Monty said, returning Vi's stare with an unwavering stare of his own. "The minor elder rune I possess will allow me to create the passage."

"Does Hades know of your intentions?"

"It is better to ask for forgiveness than permission," Monty said. "No, he does not. At least not yet. He will the moment we arrive."

"Mage Montague...you are insane," Vi said with a wide smile of approval. "We shall ride into Hell tonight!"

The four valkyries raised a fist and shouted a battle cry in a language I couldn't understand.

TWENTY-THREE

"I will create the gateway first," Monty said. "Then we open the door."

"I thought Jimmy sealed it from the outside?" I asked, looking at the large Australian Buloke door. "You can unseal it from the inside?"

"It can be opened if you know how," Monty said with nod. "I wanted him to feel we had an extra measure of safety."

"How are they going to access the door?" I asked. "The Randy Rump is outside that door. If Tellus comes through there with his mages and Verity in tow, there won't be a Randy Rump."

"The gateway will extend past the Randy Rump," Monty said. "It will create a detour through the Rump and into this room, where the gateway will be open."

"What if he blasts us on sight?"

"He could have done that at the Argosy, but he didn't," Monty said. "No, I think he will want to demonstrate his superiority first. His kind always does."

"You play a dangerous game, Mage Montague," Vi said.

"But I have to agree, men of power enjoy nothing more than the sound of their own speech."

"Too busy talking when killing is called for," Maul said. "This is why they fall before us in battle. That, and my hammer, of course."

"Of course," I said. "Are we jumping in before he gets here, or are we waiting until he makes his grand entrance?"

"Once he is in the gateway, he will sense my energy signature," Monty said. "I will amplify mine—while dampening yours as best as possible—to lure him to me. As soon as he gets into the gateway, we will cross over. Simon, you will remain behind for a few moments to make sure he follows us in."

"Is this is the part where I get killed?"

"This is the part where he tries," Monty said. "Make sure of your positioning. Do not form Ebonsoul or unleash any abilities."

"That would give away my part of the elder rune, right?"

"And very likely get you killed on the spot."

"Something I'd like to avoid if possible."

"I would hope so," Monty said. "Once through the gateway, we can't come back to retrieve you—only your hellhound can do that, and we're saving that contingency for an emergency. Did you explain it to him?"

"He knows," I said, glancing down at my hellhound as I rubbed his head, "and expects extra doses of meat if we make it through this."

"Tell him that if we get through this battle intact, our first stop will be Ezra's, and he can eat until he is satiated or bursts, whichever comes first," Monty said with a tight smile. "Is everyone clear on their roles?"

"Got it," I said with a nod. "Make sure I'm standing in the right place, push Tellus' buttons, and get blasted to Hell. Sounds simple enough."

"Colorful, but correct," Monty said, shaking out his hands. "Is everyone ready?"

"Nightwing stands at the ready," Vi said. "Tonight, we become death and despair." They all formed their weapons of darkness. "Tonight, we become the darkness, swallowing the light." I saw all of their wings appear and unfurl. "Tonight, they will fear and fall before us."

For a brief second, I almost felt sorry for Tellus and the mages who would encounter the valkyries.

Monty gestured and I felt a wave of energy wrap around me. He was actively dampening my energy signature. It felt like I had been surrounded by a blanket of warm energy.

The next moment, he activated the energy within himself and began to glow. It wasn't as bright as before, but it was still uncomfortable to look at him directly.

With our energy signatures adjusted, he moved to the door and pressed some of the runes inscribed in the surface in a specific sequence. With a satisfied nod, he moved back to the far wall and began to gesture again.

This time, I could feel the energy coming off of him. He was reading like more than a mage. If I didn't know better, I would have thought he was an Archmage.

"Monty—?"

"It's all a deception," he said, without looking at me. "One last set of sequences and we will be ready."

He paused and closed his eyes for a few seconds before he stared at the Valkyries.

"He is close," Vi said. "He brings many with him."

Monty nodded.

"All of them will wield energy in some way," Monty said. "This last sequence will set them upon us."

"Good," Nan said. "We've done enough talking and planning."

"Agreed," Maul said, swinging her hammer. "Finally. I tire of this waiting. There is killing to be done."

"Finish it, Mage Montague," Vi said. "Let us embrace death this night."

Monty began forming the last sequence needed to form the gateway.

TWENTY-FOUR

Bright white light flowed from his fingers as he gestured.

The runes around the room exploded with blue and violet light. Behind us, a large vertical portal formed, taking up the entire wall. It flowed forward, creating a rectangular tunnel with a swirling vortex leading to the domain Monty had chosen.

The bright white vortex grew in intensity until it was everything, blinding me. When I could see again, the Randy Rump was gone. We stood in an open field of grass, with a swirling vortex of power standing behind us, filled with golden and violet energy.

The vortex itself was immense.

It was as if the wall had expanded to ten times its normal size and now contained a hurricane of power swirling around inside of it. Staring at it made me feel as if I were falling into a whirlpool of energy.

I forced myself to look away as I sensed the oncoming group of mages. I fixed my gaze on the front of the group and saw him leading the charge.

Tellus.

I didn't expect him to be leading the group, but it made sense, and fit with his profile. He wouldn't let anyone else reach us first; his pride wouldn't allow it. This was *his* accomplishment—*he* would get the elder rune back, and *he* would kill us in the process. He would show everyone how powerful he was.

Behind Tellus, in the distance, I could see the large group of mages advancing on us. It wasn't exactly an army—closer to a battalion—but it was still more than the seven of us. They looked small, almost unreal, due to the distance between us.

They were moving fast and getting larger by the second, but Tellus would reach me first. They wouldn't catch up to Tellus for at least ten to fifteen minutes.

"He's coming," Monty said, his jaw set. "He'll be here inside two minutes."

"Why is the large group so far away, but Tellus is so close?"

"Tellus is stronger, and probably an accomplished teleporter," Monty said. "He's using his ability to close the distance, but there are limiters in place here even for him. It must be frustrating to no end, don't you think?"

"You are a very devious mage," I said with a smile. "He is going to get here all pissed…that's perfect."

"I'm merely putting him in the right frame of mind for you," Monty said. "Don't die."

"I'm severely allergic to dying," I said. "Besides, we're just going to have a conversation, right?"

"One in which you antagonize him into blasting you to death," Monty said, his voice grim. "Remember, he must follow you in, Simon. Or all this will have been for nothing."

"If there is one thing I'm good at, it's antagonizing people," I said. "Especially mages with their delicate egos."

"That you are," Monty said, resting a hand on my shoulder. "At the very last moment, what do you do?"

"I form Ebonsoul and get into the portal."

"Right before stepping in, not a second sooner."

"Got it."

Monty nodded and stepped close to the swirling vortex of energy along with Vi, Maul, and Braun.

"The vortex will only last for ten more minutes," he said. "You have that long to convince him your death would be a good idea."

"Ten minutes? No pressure," I said with a smile. "I can convince him of that in five."

Nan stepped close to where I stood as the small army of angry mages closed on us, getting larger by the second. She looked off into the distance, taking in the approaching mob, a fierce smile on her face and Stormchaser in her hand.

"It is in this moment, Strong, before the clashing of weapons, before death visits the field, that you must make your peace," she said. "This, right now, is the only moment of decision. Everything that follows is a product of your choice in this moment. Choose well."

She turned and they all stepped into the vortex, except Peaches.

<*Hey, boy. You need to leave now.*>

<*I go where you go.*>

<*I know, but right now you need to go without me.*>

<*I know.*> A pause. <*If you get hurt, you can call me and I will bring you.*>

<*I'll be okay. I have the best hellhound bondmate in the history of bondmates.*>

<*I am mighty. This is truth. You are my bondmate and you will be mighty too. After you eat more meat.*>

<*The Mighty Simon doesn't sound nearly as fearsome as the*

*Mighty Peaches, but thanks for the upgrade. Now, go with Monty—I have a mage to piss off.>

<*I will be waiting. Do not get lost.>*

<*I have you. I can never get lost. I go where you go.>*

My hellhound rumbled and blinked into the portal behind me. I turned and faced the oncoming destruction.

Tellus blinked in and approached. He stopped a good twenty feet away from me.

He was wearing the typical mageiform.

His suit was navy blue, almost black. It was contrasted by a pale off-white shirt and a light blue tie. I could barely see the runes on the surface of the fabric, but I knew they were there.

He kept his hair shorter on the sides than the top. Some part of him must have been channeling his inner surfer. He had finished off the ensemble with a black pair of Armani Derby shoes.

I started my mental clock. I had about eight-and-a-half minutes before the portal closed behind me.

If I was on the wrong side of it when it did, I was a dead man.

TWENTY-FIVE

"Simon Strong," Tellus said, staring at me, his dark eyes piercing through me. I could feel the anger coming off of him. I took a half step to the side and made sure I was standing directly in front of the swirling vortex. "Where is Mage Montague and the elder rune?"

I thumbed a finger behind me.

"Took you a while to get here," I said. "I thought you had to be powerful in order to be a Keeper's second?"

"I beg your pardon?"

"Well, I assumed you have to have some level of skill to work for a Keeper," I said, looking over his shoulder at the approaching mages still in the distance. "You barely made it here before them. Is that why Gault sent you to be Evergreen's second? You were too weak for him?"

"That mouth of yours is going to get you killed."

"Killed? By who?" I scoffed. "You could barely teleport *here* without stopping"—I counted on my fingers—"at least four times. Are you sweating? Is there someone stronger in that group behind you?"

"There is no one stronger here."

"Doubt it," I said. "Mage Montague is stronger than you, easily, now that he has the elder rune."

Tellus narrowed his eyes at me and scanned my energy signature. I held my breath and really hoped Monty got the dampening effect on my energy signature right, or this was going to be a short, painful conversation.

After a few more seconds, he relaxed his gaze.

"You speak boldly for someone so weak," Tellus said. "Why did Montague and your hellhound abandon you? Or are you the brave one and they fled...in fear?"

He unleashed a blast of energy in my direction. It hovered around the edges of my consciousness and I could tell he was going full throttle on the fear inducing. The suggestion of fear was there, but the compulsion I had felt earlier was gone.

"Is this the part where I'm supposed to fall apart shaking in fear of you?" I laughed. "You're a joke. To think I was scared of you before—now that I get a good look, there's nothing to be afraid of. No wonder you need so many mages to back you up." I looked around him again. "Big bad mage can't even get an elder rune back without help."

He formed a black orb of power. Arcs of red, violet, and black energy crackled around its surface. He didn't have to tell me it was deadly. I could feel its lethality from where I stood.

He let it hover in his hand as he stared hard at me.

"You dare mock me?" he said, his voice low and controlled. "No one speaks to me that way and lives."

"Mock you? You're not worth mocking," I taunted. "You should wait until your lackeys arrive. Maybe they can get the elder rune back for you, since it's clear you aren't up to the job."

"What?"

"Well, you had us in the bookstore, and you failed to act,"

I said. "You thought your little fear cloud was going to stop us in our tracks. It must have pissed you off that we got away."

I could tell I hit a nerve by the way his jaw flexed at my last words, so I did what I did best—I pushed the buttons.

"I mean, can you imagine?" I continued. "Second to the Arch Keeper and outsmarted by a simple mage and, worse, a non-mage like me. That must have stung. Had us cornered and still managed to lose us *and* the elder rune. What did Gault say? I bet he called you an incompetent, useless waste of space. I'd say he wasn't too far off."

"Those will be your last words, Strong," he said, seething with rage. "I will let Mage Montague know you died like the insignificant scum you are."

He unleashed the orb. It floated over to me slowly, promising pain and death. He made it approach me slow because he wanted to see the fear in my eyes.

I focused inward and waited. When it was ten feet away, I closed my eyes. I could still feel it, but I needed to concentrate on forming Ebonsoul.

"Prayer cannot help you now," he continued. "You are beyond hope and salvation. Die, Simon Strong."

With a flick of his wrist, the orb sped up, closing on me.

"Not tonight," I said, forming Ebonsoul in my hand. "You truly are too clueless to live."

I deflected the orb and the dampening field around me evaporated. Ebonsoul gave off a golden light and his eyes widened in recognition.

"The elder rune?" he asked, his voice filled with surprise as he formed a small constellation of deadly black orbs around his body. "Give it to me. I promise to end your life quickly, if you hand it over."

"Come and get it," I said and fell back into the portal as he unleashed the barrage of orbs at me.

"No!" I heard him scream as the vortex swallowed me.

"With me! All of you—now! With me!"

It was the last thing I heard before falling into a silent darkness.

TWENTY-SIX

A pair of enormous hands caught me before I hit the ground. Ebonsoul had vanished, but I still felt the energy of the elder rune in my body.

"I have him," Nan said, putting me down. "He looks no worse for wear. Is our enemy in pursuit?"

I nodded and staggered a few feet before falling to one knee. Peaches padded over to where I knelt and rumbled in my face before assaulting me with a tongue slap.

<Now you will feel better. My saliva will fix you.>

<I'm not broken.>

Surprisingly, I started feeling better almost immediately.

<Whoa, I do feel better.>

<I know. You are in part of my first home. I am very mighty here, bondmate.>

"He's...he's coming and he's bringing all the mages with him," I managed as I took in the scenery. "Where the *hell* are we?"

"Exactly," Monty said. "There is a time lag here. Tellus will get here soon, but we must move."

We started crossing the debris-filled wasteland.

The gray sky was covered in dark clouds, making it appear as if a storm was about to erupt above us any second. The light in this place was a gray half-light as if dawn were approaching, but as I looked into the sky, I couldn't make out a sun—or any light source, for that matter.

The next thing I noticed was the heat and the large boulders. It was as if a child had been playing with enormous rocks and had just thrown them to land anywhere.

"This place looks like an abandoned quarry," I said, looking around. "Are you sure we're in the right place?"

"I'm certain," Monty said. "Ever since Orethe left her home in Elysium to you, I've been doing some research on the different areas in this domain. This area is bad, but it is not the worst. That distinction would fall to the area guarded by Cerberus."

In the distance, I saw a large, rectangular stone structure that reminded me of Stonehenge. Everything else around us was empty wasteland as far as I could see.

"Are you sure this is the best place for a last stand?" I asked, as I stumbled forward and caught myself before introducing my face to the rocky ground. "Why do I feel like I just ran a marathon?"

"Your body is acclimating to this place," Monty said, looking around. "The hellhound saliva will accelerate the process."

"It's working," I said, feeling better by the second. "He's never going to let me live this down."

Peaches chuffed at my words.

"The mages that come through with Tellus won't be recovering as soon as you. Lacking a ready supply of hellhound saliva, they will be the first to fall."

I looked around and saw we were missing two of the valkyries.

"Where are Maul and Braun?" I asked, concerned. "Did they get lost?"

"They remained near the portal entrance," Monty said, his voice grim. "They will reduce the number of mages that come through."

"They can't face Tellus," I said, looking back at the area where I'd landed. "He still has his fear cloud."

"It won't be as potent here, but you're right," Monty said. "It will still have an effect. They won't engage him. Their job is to prevent as many mages from reaching us as possible."

I glanced over at Vi and Nan. Their faces were set in grim determination, and I understood the rest of the plan.

"They're going to stop any mages that get past Maul and Braun from getting involved with us when we face Tellus?"

"Yes," he said. "We will face Tellus in that stone structure over there. It will give us the best chance of success."

"What is that place?"

"A crucible," Monty said. "Hades uses places like these to create his Hounds."

"Like Peaches and Cerberus?"

"No," Monty said, shaking his head. "Like Corbel."

"I thought there was only one Hound of Hades," I said as the oppressive heat fogged my thoughts. "It's too hot down here, Monty."

"What did you expect when I said Hell?" Monty asked. "A tropical paradise?"

"Where is all the agony and misery?" I asked. "Where is everyone? Why are we the only ones here?"

"This part of Gehenna is patrolled by creatures I can only explain as vague humanoid beings I call demons," he said. "Fortunately, our blades are seraphs. We were able to dispatch a group that attacked us when we first arrived."

"Still feels kind of empty, though."

"That will change soon enough," Monty said, glancing

behind us. "Make haste. We need to be inside that structure when Tellus arrives."

We began to run.

It was like running through thick soup while wearing a heavy-weight vest. Each step made little progress and, for a moment, I thought I was running in place. Even Peaches was struggling.

We reached the crucible after what felt like a hundred miles. I took a few more steps before collapsing on the cool stone floor.

"I'm just going to lay here and keep this cool floor secure," I said, with a low groan. "Don't mind me."

Monty and the valkyries looked unbothered by the heat. I took that moment to examine the stone structure around me as I got to my knees.

The actual crucible was a series of large stone blocks, each about ten feet tall, eight feet wide and close to three feet thick—it resembled a rectangular Stonehenge. From what I could tell, all of the massive stones that made up the structure were covered in intricate runes and symbols. The symbols alternated pulses in bright reds and deep blues.

The entire henge was about two hundred feet long by one hundred feet wide. It reminded me of the remains of an ancient temple.

The outer perimeter of stones formed a large rectangle with spaces in between the stones to allow passage into the center, which formed a looser rectangle within the larger one. These stones were also covered in runes I didn't recognize, but pulsed white.

The ground beneath the stones was a smooth black marble, a major contrast to the ground around the henge, which was all broken rocks and dirt.

I couldn't decipher any of the runes, but I could feel the power pulsing from them. Nan gave me a look, and I managed to get into a crouch without losing my sense of balance as I caught my breath.

"No more time to rest, Strong," Nan said, lifting me to my feet and pointing with Stormchaser behind us. "The enemy approaches."

Vi and Nan took off in the direction of the approaching mages, but I didn't see or sense Tellus.

"Can you make out any of these runes?" I said, looking at some of the closest stones. "These look ancient. Was this some kind of temple?"

"Perhaps. These runes make the protorunes I'm familiar with seem recent in comparison," Monty said, stepping close to a stone and examining them closely. "I can't decipher them, but I can feel their potency. They do have a specific purpose—one we will utilize."

"Tell me they boost your energy until you become as strong as an Archmage," I said. "That would make these excellent protorunes."

"Quite the opposite," Monty said, running a hand over a group of symbols. "As long as we remain within this structure, these stones will drain your power and life force until you are left with none."

I stared at him in disbelief.

"*This* is the place you chose to fight Tellus?" I asked. "Are you insane? You want us to grow weaker right before we die?"

"This is how we even the battlefield," Monty said. "If we remain in here long enough, Tellus won't be able to draw on any of his power."

"Doesn't the same apply to us?"

"Yes, but he doesn't have an elder rune or a curse of immortality," Monty said. "That should give us a slight edge."

"You are out of your mind," I said, realizing he was right. "The chances of this working are astronomically slim."

"Better a slim chance than no chance," Monty said. "We

have faced greater odds and managed to overcome them. We need to keep our wits about us and play to our strengths."

"I don't think I could push his buttons any further," I said. "He wanted to blast me to atoms—probably still does. Why are mage egos so fragile?"

"Most mages harbor a deep-seated feeling of insecurity which is rarely, if ever, overcome," he said, staring off into the past. "Part of it is the training. Apprentice mages are forced to face their inadequacies on a daily, often hourly, basis while they are studying to become proficient. It is intensely demoralizing."

"That would explain his reaction when I called him incompetent."

"Indeed," Monty said. "To a mage of his power, that would be quite an insult, in addition to opening an old wound. Mages don't tolerate being called incompetent."

"That can't be the only reason for the delicate egos, though," I said, looking around the crucible. "I mean, this is across the board. I have yet to encounter a mage who isn't sensitive about their abilities, present company excluded."

He gave me a slight nod.

"The other reason for that is fear," Monty said. "We learn early on that our abilities can be stripped from us, whether by erasure or corruption."

"That would certainly make me twitchy."

"Imagine being able to tap into the power of the energy around us, and then suddenly losing that ability or having it ripped away. For some—most—their identity is directly tied to their power as a mage."

"That would explain most of the dark mages we've faced."

"For them, it's an unbearable, unthinkable proposition. Most of the *psychomages* you referenced are willing to do anything to hold onto that power, even if it means going dark or taking lives. They'll do anything to keep or increase their power."

"How do you deal with it?" I said. "You seem more well-adjusted than the psychomages we encounter. Aren't you afraid you will lose your ability to do the mage finger-wiggle?"

"Three reasons," he said, still looking off into the distance. "I have had excellent mentors: my father, nana, and uncle, chief among them."

He paused in thought for a moment.

"And the other reasons?"

"I am fortunate enough to be surrounded by excellent checks and balances, which prevent my ego from getting too large," he said with a small smile. "Not every mage is fortunate enough to have an *Aspis* bonded to a hellhound to keep them humble."

"We are pretty awesome, this is true," I said, rubbing my hellhound's oversized head. "What's the last reason?"

"I have lost access to my ability on more than one occasion, if you recall," he said. "While radically life-altering, it was not the end of my existence as I know it. It can be overcome."

"You've managed to separate the mage from the power."

"Precisely. I am a Montague first, and a mage second," he answered, after another pause. "I have never forgotten that lesson."

"Well, I'm glad you've made peace with being able to function in spite of not having abilities," I said. "How much time do we need for this draining effect to kick in?"

"There's no accurate way for me to tell," he said. "Time flows differently in this place, and I've never actually stood *inside* a crucible like this—I've only observed them from the outside, for obvious reasons."

"So we're facing a full strength Tellus?" I asked. "That sounds bad."

"Not quite full-strength," Monty said, forming an orb. It looked less solid than usual, and felt slightly less lethal. "Do you see a difference?"

"Your orb looks semi-transparent," I said, looking at it closely. "It feels weaker, too."

Monty nodded with a grim expression.

"The moment we set foot in this domain, our energy levels were halved."

"Which means he's coming at us at half strength."

"Which is still considerable," Monty said. "Do not drop your guard. He's close. Get ready."

"I don't see him," I said, looking around quickly. "Do you?"

Monty scanned the horizon before coming to a stop and pointing off to our side. Someone was walking toward us.

"There," Monty said, pointing at a lone figure coming our way. "He's over there and headed this way."

I turned to the direction he was pointing and saw Tellus.

Tellus wasn't looking as polished as I'd left him. His suit was ruined in a few places with visible rips in the jacket and pants, his hair was disheveled, and his tie was missing. I saw him wipe his brow a few times with his sleeve as he walked, something Monty would never do with a Zegna mageiform. Tellus was cursing as he closed on us.

"What happened to him?" I asked. "He looks shredded. Why is he walking? Why not just teleport?"

"After the limiters he faced earlier and the halving of his power here, teleporting anywhere would be foolish," Monty said. "He must have realized it would be wiser to conserve his energy if he is to face us and retrieve the elder rune."

"That makes sense, but why does he look like he danced with a lawn mower and lost?"

"Demons. The denizens of this domain don't take kindly to visitors of any sort," Monty said. "It would seem Tellus encountered some of them, and apparently he lacks seraphic weapons."

I smiled despite myself.

"Looks like someone is having a bad day," I said under my breath. "We either do this here, or we don't do it at all."

"Agreed," Monty said. "Be wary; he still poses a significant threat. Do not underestimate him."

Tellus stopped just outside the outer edge of the crucible.

"Montague and Strong," he said, his voice half a growl. "The banes of my existence. Surrender the elder rune to me, and I will make your deaths swift as I extract it. Resist, and suffer unending agony at my hands."

"He did ask nicely," I said, glancing at Monty. "What do you think?"

"He didn't say please," Monty said. "It's rude if he doesn't say please. This reflects poorly on his upbringing. It's an absolute lack of decorum."

"He's right," I said, looking at Tellus apologetically. "You could at least say, 'Please surrender, so I can kill you.' It's the polite thing to do. Any *competent* mage would know this."

Rage flitted across Tellus' face. Mage egos—so sensitive.

"It is going to *please* me immensely when I rip the elder rune from your dead bodies, and then proceed to kill Evergreen with his own rune."

"Not bad," I said, with a semi-approving nod, looking at Monty again. "He did say *please* that time. Partial credit?"

"Context is everything," Monty said, turning to Tellus. "If you truly desire the elder rune, feel free to come extract it from our cold, dead bodies."

"I don't think he's up to it," I said. "Maybe he's having performance anxiety? I mean, he couldn't even finish off Evergreen—and *he's* an old and frail Arch Keeper. No way he can handle us in the prime of our lives."

"Am I to presume that Arch Keeper Evergreen still lives?"

Monty asked. "Weren't you tasked with his elimination? I'm certain Gault will look poorly on your lack of ability to get a simple mission done."

"An oversight I will address shortly," Tellus barked. "Once I leave this godforsaken realm."

"I don't think Telly here likes walking much. He sounds upset," I said, staring at Tellus. "Must have been hard having to *actually* walk across the wasteland to find us. Those shoes aren't made for hiking."

"Very well," Tellus said, adding a few curses. "You force my hand. Never let it be said I did not give you the opportunity to die with honor."

He stepped into the crucible, unleashing a beam of black energy from his hand, forcing me to slide to the side. The beam punched a hole into and through one of the massive stones, where my head had been only moments before.

"Monty?" I said, looking at the smoking hole. "He still seems plenty strong."

"The plan remains unchanged," Monty said, gesturing and forming a lattice of golden energy around us. "Time is our ally—just make sure not to get hit."

"Oh, is *that* the plan?" I said as I dodged around the stones, avoiding beams of energy designed to punch holes in me. "Go get him, boy!"

Even though it seemed Monty and I were getting weaker, my hellhound had grown more ferocious, if that was even possible. He blinked out and pounced on Tellus, who swatted him into one of the large stones.

Peaches crashed into the stone and rolled to his feet without missing a beat, blinking out again and attacking. Tellus formed a group of orbs and slammed several of them into my hellhound.

They may as well have been orbs of smoke.

Peaches took the barrage of orbs without slowing and

leapt at Tellus again. Tellus formed a large portal in Peaches' path and disappeared my hellhound from my sight.

"Peaches!" I yelled as rage clouded my vision. "If you hurt my hellhound—"

"We must remain in the crucible," Monty called, forming several golden orbs of light and pain. "This is your hellhound in his native environment. Do you really think he's in danger here? Remain calm and focus on our objective."

"Stomping Tellus into the ground," I said, regaining control and calming down.

"I was going to say survival, but that works as well. Move!"

Monty released the orbs at Tellus and distracted him long enough for me to evade another barrage of black orbs.

Monty countered the barrage with a swipe of his hand, creating a shield to deflect them away from us and out of the crucible.

Tellus formed more orbs with a growl and unleashed them at us.

I dove behind one of the large stones as another black orb impacted where I'd been standing a second earlier. I was getting the feeling that Tellus was targeting *me* for some reason.

Monty was several stones away. I could see the casting was costing him too. His face was covered in sweat and he was breathing heavily.

"He seems particularly fixated on you for some reason," Monty said, catching his breath as he created another lattice and sent it to another part of the crucible. "Why would that be, do you think?"

"Could be something I said earlier," I answered as I calmed my breathing. "I did call him an incompetent waste of space."

"Well, that would explain his animosity towards you."

"You think?" I asked, dodging to the side as another black

orb sailed past. "You *do* realize we're over here? Why are you sending those lattices everywhere but here?"

"Insurance," Monty said, releasing another lattice to a different corner. "I hope we won't need it, but it's better to have it—"

"And not need it, than need it and not have it," I finished as I took a breather behind a large stone. "You think you can get him to focus some of that anger at you?"

"All in due time," Monty said, forming another lattice. "I need to create these while I still can. That was the last one. I hope it will be enough."

"What exactly are you doing?"

"You'll see and thank me later."

The sound of clashing caught my attention, and I looked over to where Vi and Nan were engaged in battle with both Tellus' mages and Verity. They were making quick work of the mages, but they were seriously outnumbered.

Another group had descended on both the valkyries and the mages.

Demons.

They looked like people, but were covered in a black aura of energy. They didn't have weapons, but what they did have were numbers and ferocity. They attacked without any concern for their lives—if they were alive, that is.

"They are a type of undead," Monty observed, following my gaze with his own. "We are in Gehenna, after all. The Nightwing will be able to deal with this new threat. I'm not so sure about those Arcanist mages and Verity, however."

Concern gripped my chest as I saw more and more demons race at the valkyries. They weren't going to last long like this.

That's when I heard the laughter and saw an explosion of black energy, joined by the bodies of the attacking mages and demons alike, go flying into the air, only to be bisected by an airborne Vi and her blade.

On the ground, Nan sliced through the air with Stormchaser, cutting down demons and mages with each slash. Every time they tried to close on her, she cleared the area around her with Stormchaser.

She was the one laughing.

Nightwing was going to be just fine.

"Evergreen lied to you!" Tellus called out. "He's not trying to protect the balance. By giving the elder rune to you, all he has done is upset it. If you return it to me now, I may still have a chance to right this before it's too late. Surrender, and do the right thing."

I was about to answer when Monty motioned for me not to speak. He picked up a rock and threw it against one of the stones. Tellus blasted the location of the sound a moment later, punching a crater in that large stone.

A crater, not a hole.

Monty nodded and materialized his blades, the Sorrows. A soft wail escaped them as he hefted them in his hands. As he did this, he gave me a look which I understood.

It was time to take the fight to Tellus.

I formed Ebonsoul.

TWENTY-SEVEN

Tellus looked mildly surprised when we stepped out from behind the large stones we were using as cover.

"I see you've come to your...senses."

That's when he noticed we were both holding weapons in our hands. The Sorrows were giving off a silver-and-golden energy, and Ebonsoul was a clash of its own energy: gold and red runes glowed as black and silver energy flowed around its blade.

"I'd say we have," I said. "We're not giving you the elder rune."

"You don't understand," Tellus said, before pausing and taking a few steps back. "This is madness. You can't possibly hope to defeat me with those paltry excuses for weapons."

"We can and we will," Monty said. "Do you intend to fight us barehanded?"

"You must be insane if you think I'm going to waste my time with you two," Tellus said, looking to the side. "Once Keeper Gault hears of this, it's over for you both."

"Sounds like he's scared, Monty," I said as we closed the

distance. "Why not show Gault how badass you are by taking us down yourself?"

Tellus disappeared from sight...and reappeared a second later after crashing into one of the lattices and bouncing off. He landed hard on the other side of the crucible and got unsteadily to his feet.

"I had a feeling he would choose to flee over fighting us once he realized what was happening in here," Monty said, looking at Tellus. "You should consider surren—"

Tellus formed a black blade that flowed with rust-colored energy.

"You have no idea what Gault will do to me if I return without the elder rune," Tellus said, his voice a mixture of anger and fear. "Death would be a small mercy against his wrath."

"You don't have to do this," I said. "I'm sure we could help you, or at least know someone who can."

Tellus laughed and I knew he had slipped into despair.

"Help me?" he scoffed, as he pointed at us with his blade. "You two...help *me*?"

"I think the mage is a few runes short of a full cast," I said under my breath, but loud enough for Monty to hear. "He's not going to surrender."

"I'm afraid not," Monty said, setting his jaw. "This ends here."

"Ends? Oh, no," Tellus said, shaking his head. "Even if you manage, by some miracle, to defeat me, this will be the beginning of the end for you. Gault will not stop; he will not rest. He is relentless in his pursuit and is single-minded of purpose. He *will* usher in an age of entropy."

"Not if we have something to say about it," I said. "We're going to stop him."

"Even if you could use the elder rune—and you can't—you have no hope of standing against him," Tellus said, extending a hand. "Last chance. Surrender the rune. I promise to make your deaths quick. On my word as a mage."

"He lost me at deaths," I said, without taking my eyes off Tellus. "How about you, Monty?"

"I'd have to say the 'usher in an age of entropy' line has convinced me he and Gault have lost the plot," Monty said, staring at Tellus. "This may not end now, but your part in it does."

We raced at Tellus.

Tellus recovered immediately, which made me think he was trying to throw us off by appearing off-balance. After the first few strikes and parries, I realized that Tellus wasn't just a mage—he was a battlemage.

"I've been using weapons since before either of you were born," he boasted as he parried a slash from Monty and returned a thrust, forcing Monty back, while unleashing a kick to my midsection that sent me flying back next to Monty. "At least make this interesting for me."

"We're getting our asses kicked," I said, getting to my feet. "No way is he that fast or accurate normally."

"He's using what he has left of his ability to enhance his fighting technique," Monty said. "You need to get close to him."

"Have you seen his blade? I don't want to get close to him, and Ebonsoul is a close-quarters weapon."

"Precisely. You need to cut him," Monty said. "Without his ability, I can defeat him."

"Dinner at Masa," I said as I gritted my teeth. "Full VIP treatment."

"You're arguing this now?"

"I learned from the best—my hellhound," I said. "If I'm going to get stabbed, I better have dinner at Masa waiting for me if we ever get out of here."

"Done," Monty said with a nod. "Ready?"

"Are we fighting or chatting?" Tellus mocked. "Let me guess, we're discussing the best strategy? I hear dying is a quite effective method to stop a conflict."

This time, we closed on him slowly.

"Ah, much better," Tellus said, stepping into a defensive stance. "I can tell from your expressions that you're serious now. Alone or together, the outcome is decided. You will both die by my blade."

Monty stepped in, pressing a frontal attack while I hung back and waited for an opening. Tellus dodged and parried Monty's blades as they wailed, their soft cries filling the crucible.

Suddenly, Monty stopped and slid to the side as I immediately rushed in, throwing Tellus off by a split-second.

It was all the time I needed.

Tellus reacted with lightning-fast reflexes, impaling me through my abdomen with his blade. I sliced across his hand as he kicked me back across the floor.

"That was stupid, but I expected no less from someone given too much power and too little sense," Tellus spat, looking down at me. "Why throw your life away?"

I slid back and kept my eyes on him. I felt a trickle of energy flow into me from Ebonsoul—the last of Tellus' power.

"You said, 'Alone or together,'" I said, as the pain kicked in and I clenched my jaw for a moment. "We choose together. Time for you to die." I looked at Monty. "He's done."

Monty slid back in and thrust one of his Sorrows at Tellus' midsection; Tellus managed to parry the strike, but not before Monty drew blood.

"You cut me—?" Tellus started, but had to dodge to avoid getting skewered. "You dare?"

Monty pressed his advantage.

Tellus was having a progressively worse time as Monty

began to really show him what it meant to wield a blade. Tellus slashed horizontally, but Monty ducked and cut across one of Tellus' legs. That was when I noticed that my wound wasn't healing. I reached down and drew Grim Whisper.

Tellus stumbled back and held his sword out to keep Monty away.

"I just cut your femoral artery," Monty said and stopped advancing. "You have anywhere from two to five minutes. How would you like to spend your last moments?"

"By making sure you join your friend over there in death."

My vision began tunneling in as I saw Tellus reach to his side and go for a weapon. I fired Grim Whisper twice, hitting him center mass. Tellus flew back, landing on his back. The gun in his hand fell to the side.

"Simon!" I heard Monty yell my name with urgency. "Stay with me."

"Did I get him?"

"I didn't realize your curse would be affected to such a degree in this place," he said as his voice became fuzzy. "Lay still—I'll get help."

"Make sure he's gone," I rasped, as heat flushed my body. "Monty, make...make sure."

I looked up.

The last thing I saw was a gray sky filled with angry clouds, promising a storm.

TWENTY-EIGHT

I opened my eyes.

And found myself staring into the depths of two glowing red eyes. This was followed by an enormous tongue caressing my forehead with an extra dose of drool.

<*Stop, boy. I'm fine. Stop.*>

I pushed my hellhound's massive head away, and he let me —this time.

<*You're much better now. I fixed you, again.*>

<*Thank you. Where am I?*>

<*Where the scary lady fixes the angry man.*>

I hugged him by the neck and looked around the room. It looked familiar. I was recuperating in Monty's old cell/room in Haven.

"Welcome back," a voice said from the other side of the bed I lay in. "Are you intentionally testing Kali's curse?"

Hades.

Shit.

"Hello, Hades," I said. "You know, it was a funny thing. We were on our way to Elysium, and we must have taken a wrong turn somewhere."

"If you say you should have taken a left at Albuquerque, I'll feed you to Cerberus myself," he said, with a faint smile. "In any case, you, Tristan and your hellhound were nearly executed for violating my domain."

"What about the Nightwing—are they okay?"

"Did you really think they were in any danger from Verity and the Arcanists?" Hades asked, leaning forward slightly. "They are the leaders of the Midnight Echelon. I daresay Hanna could have probably handled the entire group on her own, but she likes to share the mayhem and carnage with her sisters whenever possible."

"They made it. Good," I said, rubbing Peaches' head. "Where were you? I thought I'd lost you."

<I am your bondmate. You can't lose me.>

"He was nearly executed by his sire," Hades said, his voice serious. "I had to contain your hellhound, and renegotiate a new contract and seal with *my* hellhound. It is a good thing Persephone is as dangerous as she is beautiful."

"What?" I asked, surprised. "Why would Cerberus want to kill Peaches?"

"Peaches is not permitted to freely roam in my domain," Hades said. "Cerberus would kill him."

"Peaches can't hurt Cerberus," I said. "Not even on his best day."

"The restriction is in place because, eventually, your hellhound will become a threat to his territory, should he choose to become one," Hades answered, gazing at Peaches. "You cannot bring your hellhound into my domain without prior notice. The only exemption is travel to the home Orethe bequeathed you."

"Everywhere else is off-limits?"

"Fatally so."

"I'll keep that in mind," I said. "What did you do to Monty?"

"What do you mean, what did I do to him?"

"I know you, Hades—there's always a hand you don't show. Always," I stressed. "Is Monty in danger? Does he owe you some kind of blood debt or something? You know we were doing what was right to maintain balance in the plane."

If I was alive, I knew Monty was alive, too—but I was dealing with a god, and they weren't exactly up front about their motivations or machinations.

"Which is the only reason you three are still among the living," Hades said. "What possessed you to enter a crucible to face Tellus?"

"It was the only way we could even the odds against him," I said. "We were able to negate his power."

"And Kali's, it seems," Hades said. "Crucibles are not testing grounds for mages. It is where my Hounds are forged."

"I heard," I said. "Corbel went through that?"

"Corbel is not a mage. His experience was vastly different from yours and Tristan's," Hades said. "I can't believe Evergreen imparted his rune to you two, but it shouldn't surprise me."

"That was all his idea," I protested. "I didn't want any part of an elder rune. Do I look like I can wield some ancient rune of power?"

"No, but I suppose that was the point, wasn't it?" Hades answered. "Evergreen has managed to hide a pivotal elder rune in plain sight. It was a stroke of inspired genius."

"Didn't feel like one," I grumbled. "Now Gault is going to come for us."

"I think you have the order inverted," he said, as my hellhound plopped his head on my stomach with a low rumble. "*You* will have to go after Gault."

"Excuse me, come again?"

"He will step back for now," Hades said. "Your defeating

Tellus, as dubious as that sounds, has proven you are a worthy threat."

"I don't want to be a worthy threat, especially not to a Keeper," I said. "Can't we just give the elder rune back to Evergreen?"

"Should be possible," Hades said, leaning back and steepling his hands. "All you have to do is find him."

I groaned, closed my eyes, and put my head back on my pillow.

"Evergreen is missing?" I asked. "You don't know where he is?"

"I'm not omniscient."

"How do we find a missing Arch Keeper who probably doesn't want to be found?" I asked. "That sounds impossible."

"Missing is a strong word; hiding is probably closer to the truth," Hades answered. "And you won't find him until he wants to be found. As for you and Tristan, the world has just become a more dangerous place."

"Do you think I could just move into Orethe's place and stay there for the duration?" I asked, only half-jokingly. "Even for a century or so?"

"Do you think that will solve your current situation?" Hades asked. "You are dealing with beings that are comfortable waiting for centuries before acting. Remind me again: how long was Kali working on her plan before you upended it?"

I gave him a hard stare.

"Five thousand years," I mumbled. "A really long time."

"Say again?" he said, cupping his ear with a hand. "How long?"

"Five thousand years. Fine, I get it, I can't hide from any of this," I said, closing my eyes again. "At the very least, a vacation from the mayhem and insanity would be nice."

"In that, we are in agreement. I'll see what I can do," he said, looking up." You have guests. We will speak soon."

"Thanks," I said. "Somewhere nice and warm, more on the tropical and less on the infernal side that would be nice."

I opened my eyes, but he was gone.

Monty walked in. Behind him were four battered and bruised valkyries. Nan stepped close to the side of my bed and rested one of her huge hands on my shoulder.

"You are now almost as mighty as your hellhound," she said with a wide smile. "Congratulations."

Peaches rumbled, but didn't move his head from my stomach.

"Almost? I nearly died."

"Yes, but that was only one time," she said. "After a few more brushes with death, we will consider giving you full mighty status. Besides, I still haven't heard your new battle cry."

"Amazing," I said as they all gave me smiles, even Vi. "Did you enjoy yourselves?"

"The odds were slightly in our favor, but the demons made it enjoyable," Vi said, before growing serious. "Thank you, Mage Montague, for allowing us this moment of glory and battle. We must take our leave, but we wanted to inform you that the Nightwing stands ready to do battle at your side whenever you need it."

They all raised their right fists and placed them over their hearts, followed by a short bow. A moment later, they were gone.

"How are you feeling?" Monty asked when the room emptied. "It seems your curse has resumed working."

"Feeling much better," I said. "Why would Roxanne put me in your old cell—I mean, room?"

"So she can keep an eye on you, of course, but we need to leave," he said, glancing at the door. "Sebastian would like a word, and then we have one more stop before we can enjoy some well-deserved rest."

"Now that is what I'm talking about," I said, throwing off my sheets. "Give me a second, and I'll get dres—"

I hadn't finished the sentence when Monty gestured. I found myself in a new set of clothing. I looked down, amazed.

"Now, that was impressive," I said, looking down. "When did you learn that?"

"Really? *That* is what you find impressive?" he asked. "After everything you've seen, this is what impresses you?"

"Well, it's practical and functional," I said. "Plus, there's the upside of not blowing up anything."

"We need to go," he said. "Roxanne will have noticed even that small cast. Ready?"

I nodded and Haven vanished from sight, only to be replaced with Central Park. Peaches wandered off to smell some trees, but stayed relatively close.

Sebastian stepped into view and walked over to us. Across from where we stood, I could see the White House with the Treadwell Directive Headquarters on the top floor.

"You've made it," Sebastian said. "Good. Did you know Dexter made me promise on my word, as a Montague and a mage, that no violence would occur between us?"

"He made me promise the same thing," Monty said with a nod. "You know how he is about the family."

"True, even though he has been shunned by almost every branch of the Montagues."

"Why are we here, Sebastian?" Monty asked. "What was so urgent?"

"Urgent? Did I say urgent?"

"You said you needed me to witness an event of the utmost urgency," Monty said. "What is this event?"

"I have it on good information that Verity will eliminate the Treadwell Supernatural Directive today." He looked down at his watch. "In approximately twenty seconds or so."

"What?" I said, alarmed. "You have to get your people out of there."

"They are already gone," Monty said. "Isn't that correct, Sebastian?"

"Too true," he said. "We have proxy signatures in the offices at this moment, giving the impression of an office full of personnel."

"How can they eliminate the entire headquarters?" I asked, dubious. "That would take—"

An explosion rocked the top two floors of the White House. Every window in every office was blown out, and I could see traces of red and black runic energy wafting out of the windows.

"That," Sebastian finished. "It would seem Verity is upset at their recent losses, and *especially at* my involvement."

"H&H?" I asked. "Will they be—?"

"They are safe," Sebastian said. "Tristan, I trust you know what to do. We have relocated to the church downtown. Do not underestimate Verity. They are determined to destroy you both. I invited you here to allow you to see how committed they are."

"Thank you," Monty said. "For everything."

Sebastian waved Monty's words away.

"What's family for, if not for facing mutual enemies and crushing them beneath our heel?" Sebastian said, with a wicked smile. "I'll call you once this settles down a bit. Right now, I have several pressing matters to attend to with our relocation. No rest for the wicked, as they say."

I heard the approaching sirens in the distance getting closer. Monty formed a large green circle. Peaches and I stepped into it as we gave the White House one last, long look. Monty stepped in after us and took us home.

TWENTY-NINE

THREE DAYS LATER

"Are you sure this is a good idea?" I asked as we stood before Dex's door in our space. "Is he even strong enough?"

"Be thankful he wasn't here to hear you say that," Monty said. "This is the best solution, and will allow us to traverse the city without the Arcanists watching our every move."

"Will it work?"

"I don't know," Monty said. "He's my uncle, but he's also the Harbinger. There's plenty I don't know about him. He prefers it that way."

The door frame around Dex's door glowed a bright green and clicked open. Monty pulled the door and motioned for me to enter. I looked past the threshold and saw a brightly lit office.

"Seems innocent enough," I said.

"So does my uncle," Monty said. "Let's go."

We stepped through the threshold and found ourselves in the office of the Dean of Discipline, according to the small plaque on the desk.

Behind the desk, I saw a picture of Dex and the Morrigan standing and embracing each other as they gazed into each other's eyes.

The rest of the room reminded me of a college dean's office—if it were done in blacks, dark greens, and grays, instead of warm browns and reds. There were several bookcases lining the walls. Some of the books were recognizable; others were written in a language I couldn't understand.

There was another doorway which led to a private bathroom. Just off that doorway sat a large black sofa taking up one side of the office. Behind us was the main door to the office itself.

We stood in the center of a large, green teleportation circle, which I guessed Dexter created to allow easy access to the school from the Moscow.

The Morrigan entered the room behind us.

"Dean of Discipline?" I said, slightly awed. "I don't think any student is going to misbehave in this school."

"Welcome, Tristan, Simon, and Peaches," she said with a smile. "You'd be surprised. Some students will feel the need to test the boundaries. I am here to remind them that some boundaries are not meant to be crossed. Dexter is waiting for you in the lab—this way, please."

We travelled the empty corridors of the fortress-school sanctuary. I could see there had been plenty of work done improving the facility into a real place of learning. Several of the classrooms had state-of-the-art tech, while others had floors and walls covered with glowing runes and symbols.

It was into one of these rune-covered rooms that the Morrigan led us. She placed her hand on the door, and green runes flared to life on its surface.

"He is waiting," she said, motioning for us to enter. "Please visit when you can. We can even create an honorary teaching position for either of you, if you should wish."

"No, thanks," I said. "You don't want me teaching any classes."

"Oh, I don't know," she said, cocking her head to one side. "Basic Survival 101 would suit you well."

"I have a student, thank you," Monty said quickly. "One is more than enough."

"Speaking of which, young Cecelia shows much promise," the Morrigan said. "We will have to discuss her future with her guardian...Olga, is it?"

"It is," Monty said. "I look forward to that discussion."

"It should prove insightful," she said. "Very well, I'll leave you three to it. You'd best enter before he loses his patience."

She disappeared a moment later.

"You look forward to it?" I asked as he pushed open the door to the room. "Really?"

"No, not really, but what did you expect me to say?" he replied. "No, thank you, I'd rather not?"

"That would be unwise, lad," Dex said as we entered the room. He was doing his bohemian mage look: dress shirt, blue jeans, and bare feet. His hair was pulled back in a loose ponytail with a black raven clip holding the hair in place. "She's used to getting her way, especially when it comes to discussing the students."

We stepped into what appeared to be one of the labs. The floor, walls, and ceiling were covered in softly glowing green runes. I found most of them impossible to decipher. Monty narrowed his eyes and then opened them wide in surprise.

"These are the components to the first elder rune," he said, awe filling his voice. "It's been deconstructed and modified, but this is it. How?"

"I had a visit from an old friend," he said. "You know him as Arch Keeper Evergreen."

"How do you know him?" I asked.

"A different time, and a different name," he said, shaking

his head. "Doesn't matter now. We're here to see if we can sort this out before you get yourselves killed, or worse."

"Or worse?" I asked. "What do you mean, *or worse?*"

"Did you suffer a head blow in Hell?" Dex asked, poking my chest. "There are plenty of things worse than death. Now let me have a look at you both—stand still."

Monty and I stood side by side.

"Is there a solution?" Monty asked. "Can you remove it?"

"Are ye daft?" Dex asked, raising his voice slightly. "I'm not an Arch Keeper. Evergreen wove this into your signatures. It's elegant and complicated beyond belief; I wouldn't even know where to begin. The best I can do is hide it from all but the most powerful gazes."

"How powerful?"

"Most mages."

"Verity?"

"Unless the High Tribunal comes looking for you, aye, most of Verity as well," he said. "Archmages will be able to see that something is hidden, but they won't be able to see exactly what it is."

"Who can see what is hidden?" Monty asked. "At what level should we be concerned?"

Dexter frowned as he gave it thought.

"Well, another Keeper is going to see the elder rune—that can't be helped," he said. "Evergreen left his mark all over this cast. Hades, and beings of that level, will see right through my camouflage."

"That means Kali will see it, too," I said, disappointed. "If she looks, that is."

"If she looks, aye, she will see it too," he said with a nod. "Anyone else will only see an increase in power, but not the reason why. Any more questions?"

"I'm good," I said. "If it's just gods, Keepers, and Archmages, I can live with that."

"Agreed," Monty said. "Except that we will soon have to face Gault."

"Well, you hit the nail right on the nose," Dex said. "Nothing can be done about that except to get ready. Tell your pup to sit over there." He pointed across the room. Peaches moved silently to the location Dex pointed to, much to my surprise.

"That is a good boy," Dex said. "Right, then, there's no time like the present. Stand still and don't move an inch until I say so, understood?"

Monty and I both nodded.

Dex formed two green orbs of power and let them hover in his hands. The runes and symbols on the walls matched the color of the orbs and pulsed with power. The next moment, he squeezed his hands shut, crushing the orbs in his fists.

Then he stepped close to us and punched us both in the chest.

Instead of an impact, I felt his hand go through me. I could feel the flow of energy as he camouflaged our energy signatures.

For once, there was no pain, just a mild feeling of discomfort and a tightness in my chest. After what felt like ten minutes, he removed his hands and stepped back.

He narrowed his eyes at us and nodded with satisfaction.

"That should do it," he said. "No casting for twenty-four hours. Think you can manage that?"

"Of course," Monty said. "We'll spend the bulk of that time here, exploring your School of Battle Magic. That should keep Simon out of trouble."

"Keep *me* out of trouble? Are you serious? I'm the one who gets into trouble?"

"That's what I said."

"You're more than welcome to stay here," Dex said. "You can catch up on some lessons with your student and meet some of the other young mages who are here. The living quarters are to your right when you step out. Give me a moment, and I'll give you the grand tour. Right now, I need to disable this room."

Monty and I stood there as Dex stared at us, crossing his arms.

"That means get out," he continued, raising his voice. "I'll meet you in the living quarters. Take your pup with you and get scarce."

We quickly stepped out of the room, with Peaches bumping me in the leg and nearly knocking me into the opposite wall.

"I guess we should find these living quarters," Monty said, heading down the corridor. "I think the School of Battle Magic will be good for my uncle. He is definitely mellowing out."

"You call *that* mellowing out?"

"Definitely," Monty said, glancing behind us at the room we'd just exited. "The old version of my uncle would have evicted us from the room with orbs or violent teleportation circles, not his voice and a stern look."

"I'm just glad we can take a breather," I said. "Hades said he would look into getting us some downtime somewhere nice."

"Hades?"

"Yes, Hades."

"The god of the Underworld?" Monty asked. "*That* Hades?"

"Do you know another Hades?"

"You may want to reconsider that offer," Monty said. "Who do you think designed Gehenna?"

"You're kidding. Really?"

Monty shook his head.

"Let's go see if we can find the kitchen," Monty said. "I

could use a strong cuppa and some food before taking this tour."

"You think they have coffee brewing somewhere?"

"If I know my uncle, he's certain to have a pot going somewhere."

We headed down the corridor in search of the kitchen, putting thoughts of Keepers, mages, and runes behind us—if only for a short while.

THE END

AUTHOR NOTES

Thank you for reading this story and jumping into the world of Monty & Strong with me.

Disclaimer: The Author Notes are written at the very end of the writing process. This section is not seen by the ART or my amazing Jeditor—Audrey. Any typos or errors following this disclaimer are mine and mine alone.

Choices and conflict.

That pretty much sums up *every* M&S story, along with ample doses of property damage. This book reined in the damage a bit, even though it starts with Cece and Simon creating a hole in the Moscow, well mostly Cece, creating a hole in the Moscow.

This book begins a small arc (three books) within the larger arc of the nineteen (how are we up to 19 books?) that introduces the Terrible Trio to the Keeper and ends with the potential end of...everything.

I promise it will be fun, scary, and life-changing for our Trio. I don't want to give away the title of the next book, because even the title gives away some of the story. In order for Monty and Simon to face off against Gault, and they will have to face him, Monty (and Simon) will need to get stronger, much stronger.

Simon will have to make some hard choices, about being an Aspis, a bondmate, the bearer of a necromantic siphoning seraphic weapon, and the ever-present splinter designed to ruin everyone's day. The conversation with Michiko has to occur, as well as a blade to blade chat with a certain successor who wants Simon retired permanently so she can take the mantle of the Marked of Kali.

In LOST RUNES we met Sebastian the STRAY DOGS, or at least some of them. They have their own stories to tell. I felt it was time to introduce some of Monty's other family. We will learn more about the Treadwell's in future stories of the Treadwell Supernatural Directive and why Sebastian is the way he is and what spurred him to create the Directive.

He's not entirely good, but he's not all bad either.

In a few books, we will uncover more of Simon's history as more of his past is revealed. It was hinted at in this book (and Requiem), but it gets deeper later on.

If it feels like I'm being a bit cagey about where the stories are going, it's because I am. There are going to be some major changes in the M&S World and the conflict that is brewing is going to bring about some deaths I can't talk about…yet.

In the quest for more power, Monty & Simon will be getting more attention and most of it will be hostile. They are wading into a deeper part of the ocean that is the world of magic, and the beings swimming there feel they don't belong in these waters—starting with Gault.

We dive deeper into the nature of dark and light and secrets in the next books as Monty & Simon go after the next runes. They will have to uncover why the sects were created along with their purpose. The story will create as many questions as it answers.

Verity and the High Tribunal are feeling especially threatened by the actions of Monty & Strong and they will take drastic and permanent steps to remove them as a threat. Whether or not it will be successful remains to be seen, Cain will find a way to wield power again and he's not exactly the forgiving type.

So here we are, 19 books in and the series shows no sign of slowing down. I honestly thought this would just be a trilogy—Monty, Simon & Peaches thought otherwise.

I want to sincerely thank you for joining me in this adventure, these are by far the easiest and hardest stories for me to tell, but your being there with me for each part of this adventure makes it worthwhile.

I apologize for not being more transparent in these notes, but I do promise the next book in the series is being worked on as you read these words. I'm as anxious as you are to get to the next part of the story.

So...grab a large mug of Death Wish, jump into the Dark Goat, (shove the Sensei of Sprawl over), and strap in. We have places to go, people to see and buildings to explode.

As always, remembering the sage words of our resident Zen Hellhound Master...Meat is Life!

Thank you again for jumping into this story with me!

SPECIAL MENTIONS

To Dolly: my rock, anchor, and inspiration. Thank you...always.

Larry & Tammy—The WOUF: Because even when you aren't there...you're there.

Orlando A. Sanchez
www.orlandoasanchez.com

Orlando has been writing ever since his teens when he was immersed in creating scenarios for playing Dungeons and Dragons with his friends every weekend.

The worlds of his books are urban settings with a twist of the paranormal lurking just behind the scenes and with generous doses of magic, martial arts, and mayhem.

He currently resides in Queens, NY with his wife and children.

BITTEN PEACHES PUBLISHING

Thanks for Reading

If you enjoyed this book, would you please **leave a review** at the site you purchased it from? It doesn't have to be long... just a line or two would be fantastic and it would really help me out.

Bitten Peaches Publishing offers more books by this author. From science fiction & fantasy to adventure & mystery, we bring the best stories for adults and kids alike.

www.BittenPeachesPublishing.com

More books by Orlando A. Sanchez

The Warriors of the Way
The Karashihan*•The Spiritual Warriors•The Ascendants•The Fallen Warrior•The Warrior Ascendant•The Master Warrior

John Kane

The Deepest Cut*•Blur

Sepia Blue
The Last Dance*•Rise of the Night•Sisters•Nightmare•Nameless

Chronicles of the Modern Mystics
The Dark Flame•A Dream of Ashes

Montague & Strong Detective Agency Novels
Tombyards & Butterflies•Full Moon Howl•Blood is Thicker•Silver Clouds Dirty Sky•Homecoming•Dragons & Demigods•Bullets & Blades•Hell Hath No Fury•Reaping Wind•The Golem•Dark Glass•Walking the Razor•Requiem•Divine Intervention•Storm Blood•Revenant•Blood Lessons•Broken Magic•Lost Runes

Montague & Strong Detective Agency Stories
No God is Safe•The Date•The War Mage•A Proper Hellhound•The Perfect Cup•Saving Mr. K

Brew & Chew Adventures
Hellhound Blues

Night Warden Novels
Wander•ShadowStrut

Division 13
The Operative•The Magekiller

Blackjack Chronicles
The Dread Warlock

The Assassin's Apprentice

The Birth of Death

Gideon Shepherd Thrillers
Sheepdog

DAMNED
Aftermath

RULE OF THE COUNCIL
Blood Ascension•Blood Betrayal•Blood Rule

NYXIA WHITE
They Bite•They Rend•They Kill

IKER THE CLEANER
Iker the Unseen

*Books denoted with an asterisk are **FREE** via my website
—www.orlandoasanchez.com

ART SHREDDERS

I want to take a moment to extend a special thanks to the ART SHREDDERS.

No book is the work of one person. I am fortunate enough to have an amazing team of advance readers and shredders.

Thank you for giving of your time and keen eyes to provide notes, insights, answers to the questions, and corrections (dealing wonderfully with my extreme dreaded comma allergy). You help make every book and story go from good to great. Each and every one of you helped make this book fantastic, and I couldn't do this without each of you.

THANK YOU

ART SHREDDERS

Amber, Anne Morando, Audrey Cienki
   Beverly Collie
   Cam Skaggs, Carrie Anne O'Leary

Dawn McQueen Mortimer, Denise King, Diane Craig, Dolly Sanchez, Donna Young Hatridge

Hal Bass, Helen Valentine

Jasmine Breeden, Jasmine Davis, Jeanette Auer, Jen Cooper, John Fauver, Joy Kiili, Julie Peckett

Karen Hollyhead

Larry Diaz Tushman, Laura Tallman I

Malcolm Robertson, Marcia Campbell, Mari De Valerio, Maryelaine Eckerle-Foster, Melissa Miller, Michelle Blue

Paige Guido, Penny Campbell-Myhill

Rene Corrie, Rob Farnham

Sara Mason Branson, Sean Trout, Sondra Massey, Stacey Stein, Susie Johnson

Tami Cowles, Ted Camer, Terri Adkisson

Wendy Schindler

ACKNOWLEDGEMENTS

With each book, I realize that every time I learn something about this craft, it highlights so many things I still have to learn. Each book, each creative expression, has a large group of people behind it.

This book is no different.

Even though you see one name on the cover, it is with the knowledge that I am standing on the shoulders of the literary giants that informed my youth, and am supported by my generous readers who give of their time to jump into the adventures of my overactive imagination.

I would like to take a moment to express my most sincere thanks:

To Dolly: My wife and greatest support. You make all this possible each and every day. You keep me grounded when I get lost in the forest of ideas. Thank you for asking the right questions when needed, and listening intently when I go off on tangents. Thank you for who you are and the space you create—I love you.

To my Tribe: You are the reason I have stories to tell. You cannot possibly fathom how much and how deeply I love you all.

To Lee: Because you were the first audience I ever had. I love you, sis.

To the Logsdon Family: The words *thank you* are insufficient to describe the gratitude in my heart for each of you. JL, your support always demands I bring my best, my A-game, and produce the best story I can. Both you and Lorelei (my Uber Jeditor) and now, Audrey, are the reason I am where I am today. My thank you for the notes, challenges, corrections, advice, and laughter. Your patience is truly infinite. *Arigato-gozaimasu.*

To The Montague & Strong Case Files Group—AKA The MoB (Mages of Badassery): When I wrote T&B there were fifty-five members in The MoB. As of this release, there are over one thousand five hundred members in the MoB. I am honored to be able to call you my MoB Family. Thank you for being part of this group and M&S.

You make this possible. **THANK YOU.**

To the ever-vigilant PACK: You help make the MoB...the MoB. Keeping it a safe place for us to share and just...be. Thank you for your selfless vigilance. You truly are the Sentries of Sanity.

Chris Christman II: A real-life technomancer who makes the **MoBTV LIVEvents +Kaffeeklatsch** on YouTube amazing. Thank you for your tireless work and wisdom. Everything is connected...you totally rock!

To the WTA—The Incorrigibles: JL, Ben Z., Eric QK., S.S., and Noah.

They sound like a bunch of badass misfits, because they are. My exposure to the deranged and deviant brain trust you all represent helped me be the author I am today. I have officially gone to the *dark side* thanks to all of you. I humbly give you my thanks, and...it's all your fault.

To my fellow Indie Authors: I want to thank each of you for creating a space where authors can feel listened to, and encouraged to continue on this path. A rising tide lifts all the ships indeed.

To The English Advisory: Aaron, Penny, Carrie, Davina, and all of the UK MoB. For all things English...thank you.

To DEATH WISH COFFEE: This book (and every book I write) has been fueled by generous amounts of the only coffee on the planet (and in space) strong enough to power my very twisted imagination. Is there any other coffee that can compare? I think not. DEATH WISH—thank you!

To Deranged Doctor Design: Kim, Darja, Tanja, Jovana, and Milo (Designer Extraordinaire).

If you've seen the covers of my books and been amazed, you can thank the very talented and gifted creative team at DDD. They take the rough ideas I give them, and produce incredible covers that continue to surprise and amaze me. Each time, I find myself striving to write a story worthy of the covers they produce. DDD, you embody professionalism and creativity. Thank you for the great service and spectacular covers. **YOU GUYS RULE!**

To you, the reader: I was always taught to save the best for last. I write these stories for **you**. Thank you for jumping down the rabbit holes of *what if?* with me. You are the reason I write the stories I do.

You keep reading...I'll keep writing.

Thank you for your support and encouragement.

CONTACT ME

I really do appreciate your feedback. You can let me know what you thought of the story by emailing me at:
orlando@orlandoasanchez.com

To get **FREE** stories please visit my page at:
www.orlandoasanchez.com

For more information on the M&S World…come join the MoB Family on Facebook!
You can find us at:
Montague & Strong Case Files

Visit our online M&S World Swag Store located at:
Emandes

If you enjoyed the book, **please leave a review**. Reviews help the book, and also help other readers find good stories to read.
THANK YOU!

Thanks for Reading

If you enjoyed this book, would you **please leave a review** at the site you purchased it from? It doesn't have to be a book report... just a line or two would be fantastic and it would really help us out!

Printed in Great Britain
by Amazon